Now he unders...

Richard suddenly saw why he'd been merely stunned and not slain along with the others on the yacht. It was clear why the killer had taken the only lifeboat and deserted him. He was meant to be the accused.

Richard pressed his palm to his throbbing head. There was nothing he could do for his ex-wife, father-in-law and the pilot. He could only save himself...and hopefully his son, far away and alone.

With clumsy, cursing efforts, he was finally able to launch himself and the fragile raft into the rough seas. At first he was able to paddle some way toward the rocky shore, and the lighthouse that seemed to welcome him. But soon the raft fell apart, spilling him into the watery chaos....

Dear Reader,

Be prepared to meet a "Woman of Mystery!"

This month, we're proud to bring you another story in our ongoing WOMEN OF MYSTERY program, designed to bring you the debut books of writers new to Harlequin Intrigue.

Meet Jean Barrett, author of *The Shelter of Her Arms*.

If setting has anything to do with it, Jean Barrett claims she has every reason to be inspired. She and her husband live on Wisconsin's scenic Door Peninsula in an antiques-filled country cottage overlooking Lake Michigan. A teacher for many years, she left the classroom to write full time. She is the author of several romances. This is her first Intrigue.

We're dedicated to bringing you the best new authors, the freshest new voices. Be on the lookout for more "WOMEN OF MYSTERY"!

Sincerely,

Debra Matteucci
Senior Editor & Editorial Coordinator
Harlequin Books
300 East 42nd Street
New York, NY 10017

The Shelter of Her Arms
Jean Barrett

Harlequin Books

TORONTO • NEW YORK • LONDON
AMSTERDAM • PARIS • SYDNEY • HAMBURG
STOCKHOLM • ATHENS • TOKYO • MILAN
MADRID • WARSAW • BUDAPEST • AUCKLAND

To the best cheerleader in the business—my friend and agent, Elaine Davie

ISBN 0-373-22308-0

THE SHELTER OF HER ARMS

Copyright © 1995 by Jean Barrett.

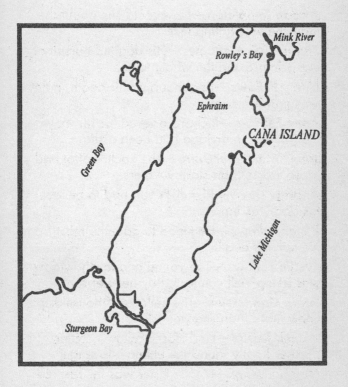

Mink River

Rowley's Bay

Ephraim

CANA ISLAND

Green Bay

Lake Michigan

Sturgeon Bay

CAST OF CHARACTERS

Richard Davis—His life was on the line, and there was a price on his head.

Jordan Templeton—How could she doubt the man she was falling for?

Sheriff Con Matthews—His dogged pursuit of Davis impressed the whole town.

Harry Fellows—Few mourned his death, many wanted his money.

Anne Fellows—Richard grieved for his ex-wife, though their marriage had been a sham.

John "Mac" MacGuire—The yacht's pilot had faced worse than stormy waters.

Andrew Davis—Richard's son had to believe his dad was innocent.

Victor Fellows—He stood to gain the most from his father's death.

Evelyn Fellows—The young and lovely widow was being well comforted by her stepson.

Sonia Gunnerson—The Fellowses' housekeeper knew more than she was telling.

Walter Jessup—Had Harry Fellows's bitter partner finally found the ultimate revenge?

Maggie Dennis—Mac's sister was the last to speak to him alive.

Dino—He was dark as a Gypsy and just as mysterious.

Prologue

Hangover, Richard thought bleakly. This has got to be a hangover.

He experienced all the classic symptoms of the condition as he slowly surfaced to consciousness: a violent headache, a sense of disorientation, the floor moving under him. There was only one thing wrong with his conviction. Except for an occasional beer, or maybe a rare glass of wine, he didn't drink.

His brain struggled with the problem, resisting the explanation for a long moment. Then, gradually, he became aware of the reality of his situation. In fact, the floor *was* in motion as the *Lady Anne* rolled in the heavy seas buffeting its hull. He was stretched facedown on the luxurious carpeting of that floor. It was another few seconds before memory permitted him to understand how he had gotten there.

He had excused himself from the salon, pleading a need to use the bathroom. The truth was, realizing that anger was getting him nowhere, he had wanted a recess to curb his mounting temper. The long passageway had offered several cabins, each accommodated with its own bathroom facilities. Lavish. Everything aboard the damn motor yacht was much too lavish.

He had selected the last cabin, as far away from that ugly scene in the salon as he could get. He recalled how he had

braced himself as he entered the room. It had been necessary. The vessel was lurching drunkenly in the stormy waters. And then . . .

He wasn't sure. Something had struck him on the back of
his skull. A vicious blow, which accounted now for his
blinding headache. Maybe a careening lamp? He twisted his
head painfully, searching the ceiling for just such a hanging
fixture. There was none. Then what had knocked him down
and how long had he been lying here unconscious?

Inhaling slowly, deeply, Richard managed to get to his
feet, where he steadied himself against the yawing of the
vessel. The bathroom was straight ahead. He staggered into
it and leaned over the sink, fighting dizziness and waves of
nausea. He expected to be sick in the marble basin, but the
weakness diminished after a minute.

The taps were gold plated. Figures, he thought bitterly.
He turned on the cold water and ducked his head, liberally
dousing his face. Reaching for one of the precisely folded
towels on the surface of the vanity, he rubbed himself
briskly.

When he lowered the towel he was startled by his reflec-
tion in the mirror over the sink. It was a face that Anne had
once told him in a careless moment was better than just
handsome because it had strength and character. Right now
it looked drawn and unhappy, the deep-set blue eyes dark
with confusion.

He started to replace the towel, and then he saw the smear
of blood on one corner. His blood. His fingers went to the
back of his skull. There was a swelling there and a slight
trickle from the wound. He wondered again what, or who,
had attacked him. It didn't make sense. Whatever their
feelings about him, the occupants of the salon would never
get physically aggressive.

He stood there, swaying with the motion of the yacht as
he made a concentrated effort to clear his mind. And this
was when he understood that something else didn't make
sense. The silence. Except for the slap and wash of the waves

battering the sleek hull, the wail of the wind, there was no sound. He should have heard the throbbing of the dual engines. They were still. Everything aboard the yacht was very still. The *Lady Anne* was without power, drifting in tumultuous waters. He had heard how unforgiving Lake Michigan could be in a storm as nasty as this one.

Something was decidedly wrong. Richard could feel it in his gut as he left the bathroom and groped his way across the cabin. He reached the gloomy passageway and stopped to listen, straining to hear the sound of voices from the salon. Nothing. He could see the door of the master cabin at the end of the passage. It had been closed when he passed it earlier. It was open now. He watched it swing rhythmically back and forth with the pitching of the vessel. Its hinges were too well oiled to creak. The silence was complete, downright eerie. He couldn't stand it any longer.

"Hey!" he shouted up the passageway, his voice sounding false to him, not his own. "Where is everyone? What happened to the engines?"

There was no answer. Deeply uneasy now, he started along the dim passage, gripping the rail hand over hand to support himself against the rocking of the yacht. He paused by the stirring door of the master cabin, glancing inside. It was empty.

He turned, facing the shallow flight of stairs to the salon. Instinct suddenly made him reluctant to climb them. But he had no choice. He had to learn what was wrong. He couldn't go on hanging here in the shadows. Grabbing the stair railing, he hauled himself up into the richly appointed, teak-paneled salon.

And now Richard knew why the *Lady Anne* was so silent.

The woman who was his ex-wife, and for whom the yacht had been named, was on the floor. Her elegant body, clad in dark slacks and a silky crimson top, lay facedown on the priceless Oriental rug. Her carefully styled blond hair was sticky with blood. She had been shot through the back of her head.

The man who was his former father-in-law, as well as his enemy, was sprawled in a deck chair, an expression of foolish surprise on his jowly face. His wide, protuberant gray eyes stared sightlessly at an antique marine painting behind the bar. The bullet hole drilled through his forehead was very round, very clean.

On one level Richard's brain, still muddled from the blow he had suffered, refused to accept the gruesome scene. They had been alive when he left them, and now they weren't alive. How could this be? There was no sanity in it, no possible logic. On another level, a far more chilling one, he couldn't deny the reality he confronted. The two people who, only a short while ago, had so coldly rejected him, denied his vital need, had been brutally, ruthlessly slaughtered.

He experienced the nausea again, sour and churning. It had nothing to do with the plunging of the yacht. It was not seasickness. It was horror.

There was no need to check them. They were both plainly dead. But for the sake of decency he went through the motions. Conquering his queasiness, he leaned first over the deck chair, and then he knelt on the rug, looking on their bodies for vital life signs that weren't there. He had stopped loving Anne long ago, but he still felt a wrenching sorrow over her death.

There was a silver yachting trophy rolling on the floor. He picked it up as he got to his feet and placed it absently on the bar. Then he used the bar to support himself, planting his fists on its polished surface. He fought his dazed mind, trying to push away the numbness, trying to think. Trying to find reason where there was no reason. *Why? Who?*

There was only one certainty. There had been four people aboard the yacht. Anne, her father, himself and the man they had simply referred to as Mac. Mac was there to pilot the *Lady Anne*. Middle-aged and amiable, he was an un-

likely candidate for a madman. But there could be no other
choice.

It was no accident, then, what had happened to Richard
in the cabin. Mac must have crept up soundlessly behind
him, striking him down. And now this homicidal maniac
was prowling somewhere on the yacht, and he had a gun.
What had triggered his rampage wasn't really important at
this moment. All that mattered was that Richard had to find
the man before he found him. But he needed a defense
against that gun. There was a possibility.

His wealthy father-in-law had once been threatened with
kidnapping. Since then he'd kept a pistol close by, calling it
his personal bodyguard. Richard didn't think he had been
carrying it when he was shot. Where was it, then? Somewhere in his cabin, the master cabin.

Cautiously he edged his way across the salon, down the
steps and into the cabin. A hurried, tense search through the
contents of the room revealed no pistol. Either it had never
been here or Mac had it.

There was a long, heavy-duty flashlight in one of the
bedside drawers. It made a poor weapon, but he took it.
Armed with the flashlight, he left the cabin and stole toward the salon. He was headed toward the bridge, searching for the man who must be waiting to ambush him. Why
hadn't he killed Richard earlier, along with the others?

The yacht continued to buck in the wild waters. He
struggled to keep on his feet and alert, and all the while he
battled at the panic that was clawing at his insides.

The salon was behind him now, then the dining room and
after it the galley. Next was a small area equipped with
lockers where various nautical gear was stored. It connected with the wheelhouse. He flattened himself against
one of the lockers, upraised flashlight grasped tightly in his
hand, and peered carefully through the window of the door.

Mac was in the wheelhouse seated on the pilot's stool, his
thick body slumped over the helm. Even from this angle

Richard could see the blood where he had been shot through the back of his grizzled head.

Like a somnambulist, Richard slid into the wheelhouse. He stared at the dead man. He stared at the control panel, then at the ship-to-shore communication. There was a reason the yacht was adrift and helpless. All of the electronic instruments were riddled with bullets.

The yacht went on tossing as he stood there in mindless disbelief, his head aching. What was the explanation? Even nightmares had explanations. But he suddenly feared this explanation more than he had ever feared anything in his life. If they were all dead, if he was the only one still here, did it mean that in some kind of blind rage he wasn't able to recollect he had murdered them himself?

His reeling brain seethed with the likelihood and then finally refused it with a silent, inner shout. *No!* Whatever his anger, he couldn't have done it. He wouldn't have done it.

That left only one other explanation. There was someone else aboard the *Lady Anne*. Someone he hadn't known about. And he had to discover him before this lunatic stalked and cornered him. The cat-and-mouse game must be resumed.

His nerves on fire, Richard carefully retraced his route, searching through the very bowels of the yacht, checking every recess where the killer might be lurking. The open deck he would save for the last. He went systematically from cabin to cabin without result. His tall, lean figure was muscular enough to match almost any adversary, but how could you fight an enemy you couldn't find?

He was back in the passageway now where he had started. The suspense was unbearable. He heard himself shouting recklessly, savagely, "Damn it, where are you? Come out where I can see you!"

There was no response to his demand. There was only the silence. Like the sinister silence of a ghost ship. The yacht went on heeling from side to side.

He reached the last cabin in the stern of the yacht. From the corner of his eye he caught a slight movement, and he whirled, flashlight still in hand. The movement came from the window, originating from somewhere outside. He crouched near the glass, scrubbing at the mist there with the heel of one hand. He peered out guardedly, identifying the movement. The trailing lines from the davits on the aft deck were whipping back and forth in the fierce wind. The *Lady Anne*'s only lifeboat with its outboard engine had been suspended from the davits. It was no longer there.

Stunned, Richard stared at the empty twin cranes. Now he understood why he couldn't locate the man responsible for the grisly carnage in the salon and the wheelhouse. The unknown assassin had fled the yacht, leaving him trapped here with the three people he had murdered.

The removal of one threat revealed another imminent danger. Across the expanse of wicked gray waters, through the murky light of the storm, he could make out the dim, low shape of the wooded coast. He knew enough about that Wisconsin shoreline to realize how cruel it could be to a vessel without power in waters this turbulent. And if the helpless yacht didn't drift onto the rocks, then it faced the risk of being dragged far out into Lake Michigan.

Flares, he thought. There had to be emergency flares somewhere on board. Without the radio there was no other way to call a distress. He flung the flashlight onto a bunk and sped toward the bow. He reached the lockers outside the wheelhouse and began tearing through them frantically.

He found the flares. He also found a deflated rubber raft and tanks of compressed air. And that was when his sense of self-preservation seized another direction as a new, sickening realization broke over him like a fever.

He couldn't use the flares. He couldn't summon help. Couldn't be found here aboard the yacht, the only survivor with three murdered bodies. They would assume he had killed them. What other conclusion could they possibly reach? He even had the motive. He didn't stand a prayer.

Now he understood it—why he had been merely stunned and not slain along with the others. Why the killer had taken the only lifeboat and deserted him. He was meant to be the accused.

Richard sank back on his heels where he hunkered by the gaping lockers, his hand pressed to his throbbing head. The strength and clarity of his mind had been affected by the blow to his skull. Maybe his mind was still not functioning sensibly. He didn't know. He only knew that he had to get off the yacht. He could do nothing now for Anne, her father or the pilot. He could only help himself. He had to reach someplace, any place that was safe where he could think calmly. Decide what he had to do. Not just for himself, either. There was someone else depending on his freedom.

Richard inflated the raft and dragged it out onto the open deck into the fury of the storm. Rain, lashed by the ferocious wind, pelted his face like needles, drenching him. He ignored the wetness. It didn't matter. Nothing mattered but reaching the shore. He didn't consider how suicidal his intention might be.

With clumsy, cursing efforts he was finally able to launch himself and the raft into the rough seas. At first he made headway, was able to actually paddle some distance toward the rocky shore. But the waves were mountainous, eventually swamping the small raft despite all his powerful struggles. In the end the punished raft came apart, spilling him into the watery chaos.

Chapter One

Jordan wasn't supposed to have a key to the lighthouse tower. Not officially, anyway. Last fall she had managed to charm a spare one out of the young coastguardsman who showed up periodically to service the automated light. She had promised him she would use the key only in the event of an emergency.

It was perhaps stretching the truth to regard her present situation as a real crisis. But, she thought, justifying her action as she fitted the key into the lock, the tower offered the only position for judging her predicament comprehensively. She needed to learn just how bad the conditions were.

The door squeaked open on the shed connecting the residence with the lighthouse proper. There was no point in fumbling for a wall switch to light the dark, damp interior. Jordan had been without power for several hours. The automatic gas generator secured in one of the outbuildings provided current only for the beacon itself. Electric lamps weren't necessary, however. Enough daylight squeezed through the small portholes in the tower to show her the way.

Groping for the rail in the gloom, she began to climb the long, spiraling stairway, her feet clanging hollowly on the metal treads. It was May and she was wearing a windbreaker, but she shivered. The place was as cold as a deep cavern, the stale air strong with the odor of mold.

Jordan had to remind herself that she loved the island in all its moods, except one. The fog, with its tragic associations, she preferred not to think about. Anyway, it wasn't the wild stuff, like today's weather, that bothered her. Storms, in fact, contributed to the maritime atmosphere she was so eager to capture for her book.

Of course, she had never counted on being stranded when she signed the lease last year, but maybe she was exaggerating her situation. She would soon find out.

She was puffing by the time she reached the pinnacle of the eighty-foot tower. The winding stairway ended there. Inner access to the glass-enclosed beacon was by an iron ladder mounting to a padlocked trapdoor over her head. She wasn't interested in that compartment, however, but in the door that opened to the cantilevered catwalk that circled the tower below the light.

The wind, still high, blasted her as she eased the door back and slipped out onto the narrow walkway. The gale robbed her lungs of air, whipped her sable hair around her face and spat raindrops at her from the last lingering clouds sailing across the late-afternoon sky. Clinging to the iron railing, she edged carefully around the tower, scanning the magnificent scene.

Lake Michigan stretched out to the horizon, a vast gray-green expanse frothy with whitecaps. Foaming surf boomed against the rockbound shore several hundred feet away, shooting spray high into the air. The bruised sky was beginning to lighten in the east, revealing a milky glow that dramatically lit the cluster of buildings composing the lighthouse station.

She looked down from the white shaft of the tower to the red-roofed, buff brick residence and the three matching outbuildings huddled around it like small offspring. The setting could, and did, qualify as a perfect tourist attraction in season. At present it was isolated and forlorn. The station hadn't been manned in years. Jordan was its only occupant.

At this particular moment, though, she wasn't interested in the picturesque aspects of the Cana Island light. It was the result of the storm that concerned her. The news she had listened to on her battery-powered radio reported it as one of the worst spring storms to ever hit the Door Peninsula. She could well believe that as she surveyed the evidence in the clearing below.

Though the stout buildings had suffered no damage except for a few torn shingles, the ground was littered with leaves, limbs and uprooted birches and cedars. She was glad to see the hardy lilac thickets had valiantly resisted the onslaught. Defying the storm, they would be heavy with bloom in another week.

None of this, which she could easily have seen from the house, had brought her up into the tower. The island was less than ten acres in extent, but its back side was thickly wooded, obstructing the scene she wanted. But now, by rounding the tower, she could easily get the view she needed over the treetops.

The tiny island was connected to the mainland by a low, rocky causeway. Jordan wasn't surprised to see the causeway flooded by the long waves breaking over it. She could spot her car parked on the other side where the road ended. To her relief it looked untouched, but it was clearly going nowhere, even if she could get to it. The road tunneling through the forest behind it was a wreckage of fallen trees, which explained why she had no power or telephone.

Nor, according to the radio, was she likely to soon recover either one. The whole peninsula was a mess, and Lord only knew when the crews were likely to get around to her remote section. They weren't apt to hurry, since the few summer cottages along the road weren't occupied as yet, and no one even knew she was here. She hadn't stopped by the local post office on her drive up from Chicago yesterday to report that she was now in residence for the season, and she wasn't about to walk the long miles back to town.

But there was no need. She had brought enough groceries with her. And even if she couldn't use her computer, she could work with a pencil by oil lamp. So, that was it. She'd just sit it out, snug and safe, and wait until they cut through to her.

Atmosphere, Jordan. Remember you wanted the atmosphere.

There was no shortage of that as she worked her way back toward the door. Even the herring gulls were obliging her. They were thick overhead, driven inland by the storm. She watched them for a moment, fascinated by the way they rode the wind so effortlessly. Wings outstretched, they wheeled above the clearing, their excited cries filling the air.

One of the white adults dropped a tidbit it had scavenged from the beach. Jordan, amused, saw a young gray gull swoop greedily after the morsel as it plummeted to the rocks. Her gaze followed the diving bird toward the thundering surf.

She never learned whether the gull successfully rescued the scrap. Its downward flight had directed her attention to another sight on the shore, something she had missed before.

Startled, she pressed against the railing, staring at the dark form wedged between two limestone boulders. It was difficult to see properly. Her eyes were tearing from the wind. She wiped at them impatiently, straining to make out the shape. Dear Lord, she wasn't mistaken. It was a human body washed up on the rocky beach.

For a long moment she was too shocked to move. Then she suddenly realized the need for immediate action. Without the telephone there was no one she could summon. If someone down there needed help, then she had to be the one to provide it. It was as simple as that.

Within seconds, she was through the door and plunging recklessly down the winding stairway. She didn't stop for anything in the house. She broke out into the open and raced across the wet grass of the clearing, pausing only once to make sure she was heading in the right direction.

She had reached the beach and was scrambling over the stony ledges when a sickening possibility occurred to her. What if whoever was down here no longer needed her assistance? She dreaded the thought of having to deal with a dead body, but necessity demanded her investigation.

She approached the two boulders. Drawing a steadying breath, she crouched between them at the side of the inert figure stretched facedown on a bed of hard shingle just beyond the surf. She gazed at him, feeling completely helpless. She had none of the skills required to tend a drowning victim, no real knowledge of artificial respiration. Where had he come from? How had he gotten here on her beach?

It doesn't matter, she told herself sharply. She couldn't go on squatting here doing nothing; she had to find out whether he was still alive. She had to touch him.

Obeying her own command, her trembling hand reached nervously for his arm. Her fingers closed over his wrist, seeking a pulse. He didn't stir, and his skin felt fearfully cold. She went on searching for a pulse and for a few ghastly seconds was unable to locate one. Then, to her immense relief, she found a beat on the back of his strongly corded wrist. She had no experience with checking pulses but, surprisingly, this one seemed reasonably even. He was alive, anyway.

But now what? He was soaked and cold and unconscious, maybe suffering shock from a serious injury. He needed to be taken inside, kept warm, possibly treated with some form of first aid. But how, in the name of all that was holy, was she supposed to get him back to the house? He was easily a solid six feet in length, and there was no way her five-foot-five frame was going to either carry or drag this rangy body the hundred yards or so to the bungalow.

Jordan sank back on her heels, frustrated by the problem. One thing was for sure. The situation didn't lack irony. She'd left Chicago for an existence meant to be quiet and uncomplicated. Then, within hours of her arrival, she'd been subjected to a wild storm, and now... Well, to put it bluntly, her landlord, the U.S. government, had failed to mention that she would be responsible for any local rescue operations. On the other hand, considering her intention was to write a book about the courageous women of the Great Lakes, there was nothing like firsthand research.

All of which, she reminded herself firmly, was doing nothing to help this poor man. There was no telling how long he had been there exposed to the wet and cold after what must have been a prolonged plunge into the icy waters of Lake Michigan. She couldn't afford to delay getting him inside. There was only one answer. He had to reach the house on his own legs. She had to rouse him somehow.

Jordan leaned forward, prepared to make the effort to roll him onto his back. She discovered, with a small gasp, the wound on the back of his skull. There was a nasty swelling, and blood caked in his hair. No wonder he was unconscious. She just hoped he wasn't sinking into a coma.

Sliding her hands under his body, she struggled with his deadweight. It didn't seem possible that flipping one helpless man could be so rigorous a task, but she was winded by the time she finally succeeded in raising him on his side. He needed only one gentle nudge then to drop onto his back. Except, as he settled against the shingle, she heard his faint groan of protest.

I'm hurting him, she thought, wincing over his pain.

Still, the groan was an indication that he was capable of being revived. Encouraged, she bent close to him, trying not to mind the frightening pallor on his lean face.

"Can you hear me?" she called.

No response.

She tried again. "Please, try to hear me. I'm going to help you, but you have to wake up."

Nothing.

The situation called for something more drastic. She lifted a hand, hesitated in regret and then with determination brought her palm down across his cheek in a sharp, stinging slap.

There was a grunt from him, but he failed to open his eyes. She cracked him again, harder this time. The blow produced a result, a very low but definite curse of outrage.

"Now can you hear me?" she shouted urgently.

There was a pause, and then to her immense satisfaction he muttered a weak but rigid, "I hear you, and if you try that again you'll be wearing a sling."

"I won't," she promised, grinning with relief. "But do you think you could get up, manage to walk? It's not far to the house, it's very close. I'll help you."

There was a slight bobbing of his square chin, which she translated as a nod, but he made no effort to move.

"Please, try," she urged.

"Yeah, all right," he mumbled.

His eyes opened then. Eyes that were a pronounced blue and rested on her face above him in deep bewilderment. She could see by the way they failed to properly focus on her that he had absolutely no idea where he was or what was happening to him.

"Come on," she coaxed. "Here, take my arm."

Jordan braced herself as he began fumbling for portions of her, seeming to grasp every part of her anatomy but her extended arm as he used her like a ladder, slowly climbing rung by rung to an upright position. It was a struggle for him just to get himself on his feet. But at last they were both standing, though he felt like a truck as he slumped against her. Both of them were breathing heavily.

"I'm cold," he complained.

"I know," she said soothingly. "But you'll be warm soon. We have to walk now. Up this way."

"Can't I ride?" he demanded hoarsely.

The man was either delirious or a comedian. "As a matter of fact," she confided, "I have a little red wagon I use to haul supplies from my car, but there's no way you'd fit in it. One foot in front of the other. You can do it."

Arm looped around him, she supported him as he began to shuffle up the beach. Together they stumbled over the rocks, finally gaining the easier ground of the clearing. Here they paused to rest before undergoing the greater distance to the house. A sudden thought occurred to her.

"Are there any others?" she wondered.

"What?" he asked groggily.

"Survivors," she explained in concern. "Are you the only one, or were there others?"

He stared blindly into space, and for a moment she thought he didn't understand and wasn't going to answer her. "No," he assured her finally. "No other survivors."

There was a grimness in his slow whisper that startled her, but she didn't pursue it. "Are you ready to go on?"

He nodded, swaying against her. She steadied him, and they started toward the house. It was an ordeal for both of them, the hundred yards seeming more like miles. Jordan, grimacing, felt as though her shoulder bones were being crushed as he leaned his considerable weight on her. She knew he was in a very weakened state, that he was making a tremendous effort to oblige her. He had a strong build, so she guessed that whatever he had undergone in the water, and maybe before that, must have been very bad.

"Almost there," she encouraged him as they dragged toward the house. There was one blessing anyway, she thought. The rain had stopped.

"We go in here," she instructed him, leading him through a lean-to that in the early days had served the keepers and their families as a summer kitchen.

They faced a shallow flight of steps up into the house itself. He was exhausted by the time they mounted them and reached the present kitchen. His knees buckled, and he started to crumple.

"No, you don't," she ordered, getting a fresh grip on him and managing to prop him up. "Not yet."

She wanted to get him into the parlor. There was a Franklin stove there and a good wood supply. Without the electric heat, it was the only place to keep him warm.

"Just a few steps more."

They passed through the kitchen and into the parlor behind it. She positioned him beside the sofa. He stood there, spent and shivering.

"Thank you," he said gravely, and then he collapsed across the sofa and passed out.

"You're welcome," Jordan whispered to his sprawled body.

She could have used a rest herself, but there was no time for that. He still needed a lot of attention. Shedding her windbreaker, she knelt in front of the stove. Within minutes she had a fire blazing in the grate, radiating waves of comforting heat into the chilly room. She went into the bedroom then and returned with an armful of blankets. Bending over the sofa, she was ready to pile blankets over his still figure when she remembered that he was wet clear to the skin. She couldn't leave him in those sodden clothes.

She was going to have to strip him.

It wasn't a task she welcomed. Her experience with undressing conscious, willing men was limited. She couldn't imagine getting that familiar with an unconscious stranger. Well, with any sort of luck he'd never know.

Steeling herself, she attacked the job with an impersonal, confident briskness that was altogether unconvincing. She started by removing his deck shoes and socks. There was no problem there. It was when she moved on to his jean jacket that she encountered trouble. The wet garment, together with his insensible state, resulted in a long, comic struggle. She was nearly winded by the time she succeeded in peeling the jacket off his frame and dropping it on the floor beside the shoes and socks in a crumpled heap.

What next? The jeans pasted to his long, athletic legs should have been the logical selection, but she avoided them and opted for his shirt clinging damply to his chest. Her fumbling fingers had the buttons halfway undone down his front when he stirred again.

"What are you doing to me?" he muttered.

Jordan could feel the color flaming into her cheeks. "Trying to get you out of your wet clothes."

"Like hell," he growled, pushing at her hands.

She straightened, glaring at him. "Okay, you want to be modest, then you do it."

He gazed at her, a blank look in his blue eyes. He was still dazed.

"Well?"

"Okay," he mumbled, "I'll do it."

Damn right he would! she thought. Dazed or not, she wasn't going to have him accuse her of trying to get intimate with him.

She stood by the sofa and watched him to make sure he didn't drop off again. It took him forever to get out of the shirt. She made no more offers to help, but she did feel sorry for him. She could sense his frustration over his weakness. He was clearly a man used to being in control, not relying on others.

The shirt was finally off, disclosing the riveting sight of hard male flesh. She swallowed and quickly dropped her gaze. He unsnapped his jeans and started to draw them down over his narrow hips. Jordan snatched up a blanket and draped it over his lower half. She was in no condition to watch him emerge in a state of rawness.

His mouth curled briefly in an amusement she tried to ignore. Then he frowned as he concentrated on wriggling out of the wet jeans under the screen of the blanket. It was quite a sight, like a molting caterpillar trying to squirm out of its tight skin.

"Help," he finally pleaded.

Taking pity on him, she knelt on the floor and succeeded in dragging the jeans out from under the blanket. To her chagrin, his shorts came with them.

She didn't need to worry about his reaction this time. He was already wrapped in the blanket and in a deep sleep of complete fatigue by the time she got to her feet. She laid another blanket over his reclining figure and then gathered up his things, spreading them to dry on chair backs near the stove.

Anything else? Yes, she remembered, the wound on his head. She would have to make an effort to treat it.

Until the power was restored, there would be no running water in the house. But there was an old-fashioned hand pump just outside the back door, and it still worked. Jordan got a kettle from the kitchen, filled it at the pump and placed it on the Franklin stove to heat. In the bathroom she rummaged through the cabinet, finding the first aid kit she had stored there last fall. She brought it back into the parlor with a towel and a washcloth. By the time she fetched a basin from the kitchen and drew a chair up close to the sofa, the water on the stove was warm enough for her purpose.

Seated on the chair with the basin close beside her, she faced the difficulty of turning his head to get at the injury. She managed to raise him enough to get a pillow stuffed under him. Then, hands on either side of his face, she carefully turned his head until the wound was exposed.

She gently cleaned the area, washing away the dried blood. Though the swelling was still considerable, the gash itself was neither wide nor deep and would surely heal without stitches. She just hoped his befuddled lethargy wasn't an indication that he was suffering from a concussion, because if he needed a doctor it was too late in the day for her to attempt walking out of here to get one. In the morning, if necessary, she would hike to town.

His thick, light brown hair was already drying. Tendrils of it curled over her fingers where they were pressed against his scalp. She was suddenly conscious of their crisp, pleasant texture brushing her skin, creating disturbing flutters in her middle.

Annoyed at the sensation, she forced herself to the more practical business of dabbing antibiotic ointment on the wound. She considered a bandage but decided his hair would present too much of a problem. She left the gash uncovered. Her patient never stirred through the whole procedure.

She was scraping her chair back from the sofa when one of the legs bumped over something. She looked down. It was a wallet. His wallet. It had managed to stay in whatever pocket he had been carrying it during his struggle in the water. But it had dropped on the floor while he undressed, and she'd overlooked it when collecting his clothes.

Jordan picked it up. The leather was soggy, the contents probably soaked. Should she? Why not? There would certainly be some form of identification in it, and she ought to know who he was, whether there was a family somewhere to be contacted. Still, she felt a little uncomfortable as she spread the wallet and investigated what it contained.

There wasn't a whole lot. A handful of damp bills, the usual credit cards and an Illinois driver's license. It was the driver's license that interested her. Richard Davis. That was his name. The card bore a Chicago address and his birth date. Richard Davis was thirty-six.

There was nothing else in the wallet, except a photograph. The shy, engaging face of a little boy grinned up at her. He was missing his two front teeth so she judged him to be six or seven years old. Did that small face bear a resemblance to the man on the sofa?

She looked up from the wallet, gazing at the face turned on the pillow. It was a strong-boned face with clear angles and planes and a blade of a nose. Not a handsome face, really, but certainly a compelling one. It bore a definite sexuality, a provocative virility that stirred her insides again.

Jordan glanced back at the photograph of the boy and felt a tenderness welling up inside her. This was absurd, crazy. They were strangers, and she had no business feeling anything but a temporary concern for Richard Davis's health.

She didn't want to go on handling the wallet. She was intruding on something that was personal and private. She laid the wallet on the table at the head of the sofa where he could easily find it.

When she checked the fire in the stove, adding chunks of wood, she discovered that there was still water in the kettle. It was steaming by now. She took the kettle into the kitchen and made herself a cup of tea. Her portable radio was on the counter. She was tempted to listen to it, but decided it was important to conserve the batteries. She would wait for six o'clock when there would be news and a weather report. She wanted to hear about any accidents on the lake that might explain why Richard Davis had landed on her beach.

She took her mug of tea and went back into the parlor, settling at the table that served as her desk under the window. She wouldn't have to bother with lighting any of the oil lamps until much later. It was that time of year when daylight went on forever. Besides, though the wind was still strong, the sky was rapidly clearing. The parlor benefited from its soft, strengthening glow.

Jordan bent over her work in the lonely silence, trying to concentrate on her notes for the book. It was a restless effort. She couldn't get her visitor out of her mind and kept glancing at his sleeping figure on the sofa. There was no use in pretending she wasn't deeply intrigued by the mystery of Richard Davis.

RICHARD OPENED HIS EYES and found himself gazing at unfamiliar surroundings. The room looked like something out of another era. It was sparsely furnished in country pieces of sturdy pine and oak, and there was a farmhouse-style paper on its walls that gave it a mood of snug cheerfulness. He didn't know where he was, but somehow he felt safe. Then he turned his head and discovered the woman writing at a table next to the window.

She was unaware of him. He studied her for a few seconds. He liked what he saw. Somewhere in her late twenties, he judged. He couldn't properly see her face because she was in profile and a curtain of silky, sable hair fell across her cheek as she bent to her work. But he could readily appreciate her figure in dark slacks and a white turtleneck sweater. It was slim and small, but the curves were definitely appealing.

She must have felt him staring at her. She glanced up, discovering that he was awake. Leaving the table, she came immediately to his side, leaning over him. He could see her clearly now. Warm brown eyes in a winsome face and a smile that was downright tantalizing.

"I see you're conscious once again," she observed. She had a husky, teasing voice that was as warm as her eyes.

Richard frowned. "I was conscious before now?"

"A couple of times. You don't remember?"

He shook his head. The last thing he could remember was struggling in the raging waters, fighting to stay alive and expecting to lose the battle.

"Well, you were out of it, all right," she admitted. "I guess you had a pretty bad time of it in the water before you crawled up on the beach. How are you feeling?"

"Like something large rolled over me." He felt stiff and sore all over, and his head still ached.

She chuckled. "Signs of recovery."

"I'll take your word for it. What is this place, anyway?"

"The Cana Island lighthouse."

"You mean the Coast Guard?" he asked quickly. Richard suddenly felt no longer safe. The horror aboard the yacht came back to him in a sickening rush, along with the panicked realization that by now he must be a wanted man.

She shook her head. "The light's automated. There hasn't been a keeper in years. I'm the only tenant now."

He had to get out of here. He had to leave. She must have contacted all sorts of people by now. They would be coming for him, and they wouldn't believe him. They would take him away in handcuffs, and he would lose any chance of clearing himself. Andrew would be all alone.

Richard started to sit up, to swing his feet to the floor. Then he realized he was naked under the blankets. "Where are my clothes?" he demanded.

"Whoa!" she ordered, pressing him flat again on the sofa. "Your clothes, which, by the way," she stressed, "you mostly removed yourself, are drying, and you're not going anywhere, even if you were in any condition to go somewhere."

The woman was bossy. "What does that mean?"

"The storm brought all the power lines down, and the road is blocked with fallen trees. We're stranded here."

"For how long?"

She shrugged. "Until they cut through to us. Certainly not before tomorrow sometime, if then."

"Telephone?"

"Afraid not. It went out with the power. Try not to worry about it," she reassured him, misunderstanding his alarm. "I know how anxious you've got to be to contact your people, but for now there's nothing we can do about it."

Richard relaxed. He was safe again. For the moment, anyway.

"Do you remember what happened to you out there in the lake?" she asked. "How you got here?"

"No," he lied.

She frowned. "I hope that doesn't mean amnesia. I guess it'll come back to you. Are you hungry? I could fix you something."

He shook his head. "I'd just like to sleep." He was feeling drowsy again. He cursed his feeble state. But he needed to sleep. He needed to recover his strength so he would be ready to leave. He had to search for the answers. Tomorrow, he promised himself. He would get away tomorrow before they had a chance to find him.

"Jordan Templeton," she said.

"What?" he murmured, settling his head against the pillow.

"My name. It's Jordan Templeton."

He didn't answer her. He shut his eyes and started to drift off. She had a soothing voice. And he liked her name. He was grateful Jordan Templeton had rescued him.

Chapter Two

"More after this," said the newscaster.

The station went to a commercial break. Jordan, perched on a stool drawn up to the counter, finished eating the sandwich she had fixed for herself. The local newscast so far had been disappointing. It amounted to repetitious reports of wind damage, power outages and scattered flooding throughout the county. There had been only one mention of any nautical accident, and that involved a fishing boat in the Green Bay waters clear on the other side of the peninsula. Nothing that could account for Richard Davis's situation.

"This just in."

The newscaster was back, and his hearty manner was suddenly subdued. Jordan, who was listening to the radio in the kitchen so as not to disturb her visitor, leaned forward with renewed interest.

"We have a bulletin on a missing craft in Lake Michigan waters off the northern half of the peninsula. The *Lady Anne,* a vintage yacht owned by Chicago industrialist Harry Fellows, is reported long overdue at the family's summer estate in Ephraim. It was last heard from early this afternoon. Repeated efforts since then to contact the vessel by radio have brought no results. Our source, a family connection, tells us that the *Lady Anne* was recently purchased by Mr. Fellows and was on its maiden run following a complete restoration and updating. Fellows, who is a familiar figure in the county, was on board with his daughter, Anne. We have yet to learn of any others who may have been accompanying them. Indications are that the Coast Guard is already conducting a full-scale search for the yacht. Stay tuned for the nine-o'clock report, when we hope to have further details.''

The weather followed, but Jordan didn't hear it. She was staring at the closed door to the parlor, thinking about the man on the other side. Was there a connection? Had Richard Davis been aboard that yacht?

Harry Fellows. She had met him once. Her grandfather had introduced her. The two men had shared a passionate interest in the marine lore of the Great Lakes, though nothing else. Harry Fellows was excessively self-important. Jordan hadn't particularly cared for him, but his extensive collection of nautical materials had impressed her.

She turned off the radio and went back to the parlor to check on her patient. He was still asleep. She didn't try to wake him, much as she wanted to hear his explanation. She fed the fire and seated herself at her desk again. But it was impossible to work. She kept thinking about the newscast, wondering if there had been some awful disaster out on the lake and whether Richard Davis had been involved in it. There was something else, something she hadn't felt before this. She was beginning to be uneasy about the man on the sofa.

The mellow light of sundown was casting long shadows in the room, and she was thinking about lighting the oil lamps, when she heard a deep sigh from the sofa. She turned her head and saw that he was awake again. She scraped her chair back and went to his side.

She tried not to sound anxious, to keep her voice even. ''Can I get you anything?''

''Thirsty,'' he said.

''How about some broth? I have a mug of it keeping hot on the stove. You should have some kind of nourishment.''

''Sounds good.''

She got the broth for him and helped him to sit up against the arm of the sofa so he could drink it. He downed the brew in greedy gulps and then handed the mug back to her, thanking her.

"How long have I been here like this?" he wondered. She hadn't noticed before how deep and rich his voice was, but there was considerable worry in it.

"A couple of hours." She made her own tone as casual as possible. "Do you think you could tell me now what happened?"

He closed his eyes and slid his long body flat again on the sofa. "Just want to sleep."

Did he? She wasn't so sure this time. Maybe he was deliberately avoiding answers. She watched him for a few seconds. His breathing was slow and even, the rhythmical breathing of deep sleep. She'd just have to wait for that nine-o'clock newscast.

DARKNESS HAD SETTLED over the island. Jordan sat on the stool in the kitchen and listened to the wind keening around the house and the steady, dull rumble of the surf on the shore. They were sounds she had always loved, lulling her to sleep in her bed, but tonight they made her nervous.

They also made her remember Dwight's last warning to her when she left Chicago. "You're essentially a city girl, Jordan," he had scoffed. "It was one thing to spend summers on the peninsula as a kid when your grandfather was alive, but you'll go crazy up there all on your own." He'd thought from the beginning that her whole intention was a big mistake. By then she'd known that Dwight Jamison was her only real mistake. So why was she letting his scornful predictions depress her now?

Maybe the insufficient light of the single oil lamp on the counter was responsible for her mood. It left the corners of the room in pools of deep shadow.

She was deceiving herself, of course. It wasn't the weather, memories or the lack of electricity that made her

tense. It was what she feared she might hear on the next
newscast, and she didn't understand her nagging apprehension. She just knew that she had this growing premonition
that something was terribly wrong where Richard Davis was
concerned.

She glanced at her watch. It was time. She bent forward
and turned on the radio. She was careful to keep the volume low. It wasn't because she didn't want to disturb the
man in the next room. Not this time. It was because she
didn't want him to know she had a radio and was listening
to it. Maybe her caution was unnecessary. Maybe she was
being imaginative. But she didn't turn up the volume.

A commercial was just ending. The newscaster came on.
There was a gravity in his voice that brought Jordan's heart
up into her throat as she strained to hear his report.

"For those of you who may have missed our eight-o'clock
interruption of the regular broadcast, I'll repeat. The missing Fellows yacht was located by the Coast Guard drifting
off Four Foot Shoal at approximately seven o'clock this
evening. Officials now confirm that there are no survivors.
Among the dead are industrialist Harry Fellows, his
daughter, Anne, and their pilot, John 'Mac' McGuire. The
Door County sheriff's department is no longer denying that
all three victims were found shot to death."

Jordan, stunned, clapped a hand to her mouth.

"In an update on this tragedy," the newscaster continued, "there is this release from the sheriff's department. It
is now verified that Richard Davis, the former son-in-law of
Harry Fellows and ex-husband of daughter Anne, joined the
yacht when it stopped at Two Rivers around noon. Davis
was not aboard the vessel when it was found tonight. The
single lifeboat was missing. This department is now looking for Richard Davis."

Jordan numbly listened as a physical description followed, along with a chilling warning that Richard Davis
could be armed and dangerous.

"We'll bring you any further developments on this situation as they come to us," finished the newscaster.

The station resumed its program of rock music. She went on sitting there on the stool, feeling very weak suddenly, her mind crawling with horrifying images of the three bodies discovered aboard the drifting yacht. It was appalling.

Richard Davis was a wanted man. They hadn't said he had murdered them, but they must believe he was the killer, that there could be no other explanation. And she was trapped with him here in her own house!

Her hand was shaking as she switched off the radio. Limp with fear, she tried to decide what to do. Without the telephone she had no way of contacting the sheriff, no way of calling for help. She was all alone with a man suspected of a brutal mass murder.

She was still without any decision when, seconds later, there was a soft thud from behind the closed door to the parlor. Startled, she slid off the stool, staring at the door.

She lost no time in snatching the radio from the counter. She thrust it into one of the cupboards behind some cereal boxes. There was one certainty, anyway. She must keep him from knowing that she had learned what had happened out on the lake. It was her only defense.

The temptation to flee out the back door and into the night was very strong. But where could she possibly go, stranded on a tiny island in the dark? It would be much better not to panic, to wait until she had a plan. She couldn't go on huddling here in the kitchen, either. She had to go into the parlor and pretend that there was nothing wrong.

Sick with dread and struggling not to show it, Jordan went into the other room. She'd left one of the oil lamps burning on her worktable. It revealed him sitting up on the sofa, hugging one of the blankets around him. He was holding a flashlight that had been on the chair near the sofa. He must have accidentally knocked it to the floor. That was the thud she had heard.

"Sorry to be so much trouble," he said. He wore a thin, crooked smile as he looked up at her. A smile that was treacherously attractive.

She gazed at him warily. He still looked a little fuzzy about things, but his color was much better and he held himself as though he felt a lot stronger. She didn't welcome his recovery now. His strength would only make him potentially dangerous to her. But she couldn't let him guess that.

"You look a lot improved," she said, amazed at her own calmness. "Is there anything you need?"

"As a matter of fact, I could use a bathroom."

"Sorry. No running water without the electricity. But there is a backhouse close outside."

"That'll do."

She watched him slide his bare feet into the deck shoes waiting beside the sofa. "Do you need any help getting out there?" she offered, praying he didn't.

"No, I'll manage."

She was relieved. She didn't want to have to touch him again, knowing what she did. It wasn't because she was afraid he would hurt her. He had no reason to. Not yet, anyway. It was because of the sensations he aroused in her every time they came in contact. She couldn't risk repeating those unsettling feelings.

It was bad enough watching his half-naked, rugged figure heaving himself to his feet, the blanket wrapped around him toga-style. Had the situation been otherwise, there would have been something oddly endearing in the sight of him like that. How was it possible to perceive a man in one moment with innocent trust and in the next to regard him as a horrible threat?

He took the flashlight and started toward the door. Then he stopped, wearing a puzzled frown.

"What is it?" she asked, striving to keep the tension from her voice.

"Just something I remembered. I thought I heard sounds in the kitchen when I woke up a minute ago, like music or voices maybe."

"It was me," she lied quickly. "I was singing."

"Oh." He directed that disarming smile at her again. "That's nice."

He left the room, and Jordan breathed in relief. Through the window she watched the wavering glow of the flashlight as he went along the path. She was grateful for his absence. It gave her the chance to consider her options. But in the end there was only one choice.

Scared though she was, she couldn't leave. She kept no boat on the island and it would be suicidal trying to cross that flooded causeway on foot in the dark, even with a flashlight. She would have to wait until morning when there was light, and by then maybe the waves would be down. She would have to stay here in the house with him and somehow find the courage to get through the long night.

There was one thing in her favor. He had no reason to be nervous about her, and she had to keep him that way. No wonder he had failed to offer any explanation about his mysterious arrival on her beach. Well, he could go on being silent. She wasn't going to press him now, risk his suspicions.

There was something else. He didn't have a weapon. If there had been a gun on him when he left the yacht, it had been lost in the waters. Not that it mattered a lot if he was capable of murderous rages. It was a dangerous situation however she viewed it, and maybe her decision to stay was a foolish mistake. But if she was very careful, stayed vigilant—

A sudden noise outside made her jump. It was all right. It was nothing but the clanging of the hand pump. He had left the outhouse and was washing his hands. He would be back in the parlor in another minute. She didn't want him to find her just standing here like this waiting anxiously. She used the opportunity to tend the fire.

She was at the stove, poker in hand, when he came back into the room and returned the flashlight to the chair. "Here," he offered, crossing to her side, "I'll do that."

"No, it's all right."

But he was insistent, taking the poker from her hand. When his hand brushed against hers, his nearness made her breath stick in her throat. It wasn't fear she felt, but it should have been. Why was she being so irrational?

She didn't want him to have the poker, though. The image of him brandishing it wasn't a pleasant one. But it would have been a mistake struggling to keep it. He'd wonder why she was so resistant. She edged away from him, watching him as he innocently stirred the fire and added wood.

"It's time I made myself useful," he said.

The glow of the flames lit his angular face. She studied his expression, looking for something sinister and finding only a quiet thoughtfulness.

She swallowed dryly as he closed the doors on the stove and turned to her. "I'm a bad guest," he said, his voice gruff with embarrassment. "I haven't shown my appreciation for all you've done, for taking me in like this. You're a pretty special woman."

What did he have to go and do that for? Thanking her in that bone-melting way? It only made it harder. She needed to get away from him.

"The special woman has had it for the day," she said lightly. "If you don't mind I'm going to say good-night."

"I think I'll turn in myself. You wouldn't imagine I'd have any sleep left in me, but I'm still tired."

"It's understandable after what you've been through," she encouraged him, hoping he would sleep through the night. "Are you all right on the sofa? There are other bedrooms upstairs, but none of them are heated or furnished."

"The sofa is fine, long enough even for me. Don't worry."

"Good night, then." She took the flashlight and started for her bedroom. At the door she glanced over her shoulder, feeling a need to check on his movements before she slipped inside.

He was bending over the table at the side of the sofa, discovering his wallet that she had placed there earlier. She stiffened in alarm. She had forgotten the wallet. He would know now that she had handled it, probably seen the contents and learned his identity. But there was nothing incriminating in the wallet, nothing that should arouse him.

"It dropped out when you were undressing," she said nonchalantly. "I'm afraid it got pretty soaked."

He nodded slowly without looking at her. "It's all right. There's nothing that won't dry."

He opened the wallet, but he didn't seem to be interested in checking its contents. The only thing that interested him was the single photograph. He seemed to forget about her as he gazed at it.

The last thing Jordan saw, and wished she hadn't seen, before she escaped into her room was the soft, vulnerable expression on Richard Davis's face as he studied the small face in the photo.

THE OLD-FASHIONED RIM lock on her bedroom door no longer worked. There had never been any need to lock the inside doors. Even though she'd been alone, she had always felt safe. Until now.

With the aid of the flashlight she quietly wedged a chair under the knob of the closed door. It was probably an ineffective barrier, but at least it gave her a semblance of security.

There was no question of undressing and going to bed. She meant to stay as alert as possible through the night. The room was cold. With the door shut, the stove was unable to provide heat. She took the quilt from the bed and bundled into it.

There was a comfortable rocking chair under the window. She settled into it. Her position allowed her to keep an eye on the door. There were no sounds from the parlor. The silence in the house should have been reassuring, but knowing what she did, it only added to her strain.

Dwight Jamison's self-assured voice inside her head mocked her again. "You've got no business staying there all alone, Jordan. The place is too remote. In a situation like that, a woman on her own is just a sitting target." Dwight had hated the island. Last fall, after signing a year's lease on the lighthouse and before she made the decision to take a leave of absence from the magazine and spend the summer here, she had invited Dwight to join her for one of her weekends on the island. It had been an awkward two days. He had been restless and disapproving. That was when she had begun to realize how ill suited they were to each other. She hated to think now that Dwight had been right about her existence here.

Jordan went on sitting there in the dark, holding the flashlight in her lap, ready to leap to her feet if there should be any sudden noise from the other room. Her mind churned with questions about the man on the other side of the door.

The radio had indicated the lifeboat was missing from the *Lady Anne,* the assumption being that Richard Davis had fled the yacht in it. But he hadn't arrived on her beach in the lifeboat. Possibly it had capsized in the stormy waters. In any case, it wasn't important. For her, only the question of his guilt mattered.

Maybe she was judging him wrongly. She kept remembering the expression on his face, tender, cherishing, as he gazed down at the young face in the photograph in his wallet. How could a man capable of such moving devotion to a child be evil, a mass murderer? But she knew it was possible, that the Jekyll-and-Hyde personality of a psychopath could strike in a blind rage and then afterward revert to a gentle innocence that failed to even remember he had killed. Maybe Richard Davis was such a personality.

There were other images that haunted her as she waited in the rocker. The shape of his craggy face smiling at her so warmly. The feel of his solid body slumping against her helplessly. The brush of his hand on her skin stirring sweet longings deep inside her. They were dangerous images, jeopardizing her safety. If she surrendered to them, failed to remember that he was wanted for a shocking massacre, she could become his next victim. She had to fight those images, resist them for the sake of her own survival.

Jordan shivered and drew the quilt around her more snugly. Her body, unable to bear the prolonged stress, gradually relaxed. She dozed fitfully, suffering hideous nightmares. Between naps she used the flashlight to consult her watch. The long hours of the night crawled by agonizingly. She wondered if morning would ever come.

She dropped off again, and then sometime later she came awake with a start. The room was still dark. She leaned forward in the rocker, rigid, listening. Yes, there was a rustling in the next room. He was stirring.

Heart thudding against her ribs, Jordan eased her stiff body out of the rocker and crept toward the door. She laid her ear against the panel, straining to hear what was happening on the other side. One of the old parlor floorboards creaked softly, betraying his careful movements. She waited tensely, expecting to find her doorknob turning furtively. But there was silence now. Nothing.

She couldn't stand not knowing what he was doing. She had to risk cracking the door to learn why he was stalking through the house. Her imagination would go crazy otherwise.

Hardly daring to breathe, she slipped the chair away from the doorknob. Then, with the quilt clutched around her, she slid the door back a few inches and peered fearfully through the opening. The lamp was still burning on the table where she had left it for him, its weak glow lighting the room.

He was just returning from the kitchen. He came to a halt, discovering her through the narrow opening. He smiled at her sheepishly.

"Sorry if I woke you," he apologized. "I was putting more wood on the fire, and then I went into the kitchen to find a drink of water."

Jordan found she could breathe again. "Oh," she said.

He gazed at her questioningly, aware of her tautness. "You okay?"

"Yes, fine," she assured him hoarsely. "Did you get your water?"

"There was a bottle on the counter. Hope it was all right to use it."

"Yes, I filled it from the hand pump."

There was an awkward pause, and then he shifted the blanket around his potent body and nodded. "Well, good night."

She closed the door and fixed the chair under the knob again. She was shaking as she went back to the rocker. She couldn't stand it. This mixture of fear and sexual awareness of him was awful, all wrong. And waiting for morning was no better, each minute dragging by like an hour. She leaned back in the rocker, shutting her eyes, but she knew there was no way she could rest.

JORDAN WAS AMAZED when she opened her eyes again to see the first gray light of daybreak stealing into the room. She must have slept after all.

It was time.

Pushing up from the rocker, she dropped the quilt onto the bed and began to make her preparations. There was a sharp chill in the room. The air outside would be colder. She changed into jeans and a warm, bulky sweater. She added her windbreaker, slipped into a pair of stout walking shoes and she was ready.

Stealing to the door, she listened. The parlor was silent. Presumably he was still asleep. She moved to the window and quietly began to raise the sash. She grimaced as the old wood squeaked. She paused to listen again. Nothing stirred in the other room. She went back to lifting the sash. It went up smoothly this time.

When she swung her leg over the sill, glancing back at the door one last time, she experienced a quick pang of regret, the illogical feeling that she was running out on him. But it was a reckless emotion she couldn't afford.

The drop to the ground was not far. She landed softly in the damp earth. There was no point in trying to lower the window behind her. She took off through the shadows around the side of the house, using the lilac bushes as a cover. When the bushes ended she had no choice but to move out into the open in order to cross the clearing. Two of the parlor windows overlooked the clearing. She could only pray that he wasn't standing at one of them as she sprinted across the dewy grass.

With relief she gained the concealing trees on the other side. She looked back over her shoulder. The clearing was silent and still. The wide track in front of her curved through the woodland and she followed it, stepping over torn limbs. The results of yesterday's storm were everywhere. But today the sky would be clear. The pure, crisp air was alive with bird song, the horizon tinted pink with the promise of sunrise.

Jordan's heart sank as she emerged from the trees on the back side of the island. The wind was down, and she had hoped to cross a dry causeway. But the waves, though sluggish now and much lower, were still piling over the stony ridge.

She had no choice but to wade across the causeway. A tricky, time-consuming business but necessary if she was to hike out of here and find a telephone somewhere that still worked. She sat on a flat boulder and began to remove her shoes.

THE FIRST SIGNS OF DAWN were lighting the parlor windows when Richard came awake. He lay there for a moment on the sofa, testing his recovery. As far as he could tell, he was fully recuperated. No headache, no grogginess, no more soreness in his limbs. He gingerly fingered the lump on the back of his skull. It was still a little tender, but the swelling had lessened considerably. His long hours of sleep had restored his body to a clearheaded strength.

It was time for him to move on. He couldn't stay and risk involving the woman in the next room. He might already have compromised her. She could be accused of aiding a fugitive. He deeply regretted that possibility, even though he'd had no choice in the matter.

Well, he'd be on his way just as soon as he could. He had no idea where he was going or what he was going to do. He just knew that he had to stay free until he could figure out some way to extricate himself from this ghastly business. It was too late now to go to the police. They'd never believe him. Everything pointed to his guilt.

Determined, Richard swung his long legs to the floor and got to his feet. The room was cold. He padded to the stove and made a fresh fire. The lamp was still burning on the table. He blew it out and then began gathering his clothes from the chair backs. They were fully dry now, though the jeans were like cardboard. They'd soften up with wear.

He dressed quietly in the gloom, careful not to disturb Jordan in her bedroom. Her door was closed. He figured she was still asleep.

He had a longing for a bath and fresh clothes, and he was conscious of a stubble on his jaw. Forget it. They weren't important. He'd have to get used to himself like this. Something told him it might be a while, maybe a *long* while, before he enjoyed ordinary comforts again.

His gaze went back to the bedroom door as he recovered his wallet from the table and pocketed it. He'd have to offer her some kind of explanation before he left. He couldn't just take off and leave her wondering, though he knew she'd hear the truth soon enough. The thought of what she would think about him when she learned what had happened out on the lake made him tense.

It didn't make any sense, but he hated the thought of leaving her. It was more than just a physical attraction, strong though that was. She was warm and caring, and she had stirred something in him. Something he hadn't felt in a long time. But there was no point in dwelling on that. It wasn't a thing that could go anywhere, not with this nightmare hanging over his head. It would be better to just thank her and get out.

He crossed to her door, prepared to rap on it. But his courage failed him. He dreaded facing her with a lie. He'd give himself a little more time, and maybe he could come up with something close to the truth that wouldn't alarm her. Meanwhile, he was hollow inside. He hadn't eaten a thing since before noon yesterday. He didn't think she'd mind if he raided her kitchen.

Keeping as silent as possible, he went into the kitchen and closed the door behind him. With the power off, there was no way to brew coffee or scramble an egg, tempting though both would be. It would have to be something cold. Cereal, maybe. He began opening cupboard doors, investigating her supplies. He found corn flakes.

He drew the cereal box off the shelf, and that was when he discovered the portable radio concealed behind it. At first he was simply puzzled, wondering why a radio was hiding behind cereal boxes. It wasn't until he slid the radio out of the cupboard and realized it was a battery model, not dependent on house current, that the truth came to him. He felt as if he'd been slugged in the gut.

If they'd found the yacht and what was aboard it, it would have been all over the news. She must have been listening to the reports last night when she was alone in the kitchen. She *knew*.

He cursed himself for a fool. Of course, way out here on her own, she'd have a battery radio. He should have realized that. But then, his muddled brain had been in no state yesterday to consider the possibility. Maybe he was overreacting. Maybe they hadn't learned yet that he'd been aboard the *Lady Anne*. If his name hadn't been mentioned, she wouldn't know he was involved.

But then, why had she withheld any mention of the broadcasts? Why had she hidden the radio? And there was another thing that he suddenly remembered. Last night when he'd said something about hearing voices in the kitchen, Jordan had claimed she was singing. She'd been nervous with him, too, at one point. Like the fool he was, he'd gone and blamed it on their growing awareness of each other.

He had to be sure, though. He couldn't just go to her and blurt it all out, panic her unnecessarily if, in fact, she wasn't yet aware of his connection with the horror on the yacht. She didn't deserve that, not after all she had done for him.

The radio might tell him.

He placed the instrument on the counter and turned it on. As early as it was, he managed to find a station that had the news. He caught the middle of the broadcast, and he heard everything he feared to hear.

"...now been established that wealthy industrialist Harry Fellows owned a Colt .38 automatic. It was a weapon of this caliber that killed all three victims. There seems to be little doubt that it was probably the same pistol carried by Fellows, although the gun was not aboard the yacht when it was searched.

"Meanwhile, the manhunt for former son-in-law Richard Davis is in progress, but efforts have been hampered by severe conditions resulting from yesterday's storm. Davis is wanted for questioning in connection with—"

Richard turned off the radio. He didn't want to listen to the rest. He had learned all he needed to know. He stood there, eyes squeezed shut, as a heavy despair settled over him.

It was true, then. Jordan must have heard all this last night. What must she be thinking about him, feeling about him? The absolute worst, of course. He had to talk to her, try to set her straight.

He turned and with quick strides hurried into the parlor.
He raised his hand and, without hesitation, banged on her
door. No response. He tried the door. Something was
blocking it from the other side. His heart dropped in his
chest as he began to understand. He put his shoulder against
the door and shoved. The chair under the knob offered little resistance. It clattered to the floor as he burst into the
room. Her bed was empty, and the window was wide open.
She was gone.

Richard didn't remember racing out of the house. The
next thing he knew he was standing out in the middle of the
clearing, desperation clawing at his insides. Andrew's welfare depended on his freedom, and Jordan Templeton was
somewhere loose out there threatening that freedom.

He swiftly scanned the clearing. Where had she gone? In
which direction? He spotted a wide track that tunneled
through the trees. It had to be the way off the island.

He took off at a fast trot, his long legs carrying him rapidly through the narrow belt of woods. There was only one
thought in his head. He had to get her back before she could
turn him in. He had to make her understand.

Chapter Three

The water was shockingly cold. Jordan gasped as the lake, still frigid after the long winter, closed around her ankles, swirled up toward her calves and threatened her knees where her rolled-up jeans were damp from the spray.

She had crossed the causeway before when it was under water, but never at this season and never when need made it so essential to reach the roadway on the far side. She wanted to hurry, to slam recklessly through the shallows to dry land. But that would be a mistake. As it was, she was fighting for her balance against the wash of the waves tugging at her legs and the stones cutting painfully into the soles of her bare feet. And all the while she was conscious of the precious minutes speeding by.

Had he awakened yet back at the house, found her gone? Was he even now searching for her?

The causeway was a hundred yards or so in length. It felt like a mile. She was halfway across now. She couldn't stand not knowing if he was behind her. She stole a moment to stop and turn, searching the track where it emerged from the woods. Empty. No sign of him so far.

But there was a sight that made her grimace with worry. Above the tops of the trees rose the tower, its graceful shaft a luminous white, the windows of its head glinting like polished mirrors. Evidence that the sun had already risen off the lake behind the woods. It was later than she thought. There was no time to lose.

Jordan pressed on. Her shoes, looped around her neck by their joined laces, swung against her like wild pendulums. The causeway dipped, the water deepening. The stones were rough, treacherous. She slipped, almost lost her footing, righted herself. Then, bit by bit, the depth lessened. It was just over her ankles. The stones were also smoother, but they were slick, too, preventing her from rushing. The waters receded. She was on dry rock.

I made it, I made it, she breathed in a litany of silent relief. Now she could hurry. She wasted no time in gaining the roadway. The sun was on this side by now, spangling the blue waters of the small crescent bay to the left, winking off the windshield of her well-traveled green Volvo.

She mourned the uselessness of her car in the situation, regretted, too, her failure to equip it with a phone. But its front fender offered a handy support for her as she struggled to replace her shoes and socks.

She kept checking the island on the other side, knowing she wouldn't feel safe until it was out of sight behind her, until she had put distance between herself and the causeway. And even then . . .

She was tying her second shoe when it happened. One second there was nothing, and in the next the rangy figure of Richard Davis was there on the opposite shore. No time for her to hide, no place for her to hide. She was in the open, and he spotted her at once braced against her car.

She straightened, heart galloping in her chest as he shouted to her. "Jordan, don't! Don't run out on me. At least let me explain. I'll stay on this side if you'll just let me talk to you."

She wasn't falling for that. She wouldn't favor him with an answer, either. There was no point in it. She began to back along the side of the car, keeping a wary eye on him. He didn't hesitate when he saw her starting to get away. He splashed into the waters of the causeway. She knew his long

legs and athletic body would eat up the distance in no time.
She didn't wait. She turned and ran.

The asphalt road tunneled through the evergreen forest,
a dark, winding ribbon that carried her around a bend and
out of sight of the causeway and her pursuer. Within minutes of her flight along its length, Jordan realized that, as an
escape route, it was a grave mistake. The road was an obstacle course of storm-felled trees and downed power lines,
hazards she had to detour around or scramble over.

It was like a war zone, she thought, and she could be one
of its victims. At this rate he would easily overtake her, and
she would be helpless to prevent him from silencing her.

She was breathing hard and battling panic as the roadway curled around the side of the bay. There were summer
cottages along here, but even if she could manage to break
in to one of them she would find no working phone. Nor did
she want to try to hide in such a place and risk being
trapped. How could she hope to evade him?

She was clambering through the tortured boughs of a
massive cedar, sorry even in her terror that the storm had
sacrificed such a splendid old monarch, when the answer
came to her. The nature preserve!

Her grandfather had introduced her to the place years
ago. It was extensive in area, thickly wooded, and the access to its depths was a rarely used footpath off the roadway less than a quarter of a mile away. Even better, the path
ended on the other side of the preserve at another county
road. There was a cabin there, the year-round home of an
eccentric. Jordan had met him once. The cabin had a telephone, and a pickup truck parked in its yard, and if neither
was of any use she was sure the old fellow's shotgun would
be.

It had been a long time since Jordan had walked the path,
and she nearly missed it. She lost frantic seconds searching
for its mouth. Almost overgrown with lush thimbleberries,
merely a thread now, but that was all to the good. With any

luck, Richard Davis would be too desperate to catch up with her to notice the path.

Her breathing ragged, she looked back down the winding roadway. He was not in sight yet, but she never doubted that he was close behind her and coming fast. She needed to disappear.

Jordan plunged through the waist-high thimbleberries, trying not to tear them, wanting to leave no sign of her exit from the roadway. The thimbleberries thinned as the cool, shadowy woods closed around her. The path widened. It was damp underfoot from yesterday's heavy rains, strewn with soggy needles, but the soft, black earth was exposed in other places. She left telltale prints in these spots and regretted them. It couldn't be helped.

Her lungs were raw now, but she didn't dare to slacken her pace. She rushed forward without pause, listening for the sound of crashing brush behind her. Where was he? How near? She heard nothing but the early-morning songs of the finches, saw no movement but the shifting patterns of sunlight on drifts of trillium already past their bloom and yellow lady's slippers just coming into flower. Sweet calls, restful scenes, and they were a mockery of her terror. Spring in all its loving glory, and she was running for her life.

She came to a fork in the path. She had forgotten the trail divided here. It was the left branch she needed. The other led to a wilderness swamp where the marsh marigolds dazzled the eye with their golden brilliance.

She chose her route and moved on. Less than a hundred yards past the fork the stillness exploded with the crackling of a brittle limb. A dark form concealed behind an uprooted hemlock leapt in front of her.

Jordan's heart went into her throat.

The shape tore across the path directly in front of her and bounded off through the undergrowth. No ambush. Not Richard Davis. Just a deer browsing on the fallen hemlock, and she had startled the animal. She sagged in relief.

She was mistaken, she instantly realized. She wasn't safe at all. There was suddenly another sound, this time behind her. The pounding of running feet. He had found the path and was following her trail!

She forced back a sob of despair. It wouldn't help. Nor at this point would further flight do her any good. He was too close. He would reach her in no time.

Well, she wasn't going to stand there and helplessly wait for him. She needed to hide. It was her only hope.

She ducked under the boughs of the toppled hemlock. There was a hollow thick with bracken. She waded through the luxuriant stuff until she was well off the path, and then she dropped flat, concealing herself among the ferns. Just in time. He came racing along the path on the other side of the hemlock. She waited for him to move on by, *prayed* he would move on by. It didn't happen. His steps slowed, stopped. She could feel him there behind the hemlock, only yards away.

Why had he stopped? Did he sense her nearness? Did he detect signs of her having left the path? There was silence. Unbearable silence. She kept still, willed herself not to breathe.

She went on hugging the forest floor, aware of its sponginess, of the tangy odors of mold and fern. Aware of a patch of dwarf lake iris, a delicate lavender blooming at the lichen-encrusted skirts of a spruce tree close by. Aware, too, of the chime of a rose-breasted grosbeak somewhere off in the woods. Again she thought of the irony of nature being ordinary while a killer stalked her. She had a desire to laugh.

"Jordan?"

She stiffened.

"Jordan," he called to her again from the path, "are you there? Come out and let me talk to you. I won't touch you, I won't come near you. I promise all I want to do is talk to you."

His voice was deep, beguiling and dangerous. Had he used that same slow, rich voice to lure the others aboard the yacht to their deaths? The voice of a deceptively virile devil. How could she have been so gullible?

There was silence again from the path. Chilling. She waited, allowing the seconds to drag on by. When she could no longer bear the suspense, she risked lifting her head to peer over the ferns.

There was a gap in the drooping limbs of the hemlock. She could see the path. It was empty. But she dared not leave her hiding place. Not yet. She had to be certain he was really gone. She strained her senses like a hunted animal, afraid that he was still lurking somewhere nearby just waiting to pounce on her.

A half minute later she caught the faint sound of him moving swiftly along the path in the distance. He must have decided in the end that she was still ahead of him. She was all right. For the moment.

Levering herself to her feet, she returned to the path, steadying herself with a fistful of feathery needles as she slid through the screening hemlock.

She checked both directions, then decided what she had to do. Continuing along the trail was out of the question. He could be waiting around any turn ahead of her. How was she to reach the cabin and help without running into him?

There was a way. She could go back to the fork, take the other path. She remembered a footbridge across the swamp at its narrowest point and then a rough trail to the back road she wanted. It was an indirect, longer route but her only chance now of staying out of his way.

She reached the turning and flew along the alternative path. The bridge was even farther than she recalled. Her lungs were burning with her urgency before she glimpsed the sunlit, watery expanse of the swamp through the trees.

Someone had laid planks along the muddy approach to the bridge. Gray and crumbling, they had been there a long time. So had the bridge. Jordan viewed it with concern as she edged her way onto its lip.

It was a rustic, weathered affair with several zigzags along its length to lend it interest for the nature observer. The bridge was intended not so much for crossing as for a leisurely viewing of the swamp's waterfowl and vegetation. For that reason, perhaps, the low structure hadn't been a priority on its builder's maintenance list. Some of the timbers were sagging in places, clearly the victims of rot. Would the thing bear her weight? There was only one way to find out.

Jordan started over the bridge, stepping around gaps, avoiding the obviously soft places. She willed herself not to hurry, to proceed with every caution. She would be all right as long as she didn't panic. The essential framework was still solid enough. At least, she hoped it was because the prospect of tumbling into all that thick, slimy ooze was enough to make her shudder.

The swamp, swollen with rain, was choked with water lilies, mossy, decaying logs and tangled grass. Just under this sprawling vegetation was deep mud as treacherous as quicksand. It was a dismal place but also fascinating. There was proof of that when, two thirds of the way across, a noisy flapping startled her. Turning her head, she watched a great blue heron rising into the air with an effortless grace. When she faced forward again, she discovered she was no longer alone. Richard Davis waited for her on the end of the bridge.

Jordan's insides tightened with alarm. All her effort had been for nothing. As careful as she had been, he must have somehow heard her and cut straight through the woods to intercept her. And now he stood there, a calm sentinel certain of her defeat. She wanted to cry in desperation.

She didn't cry, either in fear or surrender. Instead she got angry, blindly angry. How dare he terrorize her, chase her down like an animal? Well, he wasn't going to have her! She wasn't going to let him win!

They stood there in the sudden, taut stillness, measuring each other across the mere yards that separated them. She was vulnerable on the bridge. She had to get off the bridge. She started to back away, keeping her gaze locked on him.

"Jordan, wait. This is silly. You don't have anywhere left to run. You don't have a choice now but to listen to me."

Fueled by her outrage, she increased her speed. Harder and faster she backed away, straight into one of the zigzags behind her. Her full weight slammed against the angled railing. The rail was rotten. It failed to support her.

There was the fearful sound of tearing wood together with her strangled cry. Her hands beat the air, searching wildly for a solid surface that wasn't there. She went down feet first, dropping like a stone.

It was so quick none of it really registered with her. The only reality was the horror of suddenly finding herself thigh-deep in the malodorous muck that was slowly, stubbornly dragging her down like a loathsome glue. Every hideous tale she had ever heard of people being trapped in quicksand, dying by slow, agonizing suffocation, flashed through her mind. Panic clawed at her, and she began to struggle, her arms flailing at the watery surface in a useless frenzy.

"Jordan, don't! Don't fight it! You're just making it worse!"

His voice came from above her. It was steady and commanding, and she listened to it. She listened because he made sense. She stopped floundering. Her gaze lifted, searched, then encountered a pair of blue eyes that clung to hers with an intense forcefulness.

He was on the bridge in the spot where she had fallen, his long form stretched flat across its width. His right arm strained toward her, but she was out of his reach.

"Jordan, you have to help me." His voice was patient, compelling. "Just lean toward me. Do it slowly. Lean toward me and grip my hand. That's all you have to do. I'll do the rest."

She couldn't. The insidious mud was sucking her down. It was almost to her hips now. His hand was a lifeline, and she couldn't manage the simple act of clasping it. It would be trading one evil for another. But if she didn't reach for him...

Trust hung in the balance for long, precious seconds.

"Jordan, listen to me," he said softly, understanding her resistance. "You have to listen to me now and believe it. I promise you I didn't kill them. Do you understand, Jordan? *I didn't kill them.*"

She stared at him for the space of several heartbeats, shaken by his words and the realization of what she had done. Without so much as a hearing, without reason or fairness, she had both condemned and sentenced him in her mind. Though she was far from certain of his innocence, she was no longer sure of his guilt. Only one thing was clear. He was striving to save her, and it didn't matter if there was some dark purpose behind his effort. Because if she didn't trust him, she would perish. There was simply no choice in the situation. There never had been.

She obeyed his instruction, bending forward, extending her arm as far as it would go. His hand, strong and confident, grasped hers. Bracing himself, he began to haul her toward him, dragging her up out of the clinging mud. Within seconds they both stood safely on the bridge, confronting each other. His hand was still clutching hers.

"Are you all right?"

She nodded.

Richard wasn't so sure. She was wet, caked with mud from the waist down and she looked miserable. She was also trembling visibly. Fear of him? Of his intention now that he had recovered her?

Suddenly nothing was so important to him as convincing her that she had no reason to be frightened of him. "I'm not going to hurt you, Jordan," he promised her gently. "I'd never hurt you."

"I know," she whispered. "At least I think I know that much now."

But she wasn't positive, he realized. And, all things considered, he didn't blame her. Just the same, he hated knowing that she wasn't able to fully trust him. He wasn't sure why her faith should matter to him so much. It made about as much sense in this moment as the tender urge that was swelling inside him.

He couldn't help it. He looked down at her and saw a spirited face framed in sable hair and a pair of brown eyes that gazed up at him with uncertainty. Eyes that were wide and defenseless, wearing an expression that made him want to cherish her.

He didn't care that it was the wrong time and the wrong place. He could no longer stop himself. He drew her toward him, then released her hand so that both his arms were free to encircle her, to press her pliant body against the wall of his chest. And once she was secure in his arms, accepting his embrace, he did what he had been longing to do from that first minute on the sofa last night when he had opened his eyes and discovered her leaning over him, an alluring stranger wearing a warm, concerned smile.

Jordan didn't resist when his mouth angled over hers. She was too spent to fight what some part of her had been wanting all along anyway. Her mouth opened under his, welcoming his invasion. Their tongues mingled, tasted, investigated. It was a searing, consuming business, much more potent than she'd anticipated. And perhaps just as dangerous. She was sure of it when his hands shifted and began to caress the sensitive sides of her breasts.

Weak from his prolonged, loving assault, she tried to tell herself that their fiery joining was simply the result of a supercharged moment, a reaction of their tense emotions that demanded a form of release. It could have no other meaning. But the trouble was she wasn't sure.

Her senses were on a rampage when he finally released her. She needed to bring them into control. She also needed to be convinced that she hadn't made a vile mistake, that the man she'd just kissed wasn't a monster. That was why, when she found she could breathe again, she murmured anxiously, "There's just one request I have."

His blue eyes were quizzical, amused. This was hardly the response he'd expected from her. "What is it?"

One request, she thought. But his reaction to it was important to her. It could decide whether she wanted to start believing in him. "Tell me about the boy in the photograph inside your wallet."

His eyes expressed no humor now. They were totally sober, as was his voice when he told her softly, "If you haven't guessed, he's my son, Andrew. It was his mother who was murdered. I don't blame you for being scared of me, Jordan, or the police for wanting me, because the truth is, I probably have the only logical motive for being her killer."

Chapter Four

"I'm not sure I ever really loved her," Richard confided across the kitchen table while the morning sun wove patterns on the mellow pine of an old cupboard. "Whatever it was, or I thought it was in the beginning, it was over long before we were divorced. But to want her, or her father, dead? No. Not even after all that happened."

"Just what did happen?" Jordan urged. Why her understanding should matter so much to both of them, just as it had back at the bridge, was a subject neither of them was ready to define. For now, it was enough to know that she cared and that he needed her to care.

"A battle over Andrew," he said bitterly, "and I can't forgive either one of us that."

Richard paused to gulp a mouthful of strong coffee from the mug in front of him. They were back at the lighthouse and sharing a hot breakfast following her quick wash and a change into dry clothes.

He gazed at her over the rim of his mug, asking abruptly, "Did you ever meet any of them up here on the peninsula, Anne or her brother or their father, Harry Fellows?"

"I did briefly meet your ex-father-in-law," Jordan conceded, "but never his children. We didn't exactly move in the same social circles." She didn't add that she hadn't been impressed by Harry Fellows, an unattractive man with a thick waist and a self-important attitude concerned with money and power.

Richard nodded. "Then you wouldn't know the kind of family they were. Harry could be a ruthless bastard when it came to business, some of it unscrupulous, I suspect. Anne and her brother were never really into that scene themselves. They were too busy being spoiled and beautiful."

Jordan had heard about the son and daughter, the offspring of separate wives that Harry Fellows had married for the style and looks that he, himself, had never possessed. He'd been on a third wife, a young, exquisite creature, when he died. Or so Jordan heard. She had never personally glimpsed the new Mrs. Fellows, though Richard's ex-wife had once been pointed out to her at a regatta in nearby Ephraim.

A tall, elegant blonde, Anne Fellows had been one of those self-assured women who wore expensive clothes with a careless panache. Jordan could understand why Richard had wanted her. Most men would.

"I never realized any of that," he went on, "until after we were married. Maybe I didn't want to know. I was too busy convincing myself that Anne wanted me for myself and not because I was some jock who excited her."

"You were an athlete?"

"Professional soccer. I was a pretty decent player, too, until one too many injuries convinced me it was time to leave the field. That's when Anne began losing interest. Nothing glamorous about the image of an ordinary businessman. But by then we had Andrew."

Jordan could hear the deep caring in his voice whenever he referred to his son.

"I tried to make it work, for Andrew's sake," he continued. "Familiar story, huh? Maybe our marriage could have survived if it hadn't been for Harry. Harry expected to order his family's lives. Anne could never understand why I rebelled against that. After all, Daddy was so terribly generous about everything."

He smiled ruefully, the expression in his blue eyes telling her that his thoughts were suddenly elsewhere. Perhaps, she thought, dealing with old wounds. She watched him, saying nothing, and after a moment he seemed to remember that she was there across from him.

"Construction," he went on. "That was the business I started. My specialty is restoring old houses, preserving the best while making the rest fresh and modern. It was never a big outfit, but I did all right with it. It's something I'm proud of. Or what's left of it, that is."

"What do you mean, what's left of it?"

Richard, no longer hungry, pushed his plate aside. "Much as I hate to admit it," he explained, "the business was a success because of my father-in-law's influence. A chunk of his money went into the operation. Also, since reputation is everything, he had the connections to make my services popular with the right customers."

"And now they're not?"

"It all changed after the divorce. Harry pulled his support. I thought it wouldn't matter, that my work was good enough to make it on its own. I didn't realize that he was systematically seeing to it that the people who counted no longer came to me. It's been a rough year, with the outfit barely hanging on, because that's exactly the position Harry Fellows wanted me in." His mouth twisted into a wry smile. "Makes a good enough motive for murder all by itself, doesn't it?"

"He would be that deliberately vindictive, just because you and his daughter had divorced?"

Richard shook his head. "It was all because of Andrew."

"But what has your little boy to do with it?"

"Everything. Anne and I received a divided custody of Andrew. She had him during the school year. I got him for certain holidays and summer vacations and with visitation rights every other weekend. Harry wasn't satisfied with that. I found out just the other morning that Anne, with his backing, was bringing me back to court. They intended to prove my financial situation was so bad that I should no longer be able to have my son on anything but a limited basis.''

''They could actually hope to win something like that?''

''When you can afford a battery of high-powered lawyers, anything is possible. I was out of my mind when I heard about it. Not just for my sake, for Andrew's. I didn't want my kid under the full-time influence of Harry Fellows, pampered and controlled as Anne and her brother were, exposed to phony values and shady deals.''

''So you decided to do something about it,'' Jordan guessed.

''Exactly. I thought if I could talk to Anne and Harry in private, before it came to court and without all those lawyers around, maybe I could get them to see reason. Not very smart of me probably, but I wasn't thinking *smart*. I was thinking *desperate*.''

''Is that how you came to be with them out on the lake?''

He nodded slowly, the pain of memory in his eyes. ''When I called the Chicago house yesterday morning, Harry's secretary told me that he and Anne were already on their way to the place up here and not expected to return until the case went to court. The yacht had just been restored, and Harry wanted to see what it could do on a long run. He had a real passion about boats, the more impressive the better.''

''But if the yacht had already sailed—''

''I intercepted it. I learned it was stopping at Milwaukee and then again at Two Rivers for lunch. I didn't think about what I was doing. I just jumped into my car and drove. I missed the yacht in Milwaukee, but I caught up with them at Two Rivers.''

Jordan remembered now hearing on the radio that Richard had been reported boarding the *Lady Anne* at Two Rivers.

"I was ahead of them this time," he said, "but I waited around until just before they were ready to leave. I thought if I showed myself before then they might refuse to talk to me. But once the yacht was under way again and I was suddenly on board with them, there was the chance that they would be willing to listen."

"A captive audience, you mean?"

"Something like that. Anyway, I didn't put in an appearance until they were casting off. And then I made the mistake of my life. I went aboard the *Lady Anne* and straight into hell."

Richard paused to take another swig of coffee, downing it quickly as if the stuff were something potent enough to give him the courage to go on with his story. Jordan waited patiently, knowing how difficult it must be for him to relive the horror aboard the yacht.

He wiped his mouth with the back of his hand, lowered the coffee mug, then continued. "They weren't happy to see me. Well, I expected as much, that neither Harry nor Anne would want me on board. And of course it was plain they didn't. I assumed it was because of our fight, but now I think there might have been another reason."

"What?"

He shook his head. "I don't know. Whoever killed them, I suppose. He had to have been on board the whole time."

"You mean someone they were keeping under wraps and didn't want you to know about?"

"Maybe. I remember Anne was nervous about my being there. I figured that was because she didn't want a scene with me, but what if—"

"It was because she was afraid you would discover their unknown passenger." Jordan completed the speculation for him. "*Did* you see anyone else?"

"Just the man they called Mac, who was piloting the yacht for Harry. I don't remember hearing the rest of his name. I do know I was kind of surprised there was no other crew, but I didn't pay much attention to all that. I was too busy convincing Harry not to turn around and put me ashore. I thought he probably would do just that, but I kept insisting, and in the end we sat down in the salon to thrash it out."

"Did they listen to you?"

"If you can call it that, yes. Anne didn't have much to say. As usual, she sat there looking ornamental and let her father do the talking for her. Not that Harry had a whole lot to say, either, except for one arrogant refusal after another. The whole time he stayed in that deck chair of his polishing the damn yachting trophy he was so proud of and smiling at me while I squirmed."

Jordan watched Richard unconsciously rub the coffee mug between his hands, as if echoing Harry Fellows's action with the yachting trophy aboard the *Lady Anne*.

"I didn't get anywhere with my arguments," Richard said. "I just kept getting more frustrated, more angry."

Angry enough to kill, Jordan thought. The wicked thought slipped into her mind before she could prevent it. As if to deny its possibility, she quickly said, "You must have been sick about it."

"I didn't want to lose Andrew, but I knew that could happen if I didn't get them to see reason. I thought maybe if I cooled off for a few minutes I'd stand a better chance of winning some ground with them. That's when I excused myself to use one of the heads."

Richard's brow furrowed in recollection. "There was a passageway in the stern down behind the salon. I started to open the first door there and Harry called out something like, 'Not that one. There's a problem with the plumbing in that cabin. Use one of the others.'"

"The unknown passenger." Jordan realized the truth, a note of excitement in her voice. "He must have been hiding in there the whole time, and Harry didn't want you to see him."

"Probably. I wish I could say I sensed a presence behind that door, or heard something. I didn't. I was too busy trying to control myself. Not just emotionally, either. We were into rough waters by then and rolling pretty badly. I remember how long it took me staggering like a drunk down that passageway because I suddenly wanted to get as far away from that scene in the salon as I could. Nothing but the last cabin would do. I got there just as the yacht seemed to do a somersault plowing into a big wave. I did one, too. At least, that's what it felt like when something slammed into the back of my head. I didn't know anything after that until I woke up later on the floor."

"And that was when—" Jordan couldn't say it.

Richard said it for her, his voice grim. "I found the others, yeah."

He described the chilling events for her, how he had stumbled back to the salon and discovered the carnage of their sprawled bodies—Anne and her father and afterward the pilot at the helm. How he had stalked a murderer who by then was no longer aboard and how, finally, he had escaped from the yacht himself in the rubber raft.

Jordan was there with him on the *Lady Anne*, beating through the heavy seas, sharing the tension and fear and stunned disbelief. Recovering the fallen trophy from the floor, searching the master cabin for a weapon that was gone, later fighting to stay alive in the cold, violent waters of the lake. She smelled the same odors of death and damp, heard the wail of the storm as he had heard it, crept beside him through the bowels of the wildly plunging vessel.

She, too, felt an emotional exhaustion when the story was ended, when he had finished telling her everything and sat there in a limp silence, ignoring the coffee that was now cold in his mug.

Jordan, watching him, could tell that his mind was on his son again. "Where is Andrew now?" she asked him softly.

"At his school in Chicago, I hope. I've tried not to let myself think what he might have been told. I can't go to him. That's the worst part. I can't go to him, and I keep wondering when and how I can be with him again."

He can't be guilty, Jordan thought. He can't be the kind of man he is and be capable of a cold-blooded, savage slaughter. He loves his son, he saved me from the swamp, he shared a story far too real and moving not to be believed.

But none of that, she realized uneasily, either separately or collectively, was evidence of his innocence. She had absolutely no way of knowing whether anything he had told her was the truth. He could be a convincing liar and she a fool, letting her attraction for him betray her into a potentially dangerous situation.

Jordan hated her lingering shreds of doubt, her inability to fully trust him. She wanted to be on his side now without any shadows standing in the way because there was one thing that was indisputable. He was in a desperate position, and he needed someone to believe him and to help him.

She didn't dare examine her motives. She simply tried to be that needed friend, hoping in the process to quell all uncertainties. She leaned toward him from her side of the table and said insistently, "Whoever was waiting behind that door in the cabin, man or woman, killed them and then left you to take the blame. There's no arguing with that, is there?"

"Right. Unless," he added, "you're unwilling to accept the notion that there was anyone there in the first place."

"There had to be," she said without hesitation, and she caught the glimmer of relief in his eyes and knew that he'd sensed her earlier indecision. "The question now is, Who?"

"And why."

"Exactly. And what reason did Harry and Anne have to keep his identity from you? Like, was it someone you knew?"

"Could be."

"Then we have to consider the possibilities."

"Agreed, except I'm ahead of you. My brain is raw from having already wondered over and over who could have killed them. Nothing makes sense so far."

"Some enemy of Harry's? You said he could be ruthless where business was concerned."

"Yeah, but enemies like that don't usually reach for a gun."

"The situation would have to be an extreme one," she agreed. "What about Anne's brother? Where was he when all this happened?"

"Victor? I wish I knew."

"Or Harry's wife. Or his key employees?"

"It could be any of them or none of them. I have to figure out who had the right motive."

"That's the way the professionals approach it, don't they?" she said. "They consider the possible motives and then fit them to the likely suspects. Richard, what are all the motives for murder?"

"I've never tried to catalog them. Insanity? It's what I keep coming back to with this nightmare."

She shook her head. "It doesn't work. Not by itself. It would mean some random lunatic sneaked on board without anyone's knowledge and, remembering how Harry and Anne behaved, that's not likely. So, the other motives." She began to tap her fork against the side of her plate, slowly counting them out. "Passion, revenge, fear—"

"You're forgetting the most common motive of all," he interrupted her. "Gain."

"Yes, gain. Who would benefit by their deaths?"

"There's only one person I know for sure."

"Who?"

"Me. I qualify as the perfect suspect. I had both the motive and the opportunity, and unless I can prove there was someone else who had a better motive and an equal opportunity... well, I don't stand much of a chance."

Jordan couldn't stand the look on his face. It was the grim expression of a desperate fugitive, and it tugged at her heart. "What will you do, Richard?"

"Find the murderer, of course." He got decisively to his feet. "And I can't do that by sitting here."

"You have to act soon. I wish I had an inspiration for you. Maybe if I . . ."

She started to rise. He rounded the table, gently pressing her down. "You've done enough. It's my problem. Besides, you're exhausted."

He was right. Now that she had eaten and heard his story, she was beginning to droop. Her sleepless night was catching up with her.

"You were up all night, weren't you?" he accused her.

"Well, maybe half of it," she admitted.

"Because of me," he said, and the caring expression in his eyes made her go soft inside. "Jordan, I'm sorry you had to go through that kind of terror."

She tried to make light of it. "It was something I could have lived without, I admit."

"Go to bed," he urged.

Feeling useless, she watched him as, hands thrust into his pockets, he began to pace around the kitchen. She knew from the intense expression on his face that he was attacking all angles of his situation, his frustration mounting with every second. Jordan, increasingly heavy and dull, went on sitting there. She didn't mean to drift off. She meant to go on worrying with Richard about his plight, wanted to help him plan some course of action.

The next thing she knew a pair of strong arms was around her, and she was being carried out of the kitchen. She struggled awake with a faint sense of alarm. "What are you doing?" she demanded.

"Relax," he commanded her in that mellow, soothing voice. "Nothing is happening here but a trip to dreamland."

"'S too bad," she muttered. The words were out before Jordan remembered what had happened between them back on the bridge. She could feel her cheeks go pink with embarrassment.

She heard him chuckle, but she was too tired to try correcting her slip. Her eyes closed again. Despite herself, she snuggled against him as he bore her across the parlor. He made a wonderful transport, solid and secure. It was strange. Less than two hours ago she had run from this man in wild fear, and now she was in his arms and feeling warm and safe. Very strange considering she was not altogether free of her doubts.

She felt herself being deposited on her bed, her shoes tugged off and dropped on the floor, the quilt being drawn over her. The attention was delicious. All dreamy and forgetful, she started to drift off again. Then something occurred to her, and she lifted her head and said apprehensively, "You won't walk off and just disappear, will you?"

"Go to sleep," he ordered her. "I promise to be here when you wake up."

Chapter Five

Richard watched as Jordan settled down to sleep with a sigh. There was a little smile on her mouth as she slept. It had a tremulous quality to it that did things to his insides. He remembered how that mouth had felt under his on the bridge and how close he had come to losing his self-control.

Richard had been longing to kiss her again, but he had to resist the desire. An involvement of that sort could be fatal for both of them. His mere presence here was a risk for Jordan. So why didn't he just leave? Why did he hang on? He wasn't sure.

There was only one certainty in all this. He was in a hell of a mess and facing three unpleasant choices. He could turn himself in and take his chances, which were bad and growing worse. He could simply run and keep on running, which would be an intolerable existence. Or, as he'd indicated to Jordan, he could hunt for the real killer and try to clear himself. There was Andrew to think of, and that made his third choice the only one he would settle for. At least for now.

That was the easy part, he realized as he slipped out of Jordan's bedroom, shutting the door softly behind him. The formidable part was settling on a method of tracing the killer, whose existence no one else was going to believe in. Why should they when they were convinced they already had the identity of the murderer?

Hands clenched into fists that expressed the urgency of his situation, Richard began to prowl through the house. He struggled with the problem in a fever of impatience. There had to be some way to begin his search, but the solution kept evading him.

His churning mind was half aware of his surroundings. Jordan had stamped the place with her own warmth—rag rugs on the pine floors, local watercolors on the walls, country curtains at the windows. Soothing. But not for him. He was a hunted man.

He paused at her worktable, his restless hands poking at a stack of books. He picked one up and glanced at it. It dealt with famous shipwrecks on the Great Lakes. The other volumes also had maritime themes. He wondered vaguely if she was involved in some kind of investigative project.

He tossed the book back on the table. This was getting him nowhere. He had to focus, bring himself to that essential point of action.

It was the radio in the kitchen that finally delivered the inspiration he'd been striving for. He flipped it on to catch an update on the murders. The earlier portion of the report offered nothing new. Except for one daunting thing. There was an emphasis on his capture. The search for him was intensifying, making him wonder how long he could expect to hide out before they closed in on him. But there was no sense in dwelling on that.

The breakthrough came when the newscaster ended his report with a casual comment. "Word is that the Coast Guard has towed the tragic yacht, the *Lady Anne*, into a temporary anchorage in North Bay."

For Richard this disclosure was anything but casual. As memory surfaced, his mind seized on the scrap of information with a burning excitement. This was what he'd been looking for.

He had to get back aboard the yacht. There was something there that offered him his first real hope. He'd forgotten about its existence until now. And, of course, it had never occurred to him to check for it when he'd fled the vessel yesterday. All that had mattered then was getting away.

It was only a possibility, but a strong one, and all he had. For Andrew's sake, he had to return to the yacht. The information that would help him to find the killer was waiting there on the *Lady Anne*. He could *feel* it was there.

North Bay. Where was North Bay? He needed a map of the area. He'd noticed, along with the books, rolled charts on Jordan's worktable. He went back into the parlor and found the charts. He could see at a glance that they depicted in detail all the coastlines of the Great Lakes. He quietly checked them one by one, finally locating what he needed.

Unrolling the chart that represented the peninsula here, he scanned the contents. There it was, North Bay. And not far away, either. A matter of a few miles up the coastline. With any luck he could get there and back before sundown, maybe sooner.

Luck? He couldn't count on that. All he could rely on were his wits, and they told him he was a fool to assume that all he had to do was walk on board the *Lady Anne*. The yacht had to be under some kind of police guard. He'd manage somehow to board the vessel, but first he had to reach it.

According to the chart, the bay was shallow. That probably meant the *Lady Anne* was anchored well offshore. He'd need a boat to get out to it. A small one would do, just a simple outboard. Jordan's situation and her maritime interests made it likely that she'd have one on the island.

Twenty minutes later Richard stood out in the yard, puzzled and disappointed. He had circled the entire shoreline, investigated the outbuildings. There was no craft.

All right, he'd do it the hard way. He'd go on foot, working his way along the beach and through the forest. Using that route might increase the risk of his being spotted if any searchers were close by, but an open boat was also chancy. At least there was the likelihood of cover where the woods were thick. Either way, he couldn't let the threat stop him.

He cast a fast glance toward the house. Should he wake Jordan, tell her what he intended? No, she'd only worry. Better to let her sleep. He turned and started off with a determined stride.

It was after he had crossed the causeway to the mainland side that Richard first heard the sound. Startled, he came to a stop at the edge of the woods, straining his senses to identify the noise. It was a buzzing, still off in the distance but steadily, relentlessly working this way. He knew what it was then and what it meant. Chain saws. The power crews had arrived in the area and were clearing the storm debris. They were no danger to him. Not yet.

He found out just how wrong he was before he went no more than half a mile along the shore. The humming of the chain saws seemed to fade safely behind him, and that made him careless. He was about to cross a cottage clearing when, only yards away, there was a sudden roaring that brought him to a rigid standstill.

Another chain saw just starting up. More linemen, and this time he'd almost run smack into them. He circled the clearing, tried to go on. It was no good. The power crews were out in force. They were everywhere between him and North Bay. He was almost caught by one of them, heard him shout to his partner.

"Hey, Dave, there's something running through the brush back there. You think maybe—"

"Aw, you're crazy! It's just a deer. Come on, give me a hand here."

Richard, crouching in the undergrowth, made a decision. It was a decision he hated, but it was unavoidable. Deliberately, recklessly exposing himself was no way to help himself or his son. And even if he could somehow avoid the power crews and reach North Bay, how was he supposed to get out to the yacht? Swim across the open waters in full view? He hadn't been thinking. He had let pure desperation drive him.

No choice, then. He had to return to the island. He had to wait until the linemen cleared the area. More important, he had to somehow get his hands on a boat.

Richard began to work his way back toward the lighthouse. His frustration was enormous. He had already lost a precious day since the murders. He couldn't afford to lose another.

JORDAN LIFTED HER HEAD from the pillow, aware that she had been startled awake but not understanding why. Her mind was still fuzzy with sleep, and for a moment she couldn't locate the disturbance. The door to the parlor was closed, the room silent. Then why was her heart suddenly racing?

Seconds later they came again, the sounds that had aroused her. They were outside and just across the causeway. This time she could identify them. The shouts of linemen calling to one another, the persistent hum of chain saws clearing the debris from the road.

She could tell by the position of the sunlight outside her window that it was late afternoon. Even so, she hadn't expected the power crews to reach this portion of the peninsula so soon. The isolation of Cana Island was about to end.

Richard, she thought. He would probably be frantic, thinking they were going to be invaded and his presence discovered.

Fully alert now, she sat up and swung her legs to the floor, groping for her shoes. Within seconds she was searching the house for him. He was in none of the rooms. Had he fled after all, fearing capture? Her disappointment was much keener than she'd expected.

Grabbing up her light jacket, she hurried out of the house. To her relief she spotted him off to the side of the yard. He was staring through a gap in the lilac thickets. She followed his gaze that was directed over the tumbled stone wall edging the shore, out to the blue vastness of the open lake. The waters were gently ruffled today, a peaceful scene involving the misty shoulders of headlands piling into the distance on either side and far offshore the cribs of nets laid down by the commercial fishing boats.

The taut look on Richard's face told her that he wasn't seeing any of this picturesque serenity. She was sure he was viewing the waters as they had been yesterday at this time, wild and dark, a yacht wallowing in the troughs and aboard it something hideous and unspeakable.

But as she crossed the yard to join him, she was less certain that this was the explanation for his strange expression. Maybe that haunted look was simply worry over the nearness of the power crews.

When she reached his side Jordan lost no time in offering him reassurance. "It's all right. They won't have to come on the island itself. The power is buried where the causeway begins. They'll stop on that side after they've restored the overhead lines over there. And you can see the woods on the back of the island are thick enough to keep them from seeing the lighthouse station here."

He turned his head, glancing with uninterest in the direction of the causeway. "I know," he said. Then his gaze returned to the open waters.

And this time Jordan was able to clearly understand the look on his face. It wasn't worry. It was longing. A pure, fierce longing.

"What is it?" she demanded. "What are you seeing out there?"

"It isn't what I'm seeing," he answered her quietly. "It's what I *want* to see around that far bend. North Bay is in there."

She stared at him, mystified. "North Bay? What's at North Bay?"

"The *Lady Anne*," he said. He went on to tell her all that had happened while she had been asleep.

"I see," she said slowly when he'd finished. Then she shook her head. "No, I don't see at all. Just what is it you're after on the yacht?"

"The contents of Harry's safe. Jordan, he was a fanatic about keeping records. He had files on everybody, especially his enemies. And if I can get at those files—"

"They might prove who had the motive for killing him. Yes, I can see why they would be revealing. But would such files be on the yacht itself?"

"I think so. He liked to have copies of all his important documents close to him. He'd keep them in his office, at home and on his boats. That's why there's a safe aboard the *Lady Anne.*"

"You saw it?"

"No, but I'm sure it's there somewhere. Anne and I were still married when he bought the yacht and began to have it restored. I remember he was having the safe from his last yacht transferred over to the *Lady Anne.* It's an old-fashioned, wall-type safe that he felt would be suitable on a vintage yacht like the *Lady Anne.*"

"If you do manage to get aboard and find the safe, how will you get into it?"

"I know the combination. Anne gave it to me when she wanted me to get some jewelry out of the safe that she'd left there after a cruise."

"Richard—"

"Don't say it. I know what you're thinking. That it's a real long shot. That the safe could already be cleaned out by the police or the family. But don't you see? It's all I have, and I've got to go for it. There's just one thing."

"What?"

"I'll need an outboard to reach the yacht. Something small and easy to manage."

Jordan didn't let him see how his very mention of an outboard like that made her want to shudder. She couldn't forget what had happened last summer. "I don't keep any boats here," she said, unable to prevent the tension in her voice.

"I know. I checked. But the roads should be cleared by tonight. There isn't anything to prevent you from driving into town the first thing in the morning and renting an outboard and trailer for me. I hate to ask it of you, Jordan, but there's just no other way."

"No!"

He frowned over her unexpected, rigid resistance. "You mean you can't, or you won't?"

"I just mean *no.*" She knew how her sudden stubbornness must sound to him, but she couldn't help it.

"If it's the risk to you—"

"It isn't the risk, and I don't have to explain it."

Richard's eyes took on a stormy look. He faced her squarely, his hands gripping her by the wrists. "I'm not going to play games with you," he informed her, a savageness in his voice. "I want that boat. I *need* that boat, and you're going to get it for me."

She should have been afraid, but she was only angry now. "I don't have to help you, and you're hurting me."

His cold eyes met her unrelenting gaze for a long minute. Then his steely fingers relaxed, sliding away from her wrists. "You're right," he said, his voice softening. "I don't have any right to ask you to help me. But if you won't do this for me, Jordan, will you at least consider doing it for the sake of my son?"

The tenseness melted from her in a slow sigh. "You don't play fair," she accused him softly.

"No, not when it comes to Andrew's welfare," he admitted.

"All right," she agreed. "There's a place I know of that rents outboards. I'll get your boat for you in the morning."

There was a look of gratitude in his eyes that made the breath stick in her throat. His look deepened, becoming intimate. A raw thing that thrummed between them like electricity. Compelling, impossibly sensual and wonderfully dangerous.

Jordan had never felt so vulnerable.

THE POWER CAME BACK ON just before sundown. With the electric water pump restored, they were able to take showers and do laundry. It also meant the regular kitchen was back in use, allowing them to cook on something other than the old kerosene range in the summer kitchen, where their breakfast had been prepared.

Darkness settled over the island after supper. Jordan made a fire in the parlor stove to combat the sudden chill of the evening. Richard stood at the window looking out toward the lake where the lighthouse beacon flashed its perpetual warning. She knew his mind was on North Bay, that he was impatient to reach the yacht and unable to do so before tomorrow.

He finally turned away from the window, watching her where she sat at her worktable. Their awareness of each other was strongly between them again, but that wasn't a safe thing to discuss. Not under the circumstances.

Richard chose another topic to keep his mind off tomorrow. "All those maps and research materials ... what are they for?"

She hesitated, then decided to confide in him. "The book I'm trying to write."

He looked impressed, interested. "You mean a novel?"

She shook her head. "No, the true stories of the ships and their crews that sailed these waters. With a difference. My book will deal with the courageous women who accompanied their men on the voyages or, in some cases, piloted their own vessels. Most people don't know that women were involved like that in the last century."

"Meaning it hasn't been done before?"

"That's right. I think it's worth telling. Casey did, too. We used to talk about my doing it." She paused in brief reluctance, then went on quickly. "In fact, just before he died last summer he challenged me not to keep putting it off until that distant someday."

"Casey?"

"My grandfather. I spent all my summer vacations with him in his cabin here on the peninsula while I was growing up. We—we were very close."

There was no way she could make him understand what that closeness had meant to her. Casey had offered her the only real permanence she'd ever known. That kind of security had been lacking in her existence with self-involved parents who had moved them all over the country on behalf of ambitious careers, and who never seemed interested in roots. They were down in Houston now, but another transfer was already in the works. She loved them, but it was Casey who had given her the one place she could always belong to and call her own.

Richard could sense her nervousness over the subject of her grandfather. It was more than just grief. He wondered what haunted her about her Casey and whether it had any connection with her resistance this afternoon to renting an outboard for him.

"So the book is to be a kind of tribute to your grandfather," he said understandingly.

"I hope so. Casey left me a small inheritance, and that made it possible to lease the island here when it became available last fall. I used to come up weekends before I decided on a six-month leave of absence to write the book. Of course, some people think I'm making a mistake."

One of Richard's thick eyebrows elevated with curiosity. "Now who are we talking about?"

"Dwight Jamison. He's the publisher of a Chicago lifestyle magazine. I was one of his editors. Dwight never could appreciate my love affair with the peninsula."

"Is it important that he should?"

There was a sharpness in his tone that pleased her when it shouldn't have pleased her. "There was a time when it mattered," she admitted.

"So what happens when your book is finished and a big success?"

There was a certainty in his expression that she would accomplish the book. A kind of confident support that no one had offered her since Casey, and this, too, pleased her.

"I go back to the magazine. Or maybe I don't. It depends."

Richard didn't pursue the matter. She knew he felt he had no right to. She left it that way.

There was something else that went unsaid between them. He wanted her to go to town for him tomorrow. *Needed* her to go to town. But she could sense the silent fear that had been chasing through his mind all evening. Would she fail to return? Use this opportunity to turn him in?

They had yet to fully trust each other.

Chapter Six

If We Don't Have It, You Don't Need It.

That was the slogan taped to the front window of Harvey's General Store in the small town of Baileys Harbor. Jordan's past visits to the emporium had taught her that the boast was probably not an exaggeration. From its antiquated gas pumps out front to its claustrophobic hardware center in the basement, Harvey's offered a vast range of merchandise. The summer tourists were fascinated by its passageways meandering in every direction.

As Jordan was reminded this morning, the place also qualified as a hangout for the locals. There were two of them behind her at the yard goods display while she stood at the checkout counter filling out the rental form for the boat. Not surprisingly, their eager discussion was about the events connected with the murders.

"You're kidding! This morning?"

"Yeah, this morning. Eleven-o'clock service at Bayside Church in Ephraim with burial to follow in the cemetery behind. Aggie's sister being receptionist at Morgenheimer's Funeral Home is how I know."

"But so quick after it happened! Not wasting any time, are they?"

"Well, maybe the family is figuring sooner planted, sooner forgotten, though you could never put a thing like this behind you. And can you beat it? Side-by-side plots.

Looks like Harry Fellows isn't letting his daughter get away from him even in death. Do you like this green print?"

"Not much. Too busy."

Jordan tried to look uninterested in the conversation behind her, but she absorbed the information the woman revealed.

"How long will you be wanting the boat?" the young, bearded clerk behind the counter asked her.

"I'm not sure. A couple of days."

"I'll put down three. If you want to extend that time, just give us a ring."

The women had left the yard goods and moved off to another department. Two elderly men were behind Jordan now, waiting to check out their purchases. This time it was next to impossible to look unaffected by their dialogue. They were discussing Richard.

"No sign of this Davis guy, and I hear the Coast Guard was up and down that shore all yesterday. So this morning the chopper from Sturgeon Bay is gonna join the search. That area's nothing but woods and beach—the only good way to spot anything is from the air."

"That's nuts. Assuming this bird did make it ashore, he's not gonna hang around waiting to be caught. He's got to be miles away by now, probably clear out of the county."

Richard! Jordan thought frantically. He was out there on foot somewhere along that shoreline. She had begged him to stay safely inside the house while she collected the outboard and picked up a few necessary groceries. He had refused. Had insisted that he couldn't just wait idly until she returned. With the power crews out of the area, he was sure he could reach North Bay this time. He intended to reconnoiter the yacht's situation from the land side before he attempted to approach it by water.

There was no way she could warn him about the helicopter. He was on his own out there.

But there was another way she could help him. She could attend that funeral. It was an opportunity to learn something useful. There was the strong possibility that whoever had killed Harry Fellows and his daughter was a close connection. Maybe close enough to be one of the mourners. No telling what she might observe just by being there.

Yes, why not? Her presence wouldn't seem unnatural. After all, she had once met Harry Fellows, and Casey had known him fairly well because of the maritime interest they'd shared. People would think she was there for Casey's sake. She would be just another innocent mourner.

And there was something else. Andrew. She knew the Fellows's housekeeper, who was sure to be at the funeral. She could ask her about Andrew. The woman wouldn't think it was unusual for Jordan to wonder about the welfare of a little boy so directly affected by the tragedy. She could bring to Richard the news of his son that he was so desperate to hear.

"About the trailer, Ms. Templeton?" The clerk was gazing at her expectantly.

"Sorry. Uh, yes, my car does have a trailer capability." She'd installed a hitch on the Volvo last fall when she'd brought up a load of furnishings for the lighthouse residence.

"You're all set, then. Harv will hook you up around the side."

"I have another errand to run. Could you hold the boat and trailer for a bit?"

"Be waiting for you when you get back."

Jordan paid the deposit on the outboard and hurried toward her car.

RICHARD WAS AWARE of the helicopter beating along the coastline over his head as it periodically swung inland and then out again over the water, weaving a zigzag pattern that would cover the entire area.

They were hunting for him, of course. He wasn't particularly worried. As long as he refrained from any game of peekaboo with the chopper, was careful to keep under the

dense canopy of the cedar forests that hugged the shoreline, there was no way they could spot him from the air. Not
even when they dipped down for closer looks, which occasionally they did.

He was far more concerned about any searchers on foot,
but the only threat he encountered was a resentful porcu-
pine. No power crews today, and if there were search par-
ties on land, they were busy elsewhere.

Not that his hike was an easy one. The terrain was rough
and made for slow progress. It was well past midmorning
before he reached North Bay.

He congratulated himself on his safe arrival. But he soon
learned that his satisfaction was premature. Emerging from
the trees, he found himself on a gravel track that followed
the curve of the deep bay. It was necessary to risk crossing
the lane in order to get close enough to the beach to check
the scene.

The roadway was deserted, and he managed to get down
to the shore, where he concealed himself behind some low
junipers. And that's when the unexpected occurred. He
could hear all the activity long before he saw it, lifting his
head to peer through the junipers.

Sweet Lord, he thought, it's a regular carnival!

The *Lady Anne* was anchored out in the bay, but the
yacht wasn't alone. A fleet of small craft, rowboats and
cruisers, circled the vessel like vultures. They were loaded
with sightseers eager to glimpse the scene of horror. Some
of them had cameras aimed at the *Lady Anne*. Others
shouted questions to the uniformed guard leaning over the
rail. He watched them to make sure none of the boats got
too close to the yacht.

There were curious onlookers gathered along the beach as
well, staring and pointing. Another guard was there patrol-
ling the shore, a rifle slung over his shoulder.

The turmoil was a shock to Richard after the silence of the
forest. It was also a serious frustration. Getting aboard the
Lady Anne was going to be even tougher than he'd planned,

maybe something that could be managed only after nightfall.

He had seen enough. It was time to retreat. Besides, that guard on the beach was ambling this way.

Keeping low, he backed away from the junipers until he reached the cover of the trees. Then he turned to cross the roadway. And met trouble.

A trio of senior citizens came pedaling along the lane on their bicycles. There was no way to avoid them. Even worse, the frizzy-haired woman in the lead, only yards away, recognized him immediately and didn't hesitate to raise the alarm.

"It's him!" she babbled excitedly to her companions. "The one they want! I *know* it's him! He fits the description that they've been broadcasting! Fits it perfectly!"

"Lou, are you sure—"

"Hey!" she shouted. "Hey, someone! Over here! He's over here!"

Richard swung his head to spot the alerted guard on the beach charging in his direction. Then, without further pause, he turned and plunged into the woods, dodging through the pines as he ran.

There were yells behind him and what sounded like a bullet humming past his shoulder. He never stopped. He went on crashing through the undergrowth, heading inland and away from the lighthouse.

EPHRAIM WAS A picture-postcard village popular with the summer crowds. Located on the Green Bay side of the peninsula, the town with its vintage architecture was nestled in a basin between massive limestone bluffs that embraced the broad harbor.

Bayside Church was situated against a steep hillside overlooking the islands beyond the harbor. The narrow street outside the white clapboard church was lined with parked cars, some of them representing the news media, when Jordan arrived. She felt a bit self-conscious as she found a place for her own vehicle and headed inside. She had hardly expected to attend a funeral when she dressed this morning. Jeans and a casual top weren't exactly appropriate. It couldn't be helped.

The service was already in progress, the small church packed with mourners and reporters. Jordan didn't bother trying to find a seat on one of the crowded pews. Standing at the back, where she had a total view of the proceedings, was more advantageous to her purpose.

The two flower-draped caskets in front of the altar made a startling impression, reminding her of the impact of the tragedy and that both father and daughter were being laid to rest today. However, in this moment it was the living that concerned her more.

Jordan eyed heads as the minister conducted the service. Most of them were strangers, but she was able to identify the principals in a front pew. She already knew the family housekeeper, Sonia Gunnerson, a tall, large-boned woman. Seated beside her, erect and immaculate in a dark suit, was a slender man probably in his late twenties.

Even with his face only partially visible from this angle, Jordan could tell that he was arrestingly handsome, with black hair and classic features. She knew intuitively that this had to be the dead man's son, Victor Fellows, as dark as his half sister, Anne, had been fair. Without question, Harry Fellows's first two wives had produced physically perfect children.

And his third wife?

Jordan assumed it was the widow who was seated close on the other side of Victor. Evelyn Fellows was as beautiful as her stepson. And as young. It struck her how well matched they were in looks and privileged attitudes as they sat there side by side.

Watching them together, Jordan learned something else that was interesting. Victor turned frequently to Evelyn throughout the service, placing a hand on her arm, murmuring in her ear. Merely comfort for a grieving widow? Or was there something more intimate here? He did seem overly protective. But maybe she was being imaginative, wanting to find something where there was nothing.

Jordan slowly scanned the other pews, other figures. She began to wonder why she had come. She couldn't actually hope to detect guilt on any of these faces. But the unexpected did occur as her searching gaze reached the back of the church. There, standing off to the rear side, as she was standing on this side, was someone who raised in her a faint sense of alarm.

A late arrival, he must have slipped in behind her, or she would have noticed him before this. He was imposing in his brown-and-tan uniform. He was also disturbingly official looking as he shrewdly eyed the ranks of mourners. What was the sheriff of Door County doing here? He certainly couldn't expect Richard to turn up at the funeral.

Jordan had never met Sheriff Con Matthews, but she recognized him from his campaign photos. She knew he was running for an important state office. He had all the best qualities for a successful politician—an unblemished record, wholesome good looks, a commanding presence. He also had the right connections. She remembered now reading in a county paper that Harry Fellows had been one of his major supporters. This, then, explained his presence at the funeral.

A few seconds later, when his watchful gaze collided with hers, Jordan understood her anxiety. Con Matthews had a reputation for being relentless in his pursuit of offenders. He had just lost a friend and a backer in Harry Fellows, which meant he wouldn't rest until he apprehended the killer. And Sheriff Matthews must be convinced Richard Davis was that man.

She could feel herself flushing as his eyes, probing, speculative, held hers, then reluctantly slid away. Why this interest in her? She had done nothing to betray her connection with Richard, so he had no reason to suspect her. Whatever the explanation, she was beginning to fear that Richard had a serious enemy in Con Matthews.

The sheriff had departed by the time the service ended. Relieved, Jordan watched the mourners file out of the church. There was another surprising revelation when the family rose and started down the aisle. The high back of the pew had concealed a small figure squeezed on the bench between Victor and the housekeeper. The boy was about seven years old and dressed too formally, too somberly for his age, even if this was a funeral.

Jordan knew that vulnerable young face. She had looked at it in a photograph the night before last. She had seen the same blue eyes, the same light brown hair and strong bones in the face of the man who was his father. Andrew Davis was not at his school in Chicago. He was here in Ephraim. Richard would be wild when he learned this. And she couldn't not tell him. It wouldn't be fair, when he hungered to know about his son.

Her heart squeezed painfully as the forlorn Andrew stood there waiting for the adults to accompany him to the adjoining cemetery where his mother and grandfather would be interred while his own father was hunted for their deaths. What had he been told? What confusion and anguish must he be suffering?

He needed comforting and, damn it, the adults were ignoring him. The housekeeper was speaking to the minister, and his uncle was interested in nothing but soothing the nervous Evelyn clinging to his side. Jordan longed to go to Andrew, put her arms around him, tell him that his father was responsible for none of this. But there was nothing she could do, no way she could approach him. She had never felt so angry and helpless.

Turning away, she left the church in frustration and followed the other mourners up the slope. They streamed between stone pillars into the cemetery that, like the simple country church it served, was very old. Many of the headstones under the new green of the spreading maples were crooked and mossy with age, marking the resting places of some of the area's earliest settlers. In stark contrast were the two fresh graves waiting for the remains of father and daughter. Their situation commanded a view of the Green Bay waters that Harry Fellows had always loved. At least that much of this whole sorry affair was comforting.

Jordan, still feeling conspicuous in her jeans, meant to hang back at the outer edges of the crowd. But somehow, in the jockeying for positions around the graves, she ended up in the front ranks. It was there that the housekeeper found her a few seconds later.

"Jordan. I thought that was you I spotted in the church."

Sonia Gunnerson was a friendly woman with an angular face and silvery blond hair that expressed the Scandinavian heritage common to so many of the peninsula's natives. She and her late husband, Gus, had been longtime friends of her grandfather's.

Jordan talked with her, offering her sympathy as they waited for the pallbearers to bring up the caskets.

"It's a terrible business," Sonia agreed. "We're all of us still in shock."

Jordan apologized for her clothes. "I just heard about the funeral. There wasn't time to go back and change. I've been so busy trying to get this book under way, but I did want to pay my respects."

"That's right. Casey talked about you doing a book, didn't he? And I remember Harry offering you the use of his library for your research."

Jordan had forgotten that Harry Fellows, during their brief meeting, had promised to lend her volumes from his extensive collection on the Great Lakes.

"Harry would still want you to make use of his books," the housekeeper urged. "Don't hesitate to make arrangements with me whenever you're ready to borrow them. I know the family would agree with that."

Jordan thanked her as the Fellows family arrived on the scene. Evelyn was still on Victor's arm and Andrew, wearing that lost expression, trailed beside them. Jordan consoled herself by remembering that the housekeeper was a kind woman who would look out for the boy. Not the same as having his father, but it was something to take to Richard.

There was one more unexpected occurrence in this morning of surprises. The minister was reading the graveside service when Jordan heard Sonia gasp. Her swift glance revealed that Sonia was staring across the caskets with a distracted, troubled expression on her lined face. Puzzled, Jordan followed the direction of her gaze.

No question of it. Sonia's eyes were pinned on the figure of a man watching the burial as he stood off among the trees, apart from the mourners. He was lanky, with a shock of white hair, and even from this distance Jordan could read the expression on his narrow, aging face. It was a look of intense hatred.

She could swear that the eyes of housekeeper and stranger met and exchanged a silent message. Then the tall figure turned and strode off through the headstones. Sonia's worried eyes continued to follow him until he disappeared from view.

One more unidentified piece to be slotted into a puzzle that defied all explanation.

None of it was easy. Or maybe even sane.

THERE WERE CLOUDS low on the eastern horizon as Jordan drove back across the peninsula. But for now the noonday sun was unobstructed, revealing the progress of the lilacs along the roadside. Inland like this, where it was sheltered and warmer, a deep purple was already peeping through the swollen buds. They would be in full flower within a few days.

She thought about Richard as she flashed past familiar farmlands with their stone fencelines and weathered pioneer barns. She wondered how he had made out at North Bay and whether he was safely back at the lighthouse. She hoped so. She had probably overreacted regarding the Coast Guard helicopter. He would have heard its approach and been careful to keep under cover. Still, she couldn't help worrying.

Better to occupy her mind with the funeral she had just attended, try to concentrate on its participants. Victor Fellows and his young and alluring stepmother, Evelyn. The sheriff determined to avenge his friend's death. The housekeeper and her mysterious stranger. A bewildering assortment, and perhaps one or more of them concealed a murderous secret.

But it was the image of Richard's son that stayed with her more forcefully than the others. She kept seeing his small, desolate face, kept feeling the pangs of his obvious need for his father. It was then that Jordan understood why she had insisted on going to the funeral.

She'd been wanting a reason to shed the last traces of her uncertainty about Richard, some sign that would permit her to believe in him totally and without looking back. She suddenly had that clear conviction in the form of Andrew. Remembering him there at the funeral, realizing how vital the boy's welfare was, she was committed now to saving his father on his behalf. Andrew alone was responsible for her surge of spirits. That was what she told herself, anyway, not ready to admit that the man who had washed ashore on Cana Island already had a piece of her heart.

So intent was she on her new determination to fight for Richard's vindication that she almost struck the cyclist suddenly in the path of her car. There was a bike trail emerging from the trees in the direction of Lake Michigan. The frizzy-haired woman shot from it without pause, rolling onto the highway in front of her.

Jordan's foot punched the brake. The Volvo rocked to a stop less than three feet from the bicycle. Shaken, she rolled down the window, calling anxiously, "Are you all right?"

The woman nodded at her reassuringly, returning an embarrassed, "Sorry. My fault."

Her two companions now appeared on the roadway behind her with their bikes. "Lou, be careful," one of them cautioned her. "You're still in a flutter over that character at North Bay."

"I wouldn't be if you'd stop teasing me about him. It *was* this Richard Davis they're after. Why else would he have run off into the woods like that when the officer tried to stop him?"

"I guess we'll know when and if they catch up with the guy."

The cyclists waved at Jordan in friendly fashion and went on their way. She watched them go, feeling a little sick. Richard, she thought helplessly. He'd been spotted out there, recognized. Was he still running from his pursuers? Had he managed to get back to the island? Or had the worst happened? Had he been captured?

She couldn't forgive herself for attending the funeral. She should have acquired the outboard and gone straight back to the lighthouse. She should have been there waiting for him if he needed her.

As it was, she regretted having to return to Baileys Harbor to pick up the boat and trailer, but she had promised Richard she would get them. Thankfully, she had already stopped in Ephraim for the groceries.

Under way again, she sped back toward Harvey's General Store just as fast as she safely could. There was a small, frustrating delay while the final paperwork was completed at the counter inside. But at last she had the receipt in her hand and an assurance that the rig was already attached to her car in the street.

Jordan, leaving the store in a fever of impatience, wasn't prepared for the sight of the figure leaning against the boat trailer. He was leisurely drinking a can of soda as he waited for her to emerge from the store.

She went rigid with apprehension. What was the sheriff doing here, and why did she have the horrible feeling that she was being ambushed?

She made herself move slowly toward her car, trying to look unconcerned as she watched Con Matthews stand away from the trailer, set the can of soda on the hood of his cruiser parked behind her Volvo and step forward to join her on the sidewalk. Whatever his casualness, she was convinced he was here by design, deliberately waiting for her.

"Something wrong, Sheriff?" Her voice was carefully mild, but alarming questions raced through her mind. Had he somehow connected her with Richard? Learned she'd been hiding him at the lighthouse? The sheriff had to know about the sighting at North Bay. They would have radioed him that much, anyway.

Con smiled at her reassuringly. "Why is it that when people meet an officer in uniform they immediately think they're in trouble?"

"Sorry," she said, forcing herself to be pleasant. "I didn't know I was looking nervous."

"Nothing to worry about. No violations. I was just taking a break."

She didn't believe him. His presence here was much too obvious. What was he after?

"You're Jordan Templeton, aren't you? I saw you at the funeral. You've got the place out at Cana Island."

He had been asking questions, checking up on her. "That's right," she said cautiously.

He smiled again. "Don't mind me. It's my business to know about everyone in the county. Nice spot out on the island."

"Ideal for me. I'm writing a book."

"So I heard. It's also a pretty isolated spot for a woman on her own. You know we're hunting for the man who could have landed somewhere along that shoreline, don't you?"

"He's still on the loose, then?"

"Had a report he was seen at North Bay this morning, but no confirmation on an actual identity. Yes, I'm afraid he is still out there somewhere."

Jordan felt a measure of relief. Richard hadn't been caught, then. But where was he now? Back at the lighthouse, she prayed. "Well, I haven't seen any sign of him myself, Sheriff."

"Con," he insisted. "Everybody calls me Con. It's a friendly peninsula, Jordan."

He had unusual eyes, she realized. They were pure gray and as vigilant as a wolf's, making her want to squirm. He kept gazing at her intently, as he had back at the funeral, and she couldn't forget his fearful, bulldog determination to catch the man who murdered his friend and benefactor.

"Yes," she agreed. "It's one of the reasons why I'm here."

He turned his head, eyeing the boat. "Planning on some fishing?"

This was it. He suspected her use of the boat. "No," she said quickly. "It's because of the book. I plan to investigate some of the old shipwreck sites. They tell me they're still visible in spots."

The observant eyes found her again. "You be careful out there. On the island, too. I wouldn't want anything to happen to you, Jordan."

His smile this time had a genuine warmth in it. An unmistakable warmth. And Jordan suddenly understood his interest in her. The man wasn't suspicious. He was flirting with her. That was why he had approached her.

Still, she couldn't be certain of this. Better to exercise every caution. It was an awkward situation. She didn't want to make an enemy of him by being unpleasant, but she certainly didn't want to seem to encourage him, either. She settled on an impersonal politeness.

"I appreciate your concern, Sheriff, but—"

"Con," he reminded her.

"But I don't plan on doing anything risky, Con. The only worry I have is getting my frozen stuff in there back home before it thaws." She indicated the sack of groceries in her car. It made a handy excuse. "So if you'll excuse me . . ."

He didn't try to stop her when she slid toward the Volvo, making her escape. All she could think about was getting back to the island, learning whether Richard had managed to return.

She felt easier once she was under way and heading north out of town. Until she checked her rearview mirror and learned that the sheriff's white car was trailing hers.

Jordan tensed behind the wheel, but she refused to panic. This was still the highway, after all, and he could have any one of a number of destinations in the same direction.

She waited to see what would happen after she slowed and made her turn off the highway, praying he would zoom on by with a friendly wave. It didn't happen. He was still behind her as she traveled up the first of several side roads leading to Cana Island. She began to be genuinely nervous now.

You're overreacting, she told herself. This is the same road that branches off to North Bay. That's where he's headed. He's going up to North Bay to check out that sighting in person.

But when the white cruiser failed to drop away at the North Bay fork, stayed in her mirror as she twisted through the dense forest following the shoreline, Jordan knew there was no question of Con Matthews's destination.

He was after Richard. Maybe he hadn't believed her back at the store. Maybe he had reason to think she was hiding Richard somewhere on the island. She was earnestly alarmed this time.

What could she do? It was too late to swing off into another road, pretend she had some other stop to make. It would only deepen his suspicion, since she'd indicated her intention to return directly to the lighthouse.

Somehow she had to turn him back, prevent him from getting to Richard. But no solution occurred to her, and suddenly the winding road ended at the edge of the causeway. Jordan eased to a stop, the patrol car drawing up behind her. Feeling helpless, but determined to hide her agitation, she climbed from the Volvo to confront Con Matthews ambling toward her with a pleased smile under those appraising gray eyes.

"Did I forget something?" she asked him, fighting to stay calm.

"Yes, my offer."

"Funny, I don't remember any offer."

"To help you get your boat in the water."

"But I can manage that on my own."

"Why should you when I'm here to offer a hand?" He glanced at the trailer, then at the public launching ramp that abutted the causeway. "You'll need to swing around so you can back the trailer into the water. Easy to slide her down from there."

"No, really, I didn't plan on floating it right away."

"Only take a minute with both of us handling it. Your groceries will keep that long. This way the boat will be in and waiting for you whenever you're ready to use it. And after that, Jordan—" he pinned his smile on her "—you and I will walk over to the island together, and I'll check out the premises for you."

Her insides tightened with fear. This was real trouble. "But that isn't necessary," she protested, her voice weak when she wanted it to be strong. "I told you, no one has been near the lighthouse, and I'm perfectly safe."

"I'm surprised at you, Jordan," he said matter-of-factly. "You didn't think I'd let you come back here all on your own without making sure our man isn't lurking in your area? He must be desperate by now, and I wouldn't be doing my job if I didn't see to your security."

"I don't think I like this, Con," she said stubbornly, wondering if there was any way she could keep him from crossing that causeway with her.

"You aren't going to make me come back with a search warrant, are you, Jordan?" His tone was teasing, but she knew he was serious.

If she continued to object, it would only strengthen his resolve, maybe even confirm his suspicions. "No, I have nothing to hide. I just like to preserve my privacy, is all."

"Good, because my looking around the island will safeguard that for you. Now let's see about dropping this boat into the water."

There was no way out of the situation. And if Richard was there, how in the name of sweet heaven was she going to warn him? Because if she didn't warn him, she would be leading Con Matthews straight to the man he so urgently wanted.

Chapter Seven

Panic clawing at her self-control with each reluctant step she took, Jordan led the way into the lighthouse clearing. All through the lowering of the outboard she had searched for a means to prevent the sheriff from accompanying her over the now dry causeway, had delayed as much as she dared. None of it had been any good. Con Matthews was right beside her.

There was one possibility, providing Richard was somewhere in the house and not loose on the island or still off in the woods. Con would have no reason to go inside if she could convince him the residence was secure from entry. She made a little show of extracting the house keys from her purse. There had never been any reason to lock the doors, but he didn't have to know this.

"I keep the house tight," she informed him, "but the outbuildings are open. You're welcome to poke through them and elsewhere around the island. Here, I'll take the bag. You go ahead with your search."

He had insisted on carrying the groceries for her. He passed the sack to her now. She left him heading toward the nearest storage building as she sped toward the back door of the house.

Once inside, she dumped the bag on the kitchen counter, whispering urgently, "Richard, where are you?"

Silence. Had he failed to make it back to the island? She checked the view from the window, making sure the sheriff was busy elsewhere. Then she hurried through the rooms, calling softly for Richard. He was nowhere in the house. She felt both relief and a wrenching sense of loss. Relief that his absence meant he needn't be exposed to the threat of Con Matthews on the premises. And sorrow because he was somewhere out there on his own, struggling to remain free, and she might never see him again.

Sick with worry, she went back to the kitchen. She was taking another fast look through the window over the sink when the cellar door behind her creaked on its hinges.

Jordan whipped around with a startled oath. The cellar door cracked open to disclose Richard hanging in the shadows on the upper stairs. Her knees went weak with surprise.

He was an awful sight, his clothes torn and dirty, his hands and face scratched from the bramble thickets through which he must have crawled.

Richard could see the concern on her face, but this was no time to explain about the miserable terrain he had encountered in his successful struggle to lose his pursuer.

"You're bleeding," she said.

"It's nothing. Where is he?" he demanded.

"How did you—"

" I heard your car and went out to the edge of the causeway. I was going to help you with the boat, and then I saw him there with you."

He'd been shocked when he'd seen that uniform on the burly man beside her, knowing the authority represented by that badge. For one wild moment, as his insides had twisted with pain and anger, he had actually believed she'd betrayed him. Then he had recovered his senses and made a fast retreat to the house.

"It's all right," Jordan assured him. "He's busy investigating the outbuildings. I'll keep checking the window, but you stay back."

"It is the sheriff himself, isn't it?"

"Afraid so." She began rapidly unloading the grocery sack as she talked, shoving the stuff into refrigerator and cabinets in order to cover herself if the worst happened and Con Matthews entered the kitchen. "I'm sorry, Richard. I did everything to discourage him from following me here, but he was insistent and I was afraid to flat out refuse him."

"Does he believe I'm here?"

Jordan shook her head. "I think he's just being thorough."

"How thorough?"

She understood what he meant. "Don't worry. He has no reason to come into the house. I told him I keep the place tightly locked. He's probably convinced I'd be yelling my head off by now if you were hanging around and managed to get inside."

There was a long pause while Richard went on hovering in the dimness of the stairwell. Finally he asked the question both of them had been silently worried about. "And what if he isn't satisfied, Jordan? What if, after looking through the outbuildings and the woods, he asks to check the house itself from cellar to attic?"

"Then we're in trouble. But not," she added brightly, "as much trouble as you think because I've been considering that possibility, and I have something." She snatched open a drawer in the pine cupboard, fished inside and emerged with a key dangling in her hand.

"What is it?"

"A key. It unlocks the door to the tower, and the tower is strictly off-limits to the public. Con Matthews must know that, and he wouldn't expect me to have a key. So if he does come to the house, I'll lock you in the tower and let him assume that no one could possibly have any access to it but the Coast Guard."

Richard nodded. "Let's hope it doesn't come to that. Where is he now?"

Jordan glanced through the nearest window. "On the shore. Scouting along the rocks."

"What's he looking for down there?"

"I don't know. Probably nothing."

She wished this was all over with. She realized Richard must be feeling the same. The tension was awful.

There was another pause, and then he wanted to know, "What's the guy like?"

"Determined," she answered without hesitation. Richard had a right to know exactly what he was up against. She went on to explain how Harry Fellows had been the sheriff's friend and political supporter and that Con Matthews must have sworn to do whatever was necessary to catch his killer.

Richard didn't react to this, but she knew he understood the severity of his enemy. "What's happening now?" he wanted to know.

Jordan trained her eyes on the scene framed by the window. She saw the sheriff straddling a pair of boulders. He was bending over now, examining something wedged down between the rocks. There was another thing she noticed then, and it immediately unnerved her.

The threatening overcast she had glimpsed earlier from the highway was not a cloud cover. It was one of the heavy fogs common on Lake Michigan at this season. She could see the thick mass crawling over the waters behind the figure of the sheriff, moving tenaciously this way. Within a few minutes the island would be wrapped in a clammy blanket.

Fog. How she hated it. It triggered memories of last summer. Memories that made her tremble with the same helplessness of that terrible day.

"Jordan, what's wrong?"

Richard's voice reminded her of the urgency of the moment. She made an effort to forget about the fog and its hideous associations. She concentrated on the activity of Con Matthews.

"He's . . . he's picked up something from the rocks," she reported. "I can see him holding it, but I don't know what it is. It's long and dark and kind of, well, floppy. I'm not sure he knows what it is, either, but he's certainly interested in it."

Richard was across the kitchen in a flash, peering through the glass over her shoulder. She tried to press him back.

"No! If he should look this way—"

"I have to know," he insisted. He watched Con inspecting his find, and then he swore softly.

"What is it?" she pleaded.

"Just what I was afraid it was. It's part of the raft that broke up while I was escaping in it from the *Lady Anne*. I never thought about the pieces washing ashore."

"But he can't know this is from that same raft. Besides, they think you came away in the lifeboat."

"Maybe, but he's suspicious all the same. You can see he is. He knows something is up, and—"

He broke off, pulling back from the window and dragging her with him as the sheriff turned to stare at the house.

"What now?" she wondered.

He shook his head.

"I don't think he saw us," Jordan said. "I'm going to look again. It doesn't matter if he sees me. It's only normal that I'd be wondering what he's up to out there."

"Be careful."

Jordan risked what she hoped was a casual glance through the glass. Her heart dropped. Con had left the beach and was heading purposefully toward the house.

The tower key was still in her hand. Richard asked no questions when she grabbed his arm and rushed him through the house and down the steps to the door of the shed that connected the residence to the lighthouse tower.

The stout door was unlocked without delay. Richard slid through the opening into the gloom. Before she could secure the door behind him, he faced her grimly.

"If the worst happens, I want something understood. You don't know me, never saw me before. You don't know how I managed to get in here."

"Richard, please—"

"Not until you promise," he said, holding the door against her tugging hands.

There was no time to argue with him. "Promise," she agreed.

He backed away into the dimness, his compelling blue eyes holding her gaze with a message of silent gratitude that made her heart lurch in her breast. Then she snatched the door shut and relocked it. She barely got the key back into its kitchen drawer before Con banged on the door at the other end of the house.

She could feel a treacherous flush on her face. It was more the result of that tender expression in Richard's eyes than the excitement of the moment. She had to look calm and unworried before she opened the door to Con. He was knocking again, but by the time she reached that side of the house she had her emotions under control.

Jordan even managed a cheerful smile as she opened the door to the sheriff. "Everything under control?" she asked him brightly.

He didn't return her smile. His look was serious. "It's all clear out here. I'd like to look through the house now."

"But why? I told you I keep the place locked, and there's no one here but me."

"Let's just call it a precaution, Jordan. I found something on the beach."

"Yes, I noticed." There was no use pretending she hadn't when he might have spotted her in the window watching him as he'd started for the house. "What is it?"

"Could be part of a raft that was aboard the yacht."

"That doesn't mean anything, Con. Stuff is always washing up on the island, some of it years old. Anyway, didn't I hear on the radio that this man got away in a lifeboat?"

"Probably, since the lifeboat was missing, but I'd still feel better checking the house."

There was no way of keeping him out, not without risking his further suspicion. Maybe it was better to let him search the house and send him away satisfied. That way he would have no reason to return. But it was a fearful business.

He was waiting. She had to make a choice.

"All right." She relented, stepping back and allowing him to enter.

They went from room to room. He didn't overlook the cellar and the attic. Jordan never left his side, her nerves raw with strain, her glance cutting into every corner as she worried that Richard might have overlooked some article belonging to him. But he had left no sign of himself to catch the sheriff's watchful gaze.

By the time they reached the door to the tower, she was regretting her decision to admit him into the house. She should have refused, let him think what he would about her uncooperative attitude. Now it was too late. Con tried the tower door and found it locked.

"The beacon is off-limits to everyone but Coast Guard personnel," she said quickly behind him. "Even me."

Con turned and pinned her with his calculating gray eyes. "Let's have the key, Jordan," he commanded her softly.

"I don't have a key. Only the Coast Guard can get into the tower."

He smiled at her, his hand fingering the service revolver at his hip. "Sure would hate to shoot the lock off this door, but I guess the Coast Guard would understand."

He didn't believe her! What was she going to do now?

"What's it going to be, Jordan? The key or a smashed lock?"

She knew he meant it. He would destroy the lock unless she produced the key. She felt sick with failure. Richard had listened to her, trusted her, and instead of safeguarding him all she had managed to do was corner him in a place from which there was no escape. He would have been better dropping from a window, taking his chances in the open. Now, even worse, she was about to be the means of revealing him to his enemy, when his vital freedom depended on her.

There was nothing she could do but give the key to Con Matthews. But at least she could effect a small delay, prepare Richard with a warning.

Jordan took her time returning to the kitchen and hunting up the key. All the way there and back she objected in a voice loud enough to penetrate the tower door.

"The Coast Guard isn't going to appreciate these strong-arm tactics, Con. They could consider this a violation of trust since I'm responsible for the key, and that might endanger my lease."

Nothing she said made a difference to Con. He took the key from her without an apology and turned it in the lock, spreading the door inward.

Jordan held her breath, not knowing what to expect as Con fumbled for the light switch with one hand, his other hovering over his revolver. The overhead lamps disclosed the empty shed and the iron stairway beyond spiraling up the core of the tower. There was no sign of Richard, but she knew better than to be relieved. No place in the tower could offer him an undetected refuge if Con decided to be relentless in his pursuit.

"You see," she said, trying to put an end to his effort. "Nothing."

"I'll just have a look up top."

He was going to be persistent. Richard didn't stand a chance. Jordan, just as insistent, followed Con up the curling stairway, unable to help her nervous, inane chatter. What good would it do? Richard was already warned, must know they were on their way. But she couldn't seem to silence herself.

"I don't know how you think he could possibly have gotten in here. Or why he'd even want to. And you are going to have to explain if the Coast Guard finds out we were here and starts asking a lot of questions...."

Con had no reply. He probably thought she sounded foolish. She didn't blame him.

Each step of that hollow climb felt like a dreaded sentence to Jordan. At last they were in the head, standing just below the light. Con eyed the ladder and the padlocked trapdoor under the beacon.

"You will have to shoot *this* lock off if you want to get up into the light itself," she informed him angrily, "because this time I don't have a key."

The lock was undisturbed, and she knew Richard couldn't possibly have broken in to the beacon. The sheriff knew it, too. There was only one place Richard could be. It was all that was left. Con was not about to neglect investigating it. He thrust open the door to the catwalk that girdled the tower just below the light. Jordan went after him as he stepped into the open. And wished she hadn't.

She was suddenly swallowed by her worst nightmare as she clung to the iron railing. She had forgotten about the fog. It cloaked the entire island now. Long scarves of it drifted up around the tower, licking her face, summoning unwanted memories of that tragic day last summer. She couldn't see the lake, but she could hear it lapping at the rocks far below. There were gulls, too, swooping like ghosts over the shrouded waters, their harsh cries betraying their existence.

Jordan, feeling trapped in the hated fog, went on grasping the railing, weak and giddy. Con, rounding the tower and returning to her side after his inspection, noticed her faintness.

"Are you all right? If it's the height you'd better go down."

"It isn't the height, and I'm all right."

This was insane! He had circled the tower, gazed up at the windowed beacon directly above their heads and had found nothing. There was no place left for Richard to be. So where had he gone? He couldn't have climbed down. The tower was nearly vertical, its walls offering no support for hands or feet.

Dear Lord, had he fallen? She stared over the railing, but the fog was so dense it was impossible to glimpse even a patch of the ground. Richard could be sprawled down there, his body broken, and she wouldn't know.

"We'd better get you down," Con suggested.

Her light-headedness was suddenly useful. Anything to get his mind off Richard. All she wanted was to be rid of him so she could find Richard.

Con was all apologies now as he led her down the clanging stairway. "Sorry I had to put you through all this, Jordan, but I hope you understand it was for your own protection. Not that I seriously believed he could be hanging around the place without your knowledge, but I'm not overlooking any possibilities with this guy."

They reached the bottom, passed through the shed. He locked the door behind them and handed her the key. "You okay now?"

"Fine. I just don't like fog." She walked him rapidly through the house to the outside door.

"We'll catch him, you know," Con promised as he turned to face her in the doorway. "Sooner or later, wherever he is, we'll catch him."

Jordan shivered. The fierce expression in his gray eyes made her afraid for Richard. She longed to offer some word of defense on his behalf. She didn't dare.

Con noticed her trembling. "You sure you're all right?"

She didn't want him to be concerned. She just wanted him to go. She crossed her arms over her breasts and hugged herself. "It's just the fog."

"Yeah, the fog. You get back inside, then, and warm yourself. And keep your doors and windows locked. Call us if you see anything. And, Jordan?"

"Yes?"

"Maybe I'll see you around, okay?" he said meaningfully.

She gave him a noncommittal "Yes, maybe."

Satisfied with that, he walked off through the fog. She made sure he was gone before she closed and locked the door.

Richard. She had to hunt for Richard. The key was still in her hand as she raced back to the tower door. Her fingers shook as she fitted it in the lock, swung the door inward and flipped on the lights.

Richard, to her amazement, was perched on a lower step of the tower stairway, waiting for her with his hands on his knees. Jordan sagged weakly against the shed wall.

"I don't think I could pass a stress test at this moment," she admitted.

He grinned at her ruefully. "I'm not sure I could, either."

"How did you do it? Where were you?"

His finger pointed upward. "On the service ledge outside the beacon above the catwalk. When I pulled myself up there I found it was recessed. For safe footing, I guess."

"I didn't know that."

"I was praying the sheriff didn't know it, either. I had myself squeezed as flat as I could, curled up in the depression around the light. Looks like it worked."

"All the time you were just over our heads, and I thought—"

She couldn't go on. She felt ready to collapse. Richard was suddenly aware of her emotional exhaustion. He surged to his feet, wrapped an arm around her waist and led her back to the stairway. She was grateful when he settled them side by side on one of the steps. The space was narrow. They had to squeeze together, but she didn't mind that. His closeness was reassuring.

"Better?" he asked in that husky voice that warmed her insides.

"Much," she assured him. And she meant it. The tower was dank, its rough brick walls uninviting, but she didn't mind their surroundings. Not when his strong arm was still around her, comforting and protective.

"You were wonderful, Jordan," he said, his praise making her glow. "You handled it like a pro, and I can't thank you enough. But I'm not going to chance putting you through something like this again."

The glow he had lit inside her suddenly faded. She stiffened, asking sharply, "What's that supposed to mean?"

"That I'm getting out of here. I'll take the outboard because I need it to get aboard the yacht. You can say it was stolen."

"You mean you're leaving? For good?"

"That's exactly what I mean."

She pulled away from his encircling arm and faced him defiantly. "I see. You're going to head out of here, just like that. And where do you think you'll head to? Probably straight into another one of Con Matthews's patrols just waiting for you, that's where."

"Jordan, I don't have a choice."

"But you do. Think about it, Richard. After today Cana Island is the safest spot for you to make your base while you solve the murders. Con Matthews has been over every square foot of the place and satisfied himself that you're not here. He has no reason to look again."

"Maybe, but I can't count on that. If it was just myself I had to worry about—"

"Stop worrying about me. I'm already involved by my own choice, and you can't change that. I don't regret it, and I don't want you to keep regretting it, either."

He tried again to make her see reason. "Jordan, listen to me."

"No. I'm not in any danger, because Con has no reason to suspect me. So let me help you in whatever way I can."

Stubborn, he thought. She was one stubborn woman for sure, and all he wanted to do in this moment was take her in

his arms and hold her for as long as she would let him. He
didn't dare. He settled instead for a deep sigh of surrender.

"All right, you win. I guess I'm just desperate enough to
take what I can."

She favored him with a little smile of satisfaction. "That's
better. Now let me tell you about the funeral."

"What funeral?" he asked sharply.

"The one I attended this morning." She began to tell him
where she had been and what she had seen.

"Andrew," he interrupted her impatiently. "What did the
housekeeper have to say about Andrew?"

Jordan's smile slipped. She had delayed this part, dread-
ing his reaction. "I didn't ask her, Richard," she said softly.
"There was no need to. Andrew was there at the funeral."

He looked as unhappy suddenly as she had anticipated he
would. He was also furious. "Damn them! What right did
they have to bring him up here and expose him to something like this?"

"Anne was his mother," she reminded him gently. "I
suppose they figured he ought to attend her funeral."

Richard shook his head. "He's too young to understand.
It was a mistake. I could wring Victor's neck because I'm
sure he's the one who made the decision and arranged for
it." His fist came down hard on his knee. "I can't be there
for him! That's what's killing me! There's no way I can be
there for him!"

Jordan sympathized with him, understood his frustration. She laid a hand over his tightly clenched fist, trying to
ease his torment. "For what it's worth, Richard, Andrew
was being his father's son today."

He gazed at her uncertainly. "Meaning?"

"That no matter how tough it must be for him, he's handling it." Like you, Jordan thought, admiring the tenacity
that sustained him in the face of insurmountable odds. He
was driven to prove his innocence, fighting to save himself
for Andrew's sake more than for his own. It was a quality
that touched her emotions at their deepest level.

His face softened with pride. "Yeah, he would hang in there. He's a good kid."

"That's what you have to remember then, until you're free to be with him."

His expression tightened again, his blue eyes frantic. "But in the meantime he's in the care of Victor and Evelyn. He's there in that house. And one of them could have been responsible for the murders."

She hadn't thought of that before. That Andrew could in any way be in jeopardy. It was something to be considered, something she might even be able to investigate, but for now it was important to reassure Richard.

"Sonia Gunnerson is also there," she reminded him, referring to the housekeeper. "I know her, Richard, and you must know her, too. She's a caring woman, and she'd never let anything happen to your little boy. You have to hold on to that belief."

"Since I'm being framed for three murders I didn't commit," he noted bitterly, "and have no way of removing Andrew from that scene, it's just about all I do have to hold on to. Well, I've got to clear myself. It's the only way I can get Andrew back. What else about the funeral? Did you hear anything, see anything that might be useful?"

"Not much, I'm afraid," she apologized. "Except . . ."

"What?"

"There was this older man in the cemetery. I'm sure Sonia knew him, and she wasn't happy about his being there." Jordan described the situation and the lanky, white-haired stranger who had stood apart from the company of mourners.

Richard frowned and shook his head. "Doesn't sound like anyone I've ever met."

"There's just one other thing I noticed. Victor and Evelyn. I got the impression that they were, well, unnaturally close. But that could just mean they were being there for each other in their grief. Only it did occur to me . . ."

"Go on."

"The money. Harry Fellows was a wealthy man. So who gets all that wealth?"

His broad shoulders lifted in a small shrug. "I imagine the bulk of it would be divided somehow between his wife and his children. With Anne gone, that leaves Victor and Evelyn to claim it."

The next question was one Jordan hated to ask, but it had to be faced. "And Andrew?" she said softly.

"I suppose as Harry's only grandchild he must figure in for a share of it, too, which—"

Richard broke off as he was seized by the same ghastly possibility that had struck Jordan. What if someone greedy wanted it all and was desperate enough, insane enough to eliminate all obstacles, including the other heirs?

Neither of them could bring themselves to frame in words this latest potential danger to Andrew. "I've got to prove who killed them. It's the only chance I stand of getting my son out of that situation. No one is going to believe me otherwise. And there's still only one hope for doing that."

She realized what he meant. "The contents of the safe on the yacht."

He nodded, lifting his gaze to check one of the small portholes over their head. The fog was thicker than ever, gray bands of it trailing past the glass.

"And this is the perfect opportunity," he said, "to try getting aboard the *Lady Anne*. The fog out there is as good as night, maybe better."

She had forgotten about the fog. She didn't mean to clutch his arm, didn't intend to behave like some hysteric. But her revulsion was so powerful that she couldn't help herself.

"No! You can't go out in the fog! Richard, I—I won't let you do it! Do you understand me? *I will not let you do it!*"

Chapter Eight

The violence of her objection stunned him. He stared at her fingers gripping his forearm, then at her face, which looked white and strained in the glare of the tower's naked light bulbs.

"Jordan?"

She saw the bewilderment in his eyes, and she suddenly realized how totally irrational she must seem. She loosened her fingers on his arm, made an effort to recover her composure.

"I'm sorry," she murmured. "I didn't mean to go all wild on you. It's just…well, I want you to promise me you won't go out in that outboard until the fog is lifted."

"What is it? What's wrong?"

"Fog is risky, that's all."

"There's more to it than that."

"No."

"The hell there isn't. You're shaking. Now tell me."

"I—I don't want to talk about it."

"Well, I think you need to talk about it."

Maybe he's right, she thought. Maybe she would feel better confiding in him. Anyway, she could see he wasn't going to let up on her until he learned about the demon that haunted her.

"All right," she whispered. She put her hands in her lap and laced them together tightly, as if the small action could provide her with the courage to relate that monstrous day last summer.

"I'll tell you something funny," she began. "Some people think I should be nervous staying here all on my own. That I ought to mind the remoteness or the extremes of weather that can trap me on the island, snow and ice in the winter or wild storms like the one the other day. I *should* mind all that, but I don't really. Instead . . ."

"Fog," he said.

"Foolish, isn't it? It's something soft and quiet. It shouldn't be threatening unless maybe you're out driving or navigating in it. But whenever it closes in, I get this awful feeling of no longer being in control."

"Jordan, most of us have a phobia about something, and it isn't supposed to make sense."

She shook her head vigorously. "You don't understand. I was never crazy about fog, but I wasn't unreasonable about it. Not—not before last summer."

Last summer, Richard thought. She had told him earlier that she had lost her grandfather last summer. He remembered her excessive constraint over the subject and how he had wondered then about the explanation for it.

"Your grandfather?" he guessed.

She nodded mutely.

He could feel her misery. He didn't want to subject her to this. "Jordan, you don't have to tell me," he said gently.

"Yes, I do. I want to." And she meant it. She suddenly needed to share this private thing with him, just as he had shared his own inner anguish. She needed his understanding and compassion. But it was difficult when Casey had been so important to her.

"I'm listening," he encouraged her.

"I was spending the weekend with him at his cabin," she said. "We went out on the lake in his outboard. Casey loved to fish. We were probably farther from shore than we should have been in a boat that small, but it was clear and calm. The thing is, these waters can change so quickly."

He noticed how deliberately unemotional her voice was. It was probably the only way she could get through her account of that day.

"Anyway, a fog started to roll in. A heavy one. We noticed it in plenty of time. We should have been back at the dock before it closed down on us. Except Casey couldn't get the motor started. He kept tugging the cord, but it wouldn't turn over. He was wearing himself out. I begged him to let me try, but he could be so stubborn. He wasn't about to let that motor defeat him."

If a trait like obstinacy could be inherited, Richard thought, then he understood now where Jordan got her own stubbornness.

"I know why he was being so unreasonable," she continued, remorse in her voice. "It was because of me. He knew how much I disliked fog, and he wanted to get me back before it got worse. That's why he wouldn't just sit tight until it lifted and we could signal someone, even refused to let me try the oars. What happened was so needless. If only we'd realized . . ."

She paused. He gave her time to summon the will to go on.

"His heart," she said. "His heart and all that stress. But we didn't know because there were no warnings. He'd never had any health problems, and he wasn't that old."

"An attack?" Richard asked.

Jordan nodded. "A massive coronary. It was hopeless. There was nothing I could do to help him. We were buried in the fog by then. I kept shouting, but no one heard us. And when I did try rowing, all I managed was to paddle in circles. It was horrible."

There was no way she could accurately describe it for him. How utterly lost and defenseless she had felt in that wall of vapor, how useless her cries had been. She could still taste the fog in her mouth, feel the panic clawing at her.

"He was dead by the time it was all over and they finally got to us," she finished in a wooden voice.

"Jordan, I'm so sorry."

"Want to know something ironic?" she said with a small, mirthless smile. "Here I am trying to write a book about the courageous women of these waters when I'm nothing but a coward over a little fog."

It was cold in the tower. She began to shiver. Richard didn't hesitate. He took her in his arms and held her, wanting to warm her, to comfort her. That's all he intended. He didn't mean anything else to happen.

"You listen to me," he insisted, his cheek pressed against her silky, sable hair. "If there's a woman braver or with more fighting spirit than you, then I don't know her."

She clung to him, relishing his solid warmth, the security of his protective arms as she struggled with her doubts.

Sensing her lingering misgivings, he drew back. His big hands framed her face, his eyes holding hers. "Believe it," he said. "You are the woman to write that book."

He made her feel she was capable of anything, was irrefutably convinced of it. How could she resist something as provocative as that? She didn't try, didn't even want to try. She welcomed the intimacy of his thumbs slowly, sensually stroking her cheekbones. Her wide eyes and parted mouth invited a deeper closeness.

Richard's mouth slowly, lightly joined with hers in a sweet fusion. The tip of his tongue tenderly traced the contours of her lips. As her soft sigh pleaded for more, their kiss tightened, becoming a riveting business of dueling tongues, searching hands, clinging bodies. He was conscious of her taste, rich and captivating.

This is a mistake, Jordan thought even as she strained against him. What was she letting herself in for with this explosive involvement? Had her failed relationship with Dwight taught her nothing? There had been no real hurt over Dwight, no wrenching loss. But her emotions with this alluring man were already at a dangerous level, promising a monumental heartache if he left her. And that could happen at any time because, in his menacing situation, there could be no guarantees, no counting on tomorrow.

This is all wrong, Richard thought as his hands caressed her warm flesh, seeking the arousing fullness of her breasts. He didn't want to hurt her. She was a vibrant, compassionate woman. She deserved a security he couldn't offer her. Would maybe never be able to offer her. What was he doing to her? To himself?

A crazy time to be falling in love, they both thought. Is that what was happening?

Not now, not here, Richard decided, easing away from her with a massive effort that left him painfully hard, furiously unsatisfied. But he was determined that when, and if, they made love it would be thorough and unhurried and without this mess he had landed in urgently demanding his attention.

Jordan was shaken when he separated from her and drew her to her feet. But she didn't object when he growled in frustration, "Let's get out of here."

She recognized the wisdom in leaving the tower, of returning to the house where they could settle their emotions. Back in the kitchen she was aware of the fog outside the window. It hadn't thinned.

She stared at it for a moment, shuddering. Then she turned to him and said quietly, "You're going out there in it, aren't you?"

"Jordan, I have to."

It was inevitable. "I know," she said, steeling herself to accept it, "but not looking like that. Your clothes are a mess, a real giveaway."

"Do I have a choice?"

"Yes. I kept most of Casey's things. They're upstairs. He was about the same size as you so his clothes should fit you. Well enough, anyway. I'll get them."

She was back within minutes with pants, shirt and a crewneck sweater. She handed them to Richard along with her grandfather's favorite baseball cap and his aviator-style sunglasses.

"Not much of a disguise," she said, referring to the cap and glasses, "but they should help."

He accepted her offering and started for the bathroom to clean up and change. She stopped him at the door.

"There's something I'd like to try while you're in there."

"What is it?"

"A phone call to Chicago. I thought about it while I was upstairs. Richard, I know you're hoping to find something revealing in that safe, but we have to look at other possibilities, too. And this is one of them."

She could see his interest, and she went on to explain her intention. "I have a close friend at the magazine where I worked. She specializes in investigative research. Holly has all the right connections, and there's not many questions she can't get answers to."

"Such as?"

"The dilemma of who else was aboard the *Lady Anne*. We know there was someone hiding in the master cabin, and he had to have boarded in either Chicago or Milwaukee before you joined the yacht at Two Rivers."

"Right."

"And we agree that whoever it was must be the killer."

"Go on."

"There's no guarantee anyone saw him going aboard, or would even remember if they did, but it's the sort of thing Holly knows how to dig up."

"And what do you say when she asks why you want to know?"

"She won't, not if I tell her it's all confidential for the moment. Holly is used to that. Richard, we can trust her. She's very discreet."

He thought about it for a minute. Despite his objections, Jordan was growing increasingly involved in his situation. He didn't seem able to keep her out of it. Now here was a new effort she wanted to make on his behalf. Her caring mattered to him, moved him deeply, but he didn't like these risks. The trouble was, he was too desperate to refuse her help.

"All right," he agreed, "but be careful."

She promised and went out to the kitchen to make the call. She reached Holly at the magazine, explaining to her what she wanted. Her friend agreed without question to do what she could. Then, with humor in her voice, she asked pointedly, "Care to speak to Dwight? I think he's at his desk."

Jordan didn't hesitate in her brief reply. "Not interested. And if he should ask, you haven't heard from me."

Holly laughed. Jordan had the feeling as she hung up that her insightful friend was guessing there was someone in her life now far more important than Dwight Jamison. Holly was right.

Flipping on the radio to catch the latest news report, Jordan began to make a sandwich that Richard could take with him in the outboard.

SHE WAS WAITING FOR HIM when he emerged from the bathroom. There was a sober look on her face that instantly alerted him.

"What's wrong?" he demanded. "Something with the call to Chicago?"

She shook her head. "It's gone, Richard. The yacht is gone."

"What are you telling me?"

"It was on the news just now. They've moved the *Lady Anne* out of North Bay, towed it elsewhere. I guess all the sightseers there were proving a nuisance, and it was getting too hard to protect it when it had to be anchored out in the bay like that."

"Where? Where have they taken it?"

"That's just it. They're not saying this time. I suppose to avoid a repeat of more sightseers. Richard, I'm so sorry."

His face hardened. "I'm not giving up on it. There has to be a way to find out where they've put it."

She had been considering that problem while she'd waited for him. "I think there is. No one with the sheriff's department or the Coast Guard is going to disclose that information. But they would have to have told the Fellows family where they've taken it. And what they know, the housekeeper will know."

"Sonia Gunnerson?"

"She reminded me at the funeral that Harry Fellows promised to make his library available to me for my research. It's a marvelous collection of nautical books. She renewed that offer today and assured me the family would agree. She said any time I was ready she would arrange it."

Richard understood where she was headed, and he didn't like it. "You are not going to that house."

"But the opportunity is so perfect. And even if it is, well, presumptuously soon after the funeral—Richard, no, don't look like that. Listen to me. There's more than just the yacht to find out about. If Victor and Evelyn are innocent, then they would have alibis for that day, and we need to know them."

"Certainly," he said dryly. "Are you planning to ask them?"

"You know I wouldn't. But the housekeeper is an old friend who trusts me. She loves to talk, and I can be a very good listener."

"And suppose Victor and Evelyn don't have alibis. That could make them killers, couldn't it?"

"Yes, that's the point."

"No, Jordan, the point is you would be there in the same house with two people who might be murderers and probably wouldn't hesitate to murder again if they felt threatened. Damn it, it's bad enough Andrew is there, but at least he's not trying to play detective."

"And there's another reason for my going," she reminded him, pressing her argument. "You're going out of your mind about Andrew, and I could check on his welfare for you.''

She watched his face. The emotions he struggled with were plainly written there.

"All right," he said finally and with a calmness that astonished her, "you can go to the house. But," he added emphatically, "I'm going with you."

Jordan frowned. "Richard, you can't."

"I can, and I will. I'm familiar with the place. I know ways to slip inside without being seen. And if Andrew is alone, I'll find him while you keep the housekeeper busy."

"But if someone should see you—"

"That's a risk I'm prepared to take. Jordan, I *need* to see my kid. I need to see for myself that he's all right."

It was an argument for which she had no defense.

"Besides," he said grimly, "anything threatening to you comes up while you're in there, then I'm on the spot to help you deal with it. Make the call."

She did.

Sonia Gunnerson was surprised by the immediacy of her request, but the housekeeper graciously invited her to the house. Jordan assured her that she could be there within the hour.

"THIS IS IT," Richard directed her. "Let me off here. There's the path I remember. Nobody uses it. I can cut through the woods that way and work around to the side of the house."

Jordan eased the Volvo to a stop along a stretch of forest. Just ahead was the gated driveway to the Fellows' summer estate, which was located on the shoreline bluffs north of Ephraim.

"We're agreed about it, then," she reminded him as he slid from the car. "Whichever one of us gets back to this spot first waits for the other."

He nodded and met her gaze with a look that told her to be careful. She silently wished him the same as he turned and started for the path. She waited until the trees had safely swallowed him. Then she drove on through the iron gates and along the driveway bordered by thick woods that screened the house from view.

At least the hated fog, which they had negotiated at an unnerving crawl, was far behind her. This, the Green Bay side of the peninsula, was clear and sunny, as it frequently was when the cooler Lake Michigan shoreline was fog-bound. Jordan was steady now, ready to deal with her meeting with the housekeeper.

The driveway emerged from the woods, revealing the house situated in its spacious lawns. It was one of those sprawling stone mansions from a more expansive era. Like something out of a gothic novel she thought, gripped by a sense of unease as she climbed from the Volvo.

The memory of the horror aboard the *Lady Anne* was strongly with her as she made her determined way to the massive front door. Eyeing the tall, silent windows, she was increasingly convinced that someone in this house had the answers Richard needed.

Sonia Gunnerson answered Jordan's ring. There was certainly nothing sinister about the housekeeper. Her gentle blue eyes and warm smile welcomed her.

"I'm sorry to intrude at a time like this," Jordan apologized, "but as I mentioned, the library doesn't have what I need, and you did say—"

"It's nothing." Sonia forgave her, inviting her inside. "What are old friends for? Remember," she reminisced, a faint, musical accent betraying her Scandinavian heritage, "how, when you were a girl, you and Casey would visit Gus and me when we had the farm?"

"And how much I loved your lingonberries on limpa bread."

"That's right. And now," she said, shaking her head with regret and reminding them both of recent events, "so much is changed. Well, the books. We go this way."

Sonia led her through the house. There was no evidence of the family being present. No sign of Andrew. She wondered how Richard was making out, whether he was still on his way to the house or whether he had already managed to get inside. But it was a mistake to worry about him. She needed to concentrate on her own mission.

The rooms were impressive and immaculately maintained. Jordan had learned in her work with the magazine the usefulness of a little honest flattery to win information. She employed that psychology now.

"The place is beautiful and so well kept," she said, admiring the priceless antiques.

The housekeeper was pleased. "I have good day help, of course. Not that all of it doesn't keep me busy myself. Here we are."

They arrived in the richly paneled library at the back of the house. Books stretched to the ceiling, while French doors overlooked a raised terrace with a spectacular view of Green Bay.

Jordan paused in front of a library table. Several handsome ship models were displayed on its highly polished surface. Because of her nautical interest, she hoped the housekeeper would find it only natural that she should stop to examine them.

"These are very fine," Jordan said, bending to inspect an early Great Lake schooner.

"Yes," Sonia agreed. "Harry was very proud of his models. What will happen to them now or, for that matter, the rest of the place . . . well, I don't know."

It was the opening Jordan had been looking for. "Yes, I suppose the family will have a lot of decisions to make about the property. The yacht, too, I guess."

"Probably, but that has to wait until the police release it."

"Oh, isn't it docked here?"

"No, they had it anchored at North Bay, but that turned out to be a problem. They've moved it now to Sturgeon Bay. With the sheriff's department right there, and fewer tourists down at that end, I imagine they have a better control on its security."

Success! Jordan thought, and it had been much easier than she'd anticipated. She didn't dare to ask for more, not without risking suspicion.

She turned her interest in another direction. The ship models shared the table with a collection of family photographs. She permitted her gaze to wander innocently among the grouping.

"Isn't this the little boy I saw at the funeral?"

"That's right. Harry's grandson, Andrew. A sweet child."

"It must be especially hard for him," Jordan sympathized.

"I think it is, though he's been very withdrawn about it."

Jordan's gaze moved on. And there was Richard, his rangy figure in the background of a family picnic in happier days. "Is this...?"

Sonia nodded. "Andrew's father. I guess there's no mistaking the resemblance." She lowered her voice to a confidential level. "Whatever they say, I can't bring myself to believe he did it. I liked him. He seemed like a good man to me. A very caring father."

An opinion that might prove useful to know, Jordan thought. Richard needed another friend. And now that the housekeeper was mellowed by her interest and approval, she hoped to draw other answers from her. Most important of all, where were Victor and Evelyn the afternoon of the murders? Their photographs were here on the table as well, the handsome son and the young, beautiful widow side by side in ornate silver frames. Would it look out of place to admire their pictures, lead the gossipy conversation in that direction?

Before she could decide, Sonia, to her disappointment, turned to the purpose of her errand. "But none of this is getting you the books you came for, is it? This is what you want over here."

She led her to a section of shelves near the French doors. Jordan began examining the titles. There were several volumes that she legitimately did want to borrow.

"Take anything you like," the housekeeper urged.

"I appreciate this. These are marvelous."

"Some of them are very old, of course, but I know you'll care for them. Which reminds me—John McGuire had a collection of original ship logs. I remember how Harry envied him those logs. They would be wonderful for your research. I imagine his sister must have them with the rest of his things. You could probably arrange to use them."

Jordan, preoccupied by a book on logging vessels, murmured, "Who?"

"John McGuire. I don't guess you or Casey ever met him. He never visited the peninsula. Harry knew him in Chicago. They shared an interest in the history of the lakes. Nothing much else in common, I suppose."

"I don't—"

"The man piloting the *Lady Anne*. The one who was—was killed along with them. I still have trouble saying it, much less believing it."

Mac, Jordan suddenly remembered. That was the name Richard had heard. The only name. But she recalled now that the newscasts had identified him as John McGuire.

"Yes, ship logs would be worthwhile. But how would I contact this sister?"

She tried to sound enthusiastic about the housekeeper's suggestion, but privately she wasn't very hopeful. Although such logs could be invaluable to research, she didn't suppose that John McGuire's sister could provide her with any useful information regarding the murders. He was simply in the wrong place at the wrong time. Still...

"She's right here on the peninsula," Sonia explained. "Rented a place for the season. Her brother was to join her for the summer. Harry talked him into traveling up from Chicago with them on the yacht since he hadn't found a crew yet. And Mac—that's what they called him—jumped at the chance to be on the water. He knew a lot about boats, though of course he wasn't a professional pilot. Actually, he was—''

The housekeeper was interrupted by the arrival of a thin young woman wearing a cleaning smock. One of the day helpers, Jordan assumed.

"Yes, Darlene, what is it?"

The woman hovered in the doorway, casting a nervous glance in Jordan's direction. "Uh, someone in the kitchen to see you."

"Yes?"

Darlene hesitated. "Well, I think you'd better come."

The earnest expression on her face alerted the older woman and alarmed Jordan, who thought immediately of Richard. Sonia excused herself and hurried across the room. Jordan could hear the two of them out in the hallway exchanging quick whispers. Then the housekeeper, a distracted look on her face, reappeared briefly in the doorway.

"I'm sorry, Jordan. I have to go. Please go on choosing your books."

"Are you sure?"

"Yes, take your time. I'll see about getting that McGuire woman's number for you," she promised.

She was gone then, leaving Jordan to wonder about the urgency of her departure. She prayed that it didn't involve Richard, that he hadn't been spotted in the house. There had been something familiar in the housekeeper's tense manner, though. And then she remembered. Sonia had worn that same troubled expression this morning at the funeral when she'd discovered the lanky stranger off in the trees, watching the burial with a look of pronounced hatred on his face.

Who was he? What connection, if any, did he have to this whole deepening puzzle? And could he be Sonia's visitor in the kitchen?

They were questions that occupied Jordan as she selected books and waited for the housekeeper's return. It was quiet in the library. The only sound was the hushed murmur of the shining waters in the bay drifting pleasantly through one of the open French doors.

Then, gradually, she became aware of another sound. Voices. A man's heavier tone. A woman's lighter one. They came from somewhere close outside. Jordan could hardly ignore them. There was a kind of desperation in their exchange. Something to do with Richard?

Before she could examine the ethics of her action, she found herself slipping through the French door and silently crossing the elevated terrace to the stone balustrade. There was no one in sight. It was from somewhere below that the voices originated. Ignoring the stunning view of green islands in a cobalt sea, Jordan leaned against the heavy rail and peered cautiously over the edge of the high terrace.

RICHARD FLATTENED HIMSELF against the wall in the dim service passage and listened. He heard voices. Arguing voices from the direction of the kitchen. He just hoped they stayed in the kitchen.

He'd gotten into the house through the garages. One of the overhead doors near the shrubbery border, behind which he'd crept from the woods, had been left open. Easy. So far. Now came the tough part. Locating his son. He could be anywhere in the house, maybe even out on the grounds somewhere. But first he'd try Andrew's bedroom.

Satisfied that this portion of the service wing was deserted for the moment, Richard slipped past the laundry room and headed up the back stairs. There was always the chance of meeting someone on the stairway or in the upper corridor, but he wasn't going to let this stop him.

At the top of the stairs he paused again, listening. Silence. Nor was there any sign of life in the corridor that stretched the length of the house. He stole along the broad passage, reaching the closed door of the room that Andrew always occupied. It connected with the bedroom he and

Anne had once shared, but he didn't want to think about that.

Richard pressed his ear against the panel. There was the sound of a radio inside playing softly. The country music both he and Andrew liked. His son was in there. He could sense him on the other side.

Richard was suddenly worried, afraid of Andrew's reaction. He didn't want to terrify him with his appearance. He wasn't sure what the boy might have been told. But he had to see him. He had to know he was all right.

His palms were sweating as he turned the knob and slid quietly into the room. Andrew had his back to him, was unaware of his arrival. He was seated at his desk in the bay window, making a dispirited effort with a homework assignment.

Nerves betraying him, Richard whispered huskily, "Andy?"

The small figure at the desk whipped around on his chair, his eyes wide and staring.

"It's all right, Andy. I promise you everything is going to be all right."

There was no hesitation. Andrew shot across the room with the speed of an arrow and straight into his arms. Father and son hugged, clinging to each other.

At last Richard held him away, searching his face. "You okay?"

Andrew nodded.

"Sure?"

"Yeah."

They sat on the edge of the bed, Richard's arm draped around his thin shoulders, and talked. "I don't know what you've heard, Andy," his father said as gently as he could. "About your mother and grandfather, I mean, and how— how I was responsible. I wasn't responsible, and I want you to remember that. I want you to *always* remember it."

"I know. Dad, when are you coming home?"

There was no way he could explain, no way he could make him understand. He was too young, and Richard hated what all this was doing to him. "I don't know," he said honestly. "There are some things I have to try straightening out first."

"Couldn't I be with you while you straighten them?"

"I wish. Hey, don't look like that. I'm working on our being together. Just as hard as I can."

"You'll have to come for me at school in Chicago," Andrew informed him. "Uncle Vic is sending me back on the plane from Gramp's company."

"When?"

"Last thing this afternoon. Only I'm not going to be just a day pupil this time. They're going to board me there like a lot of the others."

Richard was relieved. School was the safest place for Andrew to be. He knew the staff, knew how carefully they would protect him.

"Then that's good," Richard assured him. "I'll know just where to find you. Now I want you to tell me one last time—is everybody here treating you—"

The door burst open without warning. One of the day staff in the house, a stout woman, swung into the room saying cheerfully, "Well, young man, are you ready to pack those—"

Discovering Richard, she froze. "What in—Who are you?" she demanded. "How did you get in here?"

Richard turned to his son, offering a fast, loving goodbye. "Don't forget what we talked about. See you soon, Andy."

"See you, Dad."

Richard was off the bed then and striding past the woman, who tried to stop him with a loud, "Hey, wait, you! You've got some explaining to do!"

She was shouting after him by the time he reached the corridor. He didn't pause or look back. He quickened his step, and when he neared the stairs he started to run.

DIRECTLY BELOW JORDAN, on a lower level, was an ornamental iron gazebo. In fact, she was able to gaze right through the domed roof since it was composed entirely of scrolled grillwork. There was a stone bench inside, and two figures were huddled on it side by side. She was looking onto their heads.

At first she couldn't be sure of their identities, though she knew they weren't Sonia or her visitor. Then, by stealthily shifting her position, she had a better view through the wrought-iron tracery.

No mistaking them now. Hair so black it had a blue sheen to it. And the head beside it a striking red-gold. It was Victor and Evelyn.

They were so engrossed in their conversation that Jordan was able to listen to them undetected. The cultured voice of Harry Fellows's young widow was unhappy, worried.

"I can't help it," she said. "I'm afraid all the time."

Victor's voice was soothing, protective. Just as it had been for her at the funeral this morning. "But that's done with," he assured her, his hand covering hers. "We don't have to hide anymore."

"You don't understand. I can feel people watching us, wondering. What if someone should—"

"Shh." He hushed her, raising her hand to his mouth, kissing her palm. "I'm here for you. I'll always be here for you. That's all you have to remember."

It was true, Jordan thought. What she had suspected since the funeral was plainly true. Stepson and stepmother were involved in a love affair. How long had it been going on? Had Harry Fellows learned about his wife and his son? Threatened them?

"It's not that easy, Victor." Evelyn pulled her hand away, her voice trembling. "Someone will find out. We can't go on keeping it secret."

"So what if they do?"

"But they'll think the worst. We may not be the only ones who knew the truth about Harry. They'll think the worst, and we could lose everything."

"Sweetheart," he assured her with a low sigh, "you don't seem to realize. He can't hurt us now. My father can't hurt us. That's all been taken care of. We're free."

Dear Lord, was she hearing a motive for the murders? What could even be an admission of guilt? Maybe. One thing was clear. The couple in the gazebo was protecting a secret that apparently could have serious consequences for both of them.

Jordan longed to know what that secret was. Hoping to hear it revealed, she strained eagerly against the balustrade. The pressure of her full weight disturbed the old mortar in the joint between two sections of the stone. Before she realized it, particles flaked away, drifting down through the dome of the gazebo.

Victor had his arms around Evelyn, preparing to kiss her, when the mortar bits settled on their heads like gray ashes. Jordan, knowing that her presence was about to be betrayed, whipped back out of sight with a stifled gasp.

She heard Evelyn's exclamation of alarm down in the gazebo. "What is it, Victor? What's wrong?"

Jordan didn't wait to hear Victor's reaction. Getting away before she was discovered was all that mattered now. How could she have been so careless?

Silently she fled from the terrace, scooped up her purse and the chosen books from the library and rushed toward the front door. In the entrance hall she ran smack into the day helper, Darlene.

"This is for you," the young woman said, pressing a slip of paper into her hand.

Jordan, anxious about her escape from the house, glanced at the paper in puzzlement.

"Ms. McGuire's phone number," Darlene explained. "Sonia sent it to you. She said to let you know she's sorry she can't come back herself to tell you goodbye."

"Is she all right?"

"Well, between you and me," Darlene confided, "I think she's a bit upset right now, but it's not surprising with everything that's been happening. You get what you needed?"

"Yes. Tell her thanks." Jordan hastily folded the scrap of paper, slid it under the cover of one of the books and promptly forgot about it. "I'll let myself out."

Before she could do just that, a heavyset cleaning woman appeared at the top of the main staircase. Leaning over the rail, she called down excitedly, "Darlene, call the cops! It's *him!* He was in the house!"

"Who?"

"The boy's father! I found them together before he took off! Call!"

Jordan didn't delay her exit this time. She left the house and hurried toward her car. She couldn't afford to be overtaken by Victor, detained by him. She needed to be ready to help Richard get away from the estate. Where was he now? What was happening to him?

She kept scanning the lawns and woods as she pulled away from the house and headed up the driveway. And then she saw him. A tall figure barely visible behind the shrubbery border as he came away from the service wing. He was hurrying in the direction of the woods.

This was no good. By the time he reached their rendezvous, a sheriff's cruiser could be arriving. They would be spotted together out on the road. She had to stop him, bring him to the car now.

There was a high cedar hedge at this point between the Volvo and the house. Jordan swung the car behind the wall of hedge and left it hidden. Then she took off across the lawns on a reckless pursuit of the rapidly retreating figure.

She didn't dare to call out to him for fear of being heard at the house. As it was, she risked observation from any one of the front windows. She longed for him to look over his shoulder, discover her out on the grounds. He never turned.

Where was he now? She caught a quick glimpse of him rounding a thicket of honeysuckle bushes near the perimeter of the woods. She quickened her step, circling after him. On the other side she came to a bewildered stop.

He was in clear sight just ahead of her as he started through the trees. Only it wasn't Richard. It was the lanky, white-haired mystery man from the funeral. Obviously he'd been Sonia's visitor in the kitchen and was leaving the house in the same furtive way that Richard had entered it. She watched him vanish into the woods.

Mystified, worried about Richard's whereabouts, Jordan turned and made her way back around the shrubbery. On the other side she came face-to-face with Victor Fellows.

Chapter Nine

His arrogant, handsome face was rigid with anger as he confronted her. "Hasn't anyone ever told you," he warned her in a tight, menacing voice, "that eavesdropping can be dangerous to your health?"

It was a cliché straight out of a bad movie. The trouble was, it was a very *effective* cliché. Jordan was scared. She was alone with Victor in an isolated spot, and if anything she had overheard on the terrace was threatening to him and Evelyn, if they *were* responsible for the murders...

It was her own fault. Richard had tried to keep her from playing detective. She hadn't listened, and now her life might be at risk.

There was only one thing she could do. Brazen it out with a cliché of her own. "I don't know what you're talking about."

"Liar. You were spying on us from the terrace."

She didn't care for his accusation, but she didn't have the right to deny it. She *had* been spying on him in his own house. Only there was no way she could explain it. All she could do was protect herself with another bluff.

"Why would I want to spy on you? I was borrowing books from your father's library. Didn't Sonia tell you?"

"Maybe."

"Well, then, that's all there is to it."

He went on eyeing her coldly. She could see him calculating the situation. Thinking how he had no real evidence she had been on the terrace, or that she had overheard anything vital, and that if he persisted in his accusation he risked her serious suspicions. On the other hand, if he let her go...

Would he let her go? Jordan worried. Just how dangerous was Victor Fellows?

Striving to conceal her nervousness, she started to edge past him. "I'm sorry if there was any misunderstanding. I'll take good care of the books."

His hand clamped on her arm. "Just a minute."

She faced him defiantly, resenting his grip but fearing it, too. "What now?"

"What were you doing out here?" he demanded.

"I thought I saw someone I knew cutting across the lawn."

"Was it?"

"I don't know. I lost him in the woods. It isn't important." She stared pointedly at his hand still holding her arm.

"Sorry," he muttered, releasing her.

"Anything else?"

"Yes. You might tell your friend of the woods that these are private grounds."

His message was clear. He was letting her know that he didn't want to find her here again, or any other intruder. Jordan was happy to accommodate him. Relieved, she hurried back to her car and away from the estate.

SHE HAD LOST RICHARD.

Jordan faced that unhappy truth as she drove back to the lighthouse hours later. She had waited at the rendezvous as long as she dared. Richard never appeared, and she was almost caught by the sheriff's patrol speeding toward the Fellows mansion.

Refusing to give up, she'd driven up and down every road and back lane in the area, searching for him. He had vanished. At last, in despair, she started for home.

Maybe he had found a phone and was even now trying to call her at the lighthouse. But two grave fears nagged at her. Either he had been caught, or he'd decided to do what he'd threatened all along. He'd pulled out to prevent her from being further implicated on his behalf. That meant he was out there somewhere on his own, and it would soon be nightfall. The image made her frantic.

It was foolish to suppose that he'd somehow managed to get back to the lighthouse without her. But Jordan clung to this faint hope as she parked the Volvo and hurried across the causeway.

Reaching the kitchen, she dumped her purse and the load of books on the chair under the wall phone and stood there listening. There was no point in looking through the rooms. The house was empty except for her. She could sense its emptiness.

She was stricken by the awful silence. Because only now, when he was gone, when she had to accept the reality of perhaps never seeing him again, did she understand just how desperately important he was to her.

She was standing there, struggling with her impossible heartache, when the phone rang.

Richard!

She leapt for the phone, almost knocking the books to the floor as she grabbed up the receiver. "Yes?"

"Hi. It's me, Holly."

Jordan felt her eyes smarting with tears of disappointment. She mustered a self-control, managing to say evenly, "Results so soon?"

"I wish, but I have been inquiring. I've talked to people at both the Chicago and Milwaukee harbors where the *Lady Anne* was docked. No one saw anyone going aboard the yacht except the people who were scheduled to be there. So it's a zero so far, but I will keep on trying."

Jordan tried to sound as though she still cared. "I appreciate it, Hol, and I promise to explain everything as soon as I can."

"You okay?"

"I'm fine." *Liar.*

"There is one other thing," Holly said unhappily.

"Dwight again?" Jordan guessed.

"Yeah. Our nosy receptionist heard me talking to you before and mentioned it to Dwight. He made me promise that when we spoke again I'd ask you if it was all right if he called. Has a proposition. Didn't say what, and I was afraid to ask."

"Tell him you delivered the message and there was no response."

"All right, but you know how persistent he can be."

"Yes, I know." What did it matter? she thought dismally. Dwight Jamison could offer her a dozen propositions, and she wouldn't be interested in any one of them. There was only one thing that mattered to her, and he was missing.

"I'll be in touch," Holly promised.

"Thanks, Hol. Talk to you soon."

Jordan replaced the receiver, wiped at her stinging eyes with the back of her hand and turned away from the phone to find her world rocked by the sight that filled the doorway across the room.

He had arrived in silence. She had not heard him enter the house. Hair rumpled and clothes dusty from the road he'd traveled, he looked as distraught as she had felt mere seconds ago. Distraught and utterly wonderful in his lean virility.

They stood there in a long silence charged with emotion, feeding hungrily on the sight of each other, both of them aware of what they had come so close to losing.

"I couldn't find you anywhere," she whispered.

"I was in such a rush to get away from that place I took a wrong turn in the woods. Ended up wandering all over before I found the right path again. By the time I got back to the road, you'd left.''

"I was driving around looking for you. That's how we missed each other. How did you—''

"Hiked.''

"All the way?''

He shook his head. "I ran into a kid and his jalopy. Helped him to change a flat. He gave me a lift most of the way. I walked the rest.''

"That was a dangerous thing to do.''

"He wasn't interested in recognizing fugitives. All he cared about was his car and how the Cubs were doing this season.''

"I thought I'd never see you again,'' she confessed.

"I did think about not coming back this time. But it was no good. I couldn't just walk away. I couldn't stand the thought of never being with you again.''

"Richard—''

"Oh, hell.''

Thrusting aside all barriers, and any lingering caution with them, he was across the room in four quick strides. Jordan hurled herself joyfully into his arms. Without hesitation or apology, his mouth claimed hers with a savage need. Her response was equally reckless.

Heat spiraled around her, weaving a rapturous cocoon as his tongue plundered the recesses of her mouth, seeking, demanding. She answered with her own enticing devices, tongue joined with his, her hands inflaming the hard contours of his body. She heard him groan low in his throat, aware of her own pleading whimpers.

How they got from the kitchen to the bedroom Jordan would never be able to say. It was as forgettable a process as the feverish shedding of their clothes. Nothing mattered, nothing was real but the consuming force that brought them together on the bed.

Whatever Richard had promised himself earlier about restraint was completely ignored as his mouth devoured her small, firm breasts. Jordan cried out in pleasure when his tongue tugged at her erect buds. Just as abandoned in turn, she found his arousal, teasing its swollen length until he was gasping with urgency.

"Sweetheart, I have to... please..."

She welcomed the solid body that settled so rightfully over hers. Her body arched wildly, meeting his hardness. Then that same rigid flesh carefully probed her softness, sliding into her moist depths until the two of them were merged into a molten oneness.

"It feels so—" She tried to describe it in a yearning whisper and couldn't.

Richard expressed it better when his mouth covered hers in a prolonged kiss that communicated emotions so deep and riveting that they could originate only in the cores of their souls.

She strained against him, her limbs embracing a pair of legs incredibly muscular from his years on the soccer field. Her tightening muscles fired his body into a raw action. He created a blissfulness of undulating hips and long strokes that she answered with her own wanton performance.

Together they scaled the heights, striving for a mutual pinnacle. They achieved that and more, soaring into a cosmic blaze before tumbling into sweet oblivion.

RICHARD HELD HER in his arms, cherishing her in the mellow aftermath of their lovemaking. But already a reality that he resented intruded on their hazy euphoria.

Nothing had changed. He was still a man on the run. For all he knew, he might be a fugitive for the rest of his days. Bad enough before this, but now...

No, he didn't regret for a moment the wondrous thing they had just shared. It would be branded forever in his memory. He would treasure it whatever happened, wherever he had to go. What he did damn was his inability to offer her the commitment she deserved.

How could he possibly tell her what she needed to know, what he longed to express? That kind of declaration came with a future attached to it. Only there was no promise of a future for him. He deeply minded this for himself, but what really tormented him was how much his rash passion was going to cost Jordan. If he'd hurt her beyond—

"Don't," she whispered, turning to him.

"What?" he murmured.

"You know," she said, her fingers stirring through the hair on his chest.

God, already she could read his thoughts. He couldn't stand this. He couldn't stand wanting what he couldn't have.

"You don't have to say a thing," she softly assured him. "And I don't want you to feel any guilt because you can't. I understand why it isn't possible."

"Damn it," he said, his arms tightening around her angrily, "you make it sound as if it's all right, and it isn't all right!"

They would be battling over it in another minute, she realized. She didn't want their special interlude to end like that. She had to get his mind off the subject. Talk about something else. And then it hit her all at once.

Cheeks hot with sudden remorse, Jordan pulled away from him and shot to a sitting position against the brass headboard. "Oh, my Lord, I meant to tell you straight off, and then we got—well, sidetracked. The yacht, Richard! They've towed it down to Sturgeon Bay! I was able to get that much from Sonia Gunnerson, only I couldn't learn exactly where it's docked."

"Never mind. We'll find it. Sturgeon Bay isn't that big." He quickly shared with her the essence of his meeting with Andrew and then asked, "What else?"

She went on to describe for him the conversation she had overheard between Victor and Evelyn. "What do you think? Does it prove anything?"

"Only that they've been hiding something more than just their affair and they're worried about it." Richard shook his head. "I don't know. They could be involved in the murders, but there are too many missing pieces. Also..."

"What?"

"The more I think about it, something about this whole tangled mess just doesn't work. I mean, it's wrong in a kind of way I can't put my finger on."

Jordan nodded. She, too, had been feeling that there was no easy explanation, that under it all was a frightening darkness they had yet to uncover.

"Wait," she said. "There's more."

She explained about the housekeeper's unnamed visitor but was careful to omit how she had tried to follow him and that Victor had threatened her. Richard was already unhappy enough about her risks.

"The same guy from the funeral, you say?"

"Yes, I'm sure of it."

They were speculating about the man's identity and his possible connection with the murders when the kitchen phone rang. She was tempted to leave it unanswered, except it might be Holly again with some vital information.

Jordan's robe was not handy but Richard's discarded shirt was. It hung to her knees, more than covering her as she snatched it up and struggled into it on her way to the kitchen.

This time in her race to reach the phone the books on the chair, already precariously balanced from her last rush, were tumbled to the floor. She ignored them as she grabbed up the receiver with a hurried greeting.

"So you are there," said a male voice on the other end, its overconfident tone familiar to her. "I couldn't figure out whether you weren't home or just letting it ring until you decided whether you wanted to speak to me."

Jordan could feel herself tensing. "No, Dwight," she informed him firmly, "just very busy."

"Too busy to miss me?"

She had no intentions of playing games with him. "What do you want, Dwight?"

"All right, don't go stiff on me. This is just business, that's all."

"I'm on a leave of absence, remember?"

"That doesn't mean you couldn't do a free-lance piece for me. Your beloved peninsula is getting more popular with young Chicago couples as a weekend getaway. I need a story on the bed-and-breakfasts in the area. Who better than you to write it?"

"You'll have to assign it to a staffer. I just don't have the time."

"You could make the time. That book of yours wouldn't suffer from a break."

He didn't get it. He just couldn't seem to understand and accept that he was no longer important to her, either personally or professionally. But then Dwight Jamison's self-involvement had always been one of the major problems in their rocky relationship.

She tried to tell him she simply wasn't interested in his assignment but, as usual, he failed to hear her. He went on to treat her to one of his lengthy sales pitches. Better to just let him wind down before she emphatically refused. No need to do more than pretend to listen. Her full attention wouldn't have been possible, anyway.

Richard had trailed her from the bedroom and was leaning negligently in the doorway. Since she had his shirt, he was bare-chested, wearing nothing but his snug, low-slung jeans. He made a wickedly distracting sight, his half-clad figure powerful and incredibly sexy, reminding her of their sensual magic just moments ago.

Jordan was suddenly and sharply conscious of the contrast between the two men, Dwight on the phone, Richard in the doorway. Her awareness this time had nothing to do with physical attraction. It was something just as basic but far more endearing. Dwight considered her dream about the book impractical while Richard was completely supportive of her ambition. It was that simple and that wonderful.

It was in this moment that Jordan positively knew she was in love with Richard.

All soft and weak inside, she gazed at him longingly while Dwight rattled on. She offered Richard a smile as she cradled the phone carelessly against her ear. He didn't smile back. He glowered at her darkly. That's when she realized with a lurching of her heart that something was wrong.

Jordan wasted no time then in ending the conversation. She managed to convince Dwight she had no intention of doing his story. It was impossible to go into it now, but she knew she would never go back to the magazine, either, just as she knew she could not fail to write her book. Richard had done this for her. With a hasty goodbye she hung up and turned to him.

"Don't tell me," he said, his voice approaching a growl. "He wants you back in Chicago."

She could have laughed with relief. He was jealous. Richard was actually jealous. Did that mean— No, it was too early to assume something like that. Too early and the situation too complicated by his fugitive state.

"Is that what you heard?" she asked him softly.

"Sounded like it. That he wants you back at his magazine. Or maybe he just wants you back. Are you going? Sorry. I don't have the right to be asking that."

She moved toward him. "I think you do. And, no, he didn't ask me back to Chicago. He asked me to do a story, which I turned down. And if he had asked me back, I would have been even less interested. Satisfied?"

She stood close to him now, so close she could feel his seductive heat.

"Yeah," he said, his voice low and husky. "Well, almost."

The remainder of his satisfaction was achieved when he took her in his arms and kissed her. A long and possessive kiss that made Jordan yearn to tell him just how she felt. But expressing her love now would be unfair. It would only add another burden to his already impossible load.

One thing was certain. She was more determined than ever to help clear him. She had a very selfish reason now to want his freedom.

They were on their way back to the bedroom to renew their interrupted intimacy when, in their eagerness, they almost stumbled over the books scattered on the floor.

"I promised to take care of these," Jordan muttered. "This isn't a good example of my promise."

She began to collect the volumes. Richard crouched beside her to help. "What's this?" he wondered, holding out the folded slip of paper that had fallen from the book into which she had shoved it back at the Fellows mansion.

Jordan took the paper from him and stuffed it into her purse. "A phone number that Sonia wanted me to have. Actually, it's the number of John McGuire's sister."

"Who?"

"Mac. The man who was piloting the *Lady Anne*. The sister has a place up here. She's supposed to have her brother's collection of early ship logs. Sonia thought I might be able to borrow them for my research."

Richard nodded without comment. The subject wasn't immediately important. Only one thing mattered. Getting to Sturgeon Bay the first thing tomorrow and locating the yacht. Finding a way to get aboard the vessel and hoping that the safe contained something that would clear him.

It was the longest of long shots, and he knew it. He didn't care. He was prepared to do whatever would enable him to be reunited with his son.

Chapter Ten

The cherry orchards, one of the well-known symbols of the county, were in full flower as they drove south the next morning. Ranks of them stretched across the sun-washed hillsides, their frothy crowns like banks of billowing clouds. They made a dazzling display, but Jordan was too anxious to enjoy the sight.

No one indicated interest in the occupants of the green Volvo as they whipped through the forests and farmlands, and Richard slouched down in the seat as far as he could to minimize the risk of exposure. Still, she worried about his being spotted and recognized. This was a much longer trip today, and they didn't have the fog to cover them.

It was directly after they left the village of Baileys Harbor that she noticed him, silent under the baseball cap and sunglasses, carefully searching the roadsides along which they traveled, as though he were looking for something specific.

She was about to ask him what he wanted when he said quickly, "Slow down. There up ahead. That one will do."

"What is it?"

"No, don't stop. Just notice it as we go by."

They crawled past an ordinary blue pickup truck parked along the side of the road. It was empty. Presumably, the farmer it belonged to was off in his field.

"Okay, you can speed up now. Just remember the truck."

Jordan was thoroughly mystified. "What was that all about?"

"Insurance," he explained casually. "If the worst should happen, and I get identified in this car, you don't know me. I'm just someone who waved you down, claiming my pickup stalled, and you felt sorry for me and gave me a lift. A truck actually being there backs up your side of the story. Then all they can accuse you of is being careless in picking up a stranger."

She was touched by his concern for her well-being. She was also amazed that, having established an alibi for her, he was prepared to relax for the remainder of the drive. She, herself, was far from easy. It wasn't just the risks involved in this venture, either. His closeness in the car tugged at her senses, reminding her of yesterday's passionate interlude. His intimate company this morning kept her thoughts in disorder and awakened a terrible doubt. Could she be letting herself in for a severe heartache by caring so deeply for this irresistible man when he might soon be gone from her life?

But what was the point in worrying about it when she had no choice in the matter? It was too late for that. She was already committed beyond retreat. She would take what came.

That settled, she concentrated on the drive. The lilacs back on Cana Island had yet to open, but she noticed that down here they were already in bloom. Every farmyard seemed to have them in vivid shades ranging from wine red to deep purple. Springtime on the peninsula. It had never seemed so magical to her before. Or was this just because she was in love?

STURGEON BAY WAS THE SEAT of the county, a fair-size town whose mainstay was the shipyards along the waterfront. It was this area they concentrated on, figuring the yacht would be somewhere within convenient driving distance of the sheriff's department. If the vessel hadn't been released yet to the family, then the investigators must still be interested in examining it.

Jordan, keeping a wary eye peeled for any patrol car, drove slowly along the streets paralleling the harbor while Richard searched the waters. There was no glimpse to be had of the *Lady Anne*.

"It's got to be visible somewhere," he muttered in frustration. "It's too big to be under cover."

"Why don't I drive over to the other side?" she suggested, indicating the bridge that crossed the bay at the point where it narrowed into the ship canal.

Richard shook his head. "I've been able to see that side all along here. There's nothing over there that resembles the yacht."

"No," she agreed, "but we'd have a better view back across to this side. The buildings are so thick along here that in some places you can't even see the harbor."

"Right. Let's try it."

Minutes later they were parked between a pair of rusting cranes on the opposite shore and gazing back over the waters they had just crossed.

"There!" Richard announced in triumph. "Just over to the left. Can you see it?"

Jordan nodded. No wonder they had missed it on the other side. The *Lady Anne* had been tucked in a slip behind the unoccupied buildings of a shipbuilder no longer in business. It was an ideal location for the vessel from a security point of view. Because of the valuable sailing yachts once constructed there, the entire yard was enclosed by a high cyclone fence with chained gates.

"How in the world are you going to get in there?" she asked, wondering if a daylight access was at all possible.

Richard didn't answer her. He studied the situation as the squawking gulls swooped over the harbor. One thing was in his favor. There was not a single sightseer in evidence today. Either the yacht was no longer a focus of public excitement or else its current whereabouts had yet to be broadcast.

If he had to, he was prepared to steal a rowboat to reach the yacht, even swim out to its boarding ladder. But it increasingly looked as if neither measure was going to be necessary.

"What do you see?" Richard asked her. "As far as any activity is concerned, I mean."

"One guard." Along with Richard, she had been observing the routine of the lone deputy. He would spend a few minutes pacing the open deck of the yacht and then scramble ashore to stroll back and forth along the embankment before returning to the vessel.

"Exactly. One is all they need. He can patrol the boat and at the same time keep a control on that locked pedestrian gate close by."

"What are you planning?" She could tell by the determined smile on his mouth that he had settled on a course of action.

"There should be some place out of sight behind the buildings," he explained, "where I can climb over the fence. Once inside the yard, I'll work my way toward the slip. The problem, of course, is getting past the guard. Do you think you could distract him out by that pedestrian gate long enough for me to slip aboard?"

"I'll invent something," she promised him. "But, Richard, what if he isn't alone over there? Suppose there's someone else below deck?"

"Not likely. But if there is . . . well, I'll deal with it when I have to. Let's go."

THE GUARD SAUNTERED toward the gate behind which Jordan stood, wearing her most appealing smile.

Reaching the mesh that separated them, he offered politely, "Something I can help you with, ma'am?"

"About the yacht," she began.

He shook his head forcefully, mistaking her for a sightseer. "Sorry, ma'am, but the boat is strictly off-limits."

"Oh, I realize that," she assured him. "It's just information I'd like."

"Can't discuss anything that happened aboard her," he informed her solemnly.

"Naturally. I wouldn't dream of asking you to do that. But I was hoping…" She went on to explain about the book she was writing and how it was to deal with major nautical disasters on the Great Lakes.

"Anyway," she concluded persuasively, "I may be including the *Lady Anne* in one of my chapters. All I'd like now, officer, is for you to describe the yacht to me in as much detail as you can. You know, its size, number of cabins, what its interior is like. That sort of thing. The rest I can get when it becomes publicly available."

As a diversionary tactic, Jordan realized it was pretty weak. On the other hand, the deputy was young and extremely bored by the duty he'd been assigned. He was also flattered by her request. All the same, he was being cautious.

"And Sheriff Matthews knows about this book, you say?"

"You bet. We talked about it the other day."

He considered her request, then relented. "I guess there's no harm in that much. I have a pretty good eye for detail. I can probably give you all you want in that department."

Jordan, with pencil and notebook from her purse already in hand, began to scribble furiously as the deputy fed her a quantity of facts and figures. None of which she would ever use.

She was just aware in her peripheral vision of Richard sneaking aboard the yacht behind them. She kept the officer busy so he would have no reason to turn around. She also prayed ferociously.

RICHARD, TOO, PRAYED as he swiftly circled the deck, putting the superstructure of the yacht between him and the guard's field of vision. Getting over the fence and reaching the slip had been no problem. And, thanks to Jordan, he was on board the *Lady Anne*. But now he faced his first major obstacle. What if the interior had been locked up tight? How was he going to break in without arousing the guard?

He reached the door to the salon, tried it while he went on praying. It eased back without a protest. He was pleased but not ready for any state of elation. The unlocked door presented two potential hazards. It suggested that the guard needed ready access so that he could periodically check the interior. It also could mean that another deputy was inside at this moment.

Only one way to find out, Richard realized.

Senses fully alert now, he stepped into the salon, drawing the outside door shut behind him. He stood there listening carefully. Silence. He was alone on the yacht. He hoped.

He gave himself a moment while his eyes adjusted to the gloom. The curtains at all the windows had been drawn, presumably to prevent any curious glance from the outside. It had probably been done back at North Bay where the sightseers had relentlessly circled the yacht.

Richard left the curtains drawn. They would be an advantage to him, permitting him to move freely around the interior without being observed. But the shadowy half-light made him uneasy. He couldn't forget how the bodies of his ex-wife and her father had lain here less than three days ago. The images still haunted him.

Forget it, he ordered himself sharply. There are no ghosts here.

He began to search through the stillness for the wall safe.

Fifteen minutes later Richard was back in the salon where he had started, battling defeat. He'd covered the entire yacht cabin by cabin, looking behind pictures, inspecting the backs of cupboards and lockers, testing the wall paneling for any camouflaged doors. He'd checked both the obvious and the obscure places. There was no evidence of a safe.

Was he wrong? Did the safe not exist at all? No, he *knew* Harry had installed it. It had to be here somewhere. Did he still have time to hunt for it? He'd have to find out.

One of the windows in the dining room adjoining the salon offered the best view of the pedestrian gate out by the fence. He went there and peered through a narrow opening in the curtains. Jordan and the guard were still engaged in conversation, but how long could she keep him occupied before he returned to the yacht? He'd have to hurry.

It was when he drew back from the window that Richard spotted it just to his left and slightly below eye level. A louvered metal cover in the bulkhead between dining room and galley. The same kind of cover as all the others throughout the vessel that were laid over ducts feeding heat and air-conditioning to the cabins. But with a difference. This vent was oversize, larger than the others. He would never have noticed it otherwise.

Even before his fingers grasped the edge of the vent, prying at it, he was confident of what it concealed. He wasn't wrong. One good tug and the cover swung open on invisible hinges. And there it was confronting him. The safe.

Richard lost several more precious moments getting it open. He had a talent for remembering numbers, but he'd used this combination only once and that was some time ago. In the end, refusing failure and by making repeated efforts, he finally realized he had the sequence out of order. Once corrected, the safe surrendered to him.

Door open, he quickly investigated the cavity behind it. It contained two items. One of them was familiar to him. The jewel case Anne used when traveling. He examined its contents to be sure and then returned it to the safe with the jewelry untouched. It was the other he wanted. An attaché case, the kind that carried valuable documents. There was no time to try to unlock it. He grabbed it and slammed the door of the safe. His adrenaline was on overdrive. It made him careless about securing the outer vent cover. He slammed it too hard. The resulting clang of metal on metal was like a cannonade in the silence. What's more, faint though the noise must have been outside the yacht, he knew the guard hadn't missed it. He heard the sound of feet hurrying in his direction.

No time to get off the yacht. Only one choice. Snatching open a nearby locker, he dived inside, pulling the door after him. Through the louvered portion of the door he could hear the slap of feet on the deck, then the sound of the guard entering the yacht.

Squeezed to the back of the locker, hugging the attaché case against his chest, Richard listened and waited. How thoroughly would the young deputy check out the cabins? Would he investigate behind every door?

Mercifully, the worst never happened. The guard must have left the door to the deck open. Seconds later Richard was able to hear the slam of a car door out near the gate followed by the sound of surprised voices. It was enough to recall the deputy to the gate, apparently satisfied that the yacht was undisturbed.

When he was gone, Richard crept out of the locker. The exchange of voices at the gate told him that he needed to get off the *Lady Anne*. Now.

JORDAN FELT as if she were fast approaching a state of apoplexy. Keeping the guard occupied while Richard went after the safe was enough tension by itself. She didn't need the alarm of the deputy racing toward the yacht because of a suspicious noise, nor the added suspense of worrying how Richard was going to evade the man. Now, even worse, she suddenly had to deal with a new arrival on the scene.

She didn't know who was more surprised, Sonia Gunnerson or herself.

"Jordan! How nice to see you again."

Meaning, Jordan realized, what on earth are *you* doing here? She decided that things might be worse at that. This could be Sheriff Matthews she was confronting instead of the mild-mannered housekeeper.

She gave the woman the same song and dance she had offered the deputy, adding, "Of course, I would never include the *Lady Anne* in my book without the family's permission."

Sonia seemed to accept her explanation, but Jordan was taking no chances on a barrage of questions for which she had no answers. She forestalled that possibility with a rapid change of subject. "Are you feeling better today? Your helper implied that you were a little under the weather yesterday."

It was the housekeeper this time who was evasive. "Me? Oh, yes, I'm all right. I apologize for leaving you in the library like that. It's just that things have been so... well, difficult."

"I understand."

"In the house and with the family, that is," she said quickly, avoiding any reference to her unnamed visitor. "The loss is so hard on all of us. I'll forget and walk into a room expecting to see Harry or Anne there, and then it will hit me all over again."

"It can't be easy," Jordan agreed sympathetically, wondering what was happening aboard the yacht.

"That's why I'm here this morning. Victor wants several personal items collected from the yacht. I volunteered. It made an excuse to get away for a bit."

Jordan, hearing that, sent out a silent appeal. *Richard, get off the yacht. Now, before it's too late.*

Or was it too late already? The guard was heading back this way. All alone, too. Did that mean—

The young deputy reached the gate, muttering, "Probably just one of the gulls banging into a deck chair. That happened before."

Jordan permitted herself an interval of relief. Richard was still safe. But what now?

"Ma'am?" The deputy addressed himself to Sonia from behind the locked gate. The housekeeper explained her errand. He shook his head. "I couldn't take you aboard without authorization."

"Yes, I realize that. My employer made arrangements with Sheriff Matthews. He's going to meet me here. He should be along anytime."

Could it get any worse? Jordan had dared to wonder. Yes, it just had.

She flirted with the temptation to return to her car parked around the corner before Con Matthews arrived. But it was more important to remain here, keeping the guard and Sonia busy so that Richard had an opportunity to leave the yacht unobserved.

The housekeeper, prepared to chat while they waited, helped her in that direction. "How's the research coming, Jordan?"

"Slowly. I do appreciate the loan of the books." She decided that Victor couldn't have mentioned his angry encounter with her yesterday, or Sonia wouldn't be this friendly. Nor did the woman have any reason to connect her with Richard's appearance at the Fellowses' house.

"No hurry about returning them. Oh, have you called John McGuire's sister yet about borrowing those ship logs?"

The guard was uninterested in their conversation. Thankfully, however, he continued to hang at the gate instead of returning to the yacht, probably to be on the spot when the sheriff arrived.

"Not yet. I hate to intrude on her so soon after her brother's death."

"You could be doing her a favor. Sometimes people need reasons to keep busy, though she's probably already busy with a young man on the scene."

"Oh?"

"Yes, some connection or other of her brother's from Chicago. Showed up on the same day he died. She's letting him camp out in her barn, of all things. Maybe she needs the company. It must be every bit as hard on her as on the rest of us. Possibly even worse, considering she was the last one to have contact with the yacht that day.''

This was something new. Jordan was immediately intrigued. "I hadn't heard that."

"Wasn't it on the news? Well, maybe not, but I know I did hear it somewhere. Yes, the yacht has a phone, and John McGuire used it to call his sister at her home. Not long before they all died, I think."

"Something important?" Jordan asked. The deputy must not think so. He was paying no attention to their dialogue.

"Their conversation?" Sonia said. "I don't guess so, or everyone would be talking about it by now. Just the same, I think it's eerie to know she spoke to her brother like that just before it all happened."

"Yes," Jordan agreed, wondering if there was anything significant here and if she had been too quick to regard the sister's phone number as unimportant. It was something to be discussed with Richard, maybe pursued.

At the moment, however, she had another problem on her hands. A familiar white cruiser coasted to a stop behind the housekeeper's car. From it emerged the husky figure of Sheriff Con Matthews.

"Jordan! I didn't expect to see you down here." The gray wolf's eyes looked pleased at the sight of her. There was also an expression in them that questioned her presence. He expected an explanation. She gave him one.

"I had some shopping to do in Sturgeon Bay. While I was here, I thought I'd have a look at the yacht from a respectable distance. Could be a possibility for my book." Casual enough to be believable, she hoped.

He seemed to accept her excuse. Nodding, he turned to his deputy, who was already unlocking the gate. "All right, Chris, you can conduct Mrs. Gunnerson on board the yacht. Here's the list of what's permissible for her to bring away with her."

The guard and Sonia went off toward the *Lady Anne*. Jordan wanted nothing so much as to make an exit herself, but she deliberately lingered with the sheriff outside the gate. He was more interested in her company than accompanying the others to the yacht, and that could be a vital advantage for Richard. She would also be on the scene to hear any cry from the yacht, should either the deputy or the housekeeper discover a sign of Richard. She could feel the unbearable tension building inside her again.

"How's the book progressing?" Con asked her.

"It's a challenge."

"Been out to any of the wreck sites yet in the outboard?"

Jordan shook her head. "The fog yesterday prevented that. I may go out this afternoon."

"You be careful. Everything quiet on the island?"

She'd known he would get around to this. "I haven't seen any strangers, Con," she answered him truthfully. He'd just given her the opportunity to ask a question of her own. It might be useful if she could learn where the search for Richard was now concentrated. "You haven't caught the man you're looking for, then?"

The smile left his face, his jaw tightening grimly. "Not yet, but we're combing the county. Almost caught him on a couple of occasions. I'll bring him in soon. I won't give up until I do."

Jordan regretted having asked him. The relentlessness in his promise, together with the sudden intensity in those unusual gray eyes, frightened her. She shivered under his fierce gaze. "You sound so—so *personal* about it."

"Wouldn't you?" he challenged her, "if it had been your friend who was cold-bloodedly murdered?"

"I'm sorry. You were very close to Harry Fellows, weren't you?"

"I guess that's no secret," he admitted. "But he was more than just a friend. He was my chief political supporter in my race for the state senate."

"Then his death must be very hard on you," she sympathized.

"Worse than you know," he confided. "I had to be there on the yacht when the bodies were found. I had to see him and Anne like that. Those kinds of situations are always tough, but when it's someone you know..." He shook his head. "Pretty awful. It's the little things that can be the hardest. Harry had this yachting trophy he was crazy about. I was with him the night he collected it at the awards banquet. He was always polishing the damn thing. Must have been polishing it when he was shot. He was sitting there cradling it like a baby. You don't forget a sight like that."

"No," she agreed, thinking he was the wrong person to be investigating this case, that his emotions were too involved. Richard would never stand a chance.

"And that's why I won't be satisfied until Harry's killer is in my jail," Con swore.

Jordan felt sorry for him in his loss, but he wasn't being fair. And it was so frustrating! She longed to tell him about the suspects they had discovered. Victor and Evelyn Fellows, Sonia Gunnerson's mystery man, perhaps even others she and Richard had yet to learn about. But she could say nothing. Not unless Richard was caught. And if that happened, she would lose no time in sharing her knowledge.

Still, she couldn't stand to remain completely silent. She had to make some effort, however feeble, to speak on Richard's behalf. "I know it looks bad for this Richard Davis you're all after," she challenged Con, "but maybe he didn't do it. Maybe there's another explanation. I mean, the motive the media keeps reporting isn't exactly a murderous one. He just wanted to retain the custody of his son, didn't he?"

"Then I guess you haven't heard the latest."

There was something in his tone, a kind of savage certainty, that made Jordan go cold with apprehension. "What latest?"

"I'll show you." He moved to the open window of the cruiser, reached inside and came back with a newspaper that he thrust into her hands. As she held it, his fingers stabbed at the front page. Its banner boasted a damning headline. Newest Accusation in the Davis Manhunt.

"Read it," Con demanded, "and then tell me the guy didn't have sufficient motive."

Shaken by the headline, Jordan scanned the story that was accompanied by a photograph of Richard. It revealed that he benefited dramatically from the deaths of his ex-wife and father-in-law. His financially troubled construction business was in debt to Harry Fellows and his daughter. A debt that, by one of the terms of the agreement, would be canceled in the event of their deaths.

Richard, why didn't you tell me? Why did you keep silent about this?

She feared the answer. Feared it with a shock that rocked her loyalty to its very roots.

Con was watching her with those vigilant gray eyes, waiting for her reaction. Before she could form a response, the young deputy called to him from the deck of the yacht.

"Sheriff, the housekeeper is asking to take a couple of things not on the list."

"Be right there," Con assured him.

Jordan welcomed the interruption, but the tenacious sheriff was in no hurry to leave.

"Well?" he persisted.

What could she say? She wanted to vehemently deny the latest claim, to denounce both him and the media for crucifying Richard before he could defend himself. She didn't dare. Also, there was this ugly doubt nagging at her, threatening her clear judgment. She wanted Richard. She wanted him to tell her that none of it was true, that his only motive in boarding the *Lady Anne* that day had been Andrew.

Where was he? Surely at the Volvo by now. He must have managed to slip away off the other side of the yacht. If he was still aboard, or had left any sign of his presence, the deputy and Sonia would have raised an alarm by now. She had to get back to her car.

"You'd better go," she urged Con, edging away from him along the sidewalk.

"Can I call you? Maybe we can get together."

"I'm going to be pretty busy."

He didn't discourage that easily. "We'll see," he promised.

Jordan left it at that. She couldn't afford to alienate him. Her nerves were in a raw state as she turned and hurried away. She was still clutching the newspaper.

"EASY," RICHARD MUTTERED from his slouched position beside her as Jordan charged onto the highway, narrowly missing an oncoming minivan. "All we need now is a patrol car on our tail."

He was right. She was driving recklessly in her eagerness to put Sturgeon Bay behind them since finding him crouched down in the Volvo waiting for her.

Jordan slowed to a safe speed and checked her rearview mirror. There was no sign of any pursuit.

"It's all right," she said. "We're out of town. You can sit up now."

He eased himself to a more comfortable position and began to examine the lock on the attaché case in his lap. He had already briefly described for her his adventure on the yacht and how in the end he had managed to lower himself from the concealed side and to climb back over the fence behind the buildings. She had no other questions for him. None, anyway, that she'd found the courage yet to ask.

Jordan concentrated on her driving, but she had never been so aware of him. His big, tanned hands clasping the vital attaché case, his narrow hips, his long, muscular legs encased in the tight jeans. And the sensual, masculine warmth of him so close to her in the confines of the car. She was conscious of all these things while at the same time her stricken mind remembered the story on the front page of the folded newspaper tucked into the pocket of the door on her side.

It looked worse than bad for him now. It looked as if he might actually have— *No!* She didn't want to believe there was the remotest possibility of his guilt. She didn't want to even consider that his concern for her all along had been nothing but a careful act to enlist her support. Because if there was the slightest chance that he might have deceived her, it would make everything a cruel lie. All of it, his rugged appeal, his tender playfulness, the intimacy they had shared, would be a lie.

It couldn't be a lie! She loved him, she had faith in him. Or was he, nagged a nasty little voice inside her head, *was* he a man she didn't know at all?

"Damn," Richard said. "Without a penknife I can't work this open. Any tools in the glove compartment?"

She shook her head.

"Then the lock will have to wait until we get back to the island. I guess I can be patient that much longer." He slid the case to one side and turned his head to face her. "Do you want to tell me what's wrong?"

So he did sense her constraint. Without a word she passed the newspaper to him. He dragged his gaze away from her and turned the newspaper, exposing the front page. There was silence in the car while he read the story.

"Is it true?" she asked, keeping her eyes on the road with difficulty because what she wanted to do was study his face. "Do their deaths mean the debt against your business is canceled?"

"I don't know how they found out about it, but, yes, it's true."

"Why didn't you tell me, Richard?" she pleaded in a hoarse voice. "Why did you let me believe that the only motive you could be accused of was your battle over the custody of Andrew?"

"Because Andrew *was* my only motive in boarding the *Lady Anne*. Nothing else mattered then, and it doesn't matter now. And if that's not enough to convince you of my innocence," he went on, his face suddenly taut with anger, "if this damn story has you doubting me all over again, then pull over to the side of the road. Just pull over now, and I'll get out, and I promise you'll never have to see me again."

Jordan could feel them coming, tried to hold them off. It was no use. The hot, unwanted tears filled her eyes, coursed down her cheeks as she struggled to keep the car safely on the road.

"Oh, God," he muttered, realizing what he had done. "You're crying."

She didn't answer him. She was too busy being ashamed of her emotional tears.

"Jordan," he ordered her, this time calmly, "pull over before you get us into an accident."

He was right again. She had no business staying at the wheel. Flipping on the directional, she eased the Volvo over to the side of the highway, parking on the broad gravel shoulder.

He reached for her then, placing both hands gently on either side of her head and turning her to face him. He had removed the sunglasses, and his blue eyes gazed closely, earnestly into hers. "Listen to me, sweetheart," he implored. "The money part of it just wasn't important. I never thought about it. I didn't even remember that clause in the debt agreement until just now, it was so long ago. I can't help it if that sounds incredible, but it's true. Do you believe me?"

She nodded mutely.

"Are you sure? Because if you aren't, nothing else matters."

"I'm sure," she whispered.

"Good."

And that was when he kissed her. A slow, deep, very thorough kiss. Jordan's spirits soared. He could have been the devil himself after that kiss, and she would have trusted him. But he wasn't the devil. He was Richard Davis, the man she loved. A caring father, a decent human being, and she was furious with herself for having let any shadow of doubt cross her mind, even momentarily. Her determination to fight for his vindication had never been stronger.

Richard grinned at her, admiring the steel in her brown eyes that only seconds ago had been awash with tears. "Anything else?" he asked.

"Yes, you might pass me the box of tissues in the glove compartment. I have some serious mopping up to do here."

Chapter Eleven

Jordan sat across from Richard at the worktable in the parlor, anxiously waiting for his verdict as he sifted through the material he'd removed from the attaché case scant minutes ago.

"Anything?" she asked tensely.

He didn't answer her. He kept turning papers, many of which looked like drawings to her, though it was difficult to tell from her angle of observation. Not that his reply was necessary, she began to realize. The mounting disappointment was plain on his face.

"Specs," he finally pronounced in disgust, slapping the papers down on the table. "Nothing but specs."

"Specs? I don't—"

"Specifications," he explained. "Detailed designs and notes for the rebuilding of the *Lady Anne*."

"And that's everything?"

"Complete."

"But if that's all it is, why lock it in a case inside a safe, especially when the work on the yacht is finished?"

Richard shrugged. "That was Harry. He could make a secret out of what he ate for breakfast."

"There must be something more," she insisted, gazing longingly at the opened attaché case. "There's a pocket there inside the lid. Try that."

She was right. He hadn't investigated the pocket yet, though it looked pretty flat. He slid his fingers into the fold and withdrew a thin packet secured by a rubber band.

"Photographs!" she said excitedly.

She watched eagerly as he disposed of the rubber band and began to examine the prints one by one. He shook his head.

"Just more of the same," he reported. "All of them snapshots of the work in progress on the *Lady Anne*. A visual record, and nothing incriminating about any of them."

She shared his keen frustration. "What now?" she wondered.

He didn't respond. He was frowning over one of the snapshots.

"Richard?"

"Surprise, surprise," he murmured. He passed the photograph to her. "Take a look at this one."

Jordan gazed at the picture of two figures posed in front of the *Lady Anne* as it underwent remodeling in dry dock. One of them she recognized as Harry Fellows. His companion, who'd apparently joined him in a visit of inspection, was a stocky, grizzled man somewhere in his late forties or early fifties. He had a broad, amiable face and the kind of wise little smile that looked as though he had experienced, and accepted, human nature on all its complicated levels. Not surprising, perhaps, considering he wore a Catholic clerical collar.

She looked up from the snapshot. "Who is he?"

"Was," he stressed. "He was murdered along with Anne and Harry."

"Mac? The man who was piloting the *Lady Anne*?" She stared at him. "But, Richard, he's wearing—"

"Right. The guy must have been a priest."

Sonia, Jordan remembered. She had started to tell her this very thing yesterday when they'd been interrupted in Harry Fellows's library.

John McGuire had been Father McGuire. She found it astonishing.

Richard read her face. "Yeah, I know. It's a surprise. An interesting one, but it doesn't make it a helpful one."

"Maybe it does," she said slowly, recalling all the rest the housekeeper had shared with her both yesterday and this morning in Sturgeon Bay.

He scooted his chair around, leaning toward her earnestly. "I'm open to any suggestion," he encouraged her. "Hell, I'm *desperate* for a suggestion."

"John McGuire was on his way to join his sister here on the peninsula. Sonia told me about it, though she never said *why* he was coming to stay with her. But she did drop a few other things." Jordan went on to explain about John McGuire's telephone call to his sister, the last contact from the yacht. She included in her account the housekeeper's gossip about the unnamed young man arriving at the sister's on the day of the murders.

"And this kid had some connection with McGuire?" Richard pressed.

Jordan nodded. "That's what Sonia claimed. What do you think? Could any of this be involved with the murders?"

"Maybe. There's got to be an answer somewhere. Something in all this mess that we're overlooking."

Something, she thought. The word triggered a sudden realization.

He noticed the intense look on her face. "What is it?" he asked sharply.

"What you said just now . . . it sort of kicked in this feeling. Like there's something I did hear or see just recently, only it's not right."

"What are you talking about?"

"You know, one of those jarring little things that nag at you because it doesn't fit the pattern."

"*What,* Jordan?"

She made a concentrated effort, casting her mind back over the past several crowded days, sorting through the jumble buried in her memory. She shook her head. "Sorry. Whatever it is, if it's anything at all, I can't get a handle on it."

"I know the feeling," he said angrily. She watched him as he restlessly left the table and went to stand by the window where he looked out at the lake, as though the answer must be out there on the blinding waters.

She knew he was struggling with the problem, battling to make a choice about his next move. She tried not to be discouraged for him, but she felt more confounded than ever by the daunting puzzle that challenged them. How were they to make any sense out of a brutal crime that had too many players and too many pieces, none of which fit with any clarity? But she knew Richard would never give up until he did. Nor would she.

While she waited for him to declare his decision, she began to clear away the tools he had used to force the lock on the attaché case. They were scattered across the newspaper he had spread on the worktable to protect its antique surface. The same newspaper she had brought back from Sturgeon Bay. This was when she noticed on an inside page the photograph that, until this second, she had overlooked. It accompanied a story of yesterday morning's funeral. The camera had captured the mourners gathered at the graveside.

"Richard, look!"

He came away from the window, stopping behind her to gaze over her shoulder. "What?"

"Him." She pointed at a figure stationed behind the others. "The man I was telling you about. The one that has Sonia so worried."

Richard leaned down, peering more carefully at the thin figure with the thatch of white hair. He said nothing for a long minute as he studied the photograph. Then suddenly he announced positively, "I've seen him before."

"Where? Who is he?"

"I don't know. I just know that he looks familiar."

She swung around on the chair to face him. "Richard, think. This could be important."

"I'll try to place him, but right now I've got a priority in another direction."

"You've made a decision."

"Just about the only one available to me, what with the attaché case proving a dead end. John McGuire's sister and the kid who showed up at her place the day he died. It needs to be checked out."

"And I have the right excuse for paying her a visit. The ship logs."

"That's it. And while you get her to tell you about her brother's last phone call from the yacht, maybe even who this kid is and why he's staying with her, I'm going to have a look around the barn where he's supposed to be camping."

"Richard, that's too risky. They're not going to welcome you on the property."

"With any luck, they won't even know I was there. Look, I'm not letting you go alone, so let's not argue about it."

Jordan didn't. She could see he was driven again to do whatever was possible to clear himself. His mind and heart were with Andrew.

She left him in the parlor and went into the kitchen. The phone number Sonia had provided was in her purse on the counter. She fished it out, spreading the paper flat. The housekeeper had printed the woman's full name. Maggie McGuire Dennis. The name was followed by a local number.

Turning to the phone on the wall, she punched in the numbers and waited while it rang once, twice, three times. No answer. Refusing to give up, she persisted, letting it ring. It was after the sixth ring that the phone was finally picked up.

"Hello."

A woman's voice. Not hurried and breathless, either, like someone who's run to catch the phone. Had she sat there and deliberately let it ring, resisting an answer?

"Ms. Dennis?"

"Who's calling?"

Jordan wasn't mistaken. The woman's manner was reluctant, even suspicious. Understandable if she was grieving for her brother and didn't want to be bothered. But if Maggie Dennis did have something to hide...

"This is Jordan Templeton at Cana Island, Ms. Dennis. Sonia Gunnerson very kindly gave me your number. I'm sorry to impose on you like this, but I'm hoping you'll be able to help me out." She went on to tactfully, but persuasively, explain her need to borrow the ship logs for her research. "It's asking a lot under the circumstances, I know," she finished, "but they would be valuable to me, and I promise to be careful with them."

There was a long pause while Maggie Dennis considered her request. "All right," she agreed, her manner less stiff but still on the wary side, "I'll dig them out for you, but you'll have to pick them up right away if you need them before tomorrow. I'm not going to be available later this afternoon."

Perfect, Jordan thought. "That's no problem. If you'll give me directions, I can be there in a few minutes."

After she hung up she went back to the parlor to report her success. She found Richard leaning over the worktable, staring at the photograph in the newspaper. There was a gleam of satisfaction in his gaze.

"You've remembered!" she declared.

He turned to face her. "Jessup," he said. "That's the name. And his first name..." He struggled to pin it down. "Walter, I think. Yeah, I'm sure that's right. Walter Jessup."

Jordan didn't dare to let herself be excited, though she hoped there was potential in his recollection. "And this Walter Jessup is someone you know?"

"I never met him. I just know who he is."

"How?"

"Anne was sorting through a bunch of family pictures one day. This was right after we were married. She was planning to have a collection of them framed for our house, and she wanted my opinion about the selection. A lot of them were pictures of people I didn't know so, frankly, I wasn't much interested. But I was trying to be polite about it. You know, asking who's this one, who's that one."

"And Walter Jessup was among them?"

"Yes. He and Harry were standing together in front of the first factory Harry started. Only Harry didn't start it alone. Walter Jessup was his partner."

"What happened?" Jordan sensed there was something momentous here.

"Ruin. At least for Jessup. Anne told me about it. The factory burned, and Jessup was convicted of insurance arson. He went to prison for it. But Harry Fellows, being what he was, managed to walk away free and clear."

"Are you saying Harry was actually the one who was responsible for the fraud?"

Richard shrugged. "Well, Anne denied her father was in any way to blame. But, knowing Harry, it's certainly possible."

"Do you realize what this means, Richard?"

"Yeah, if it's true. *If* Walter Jessup did serve time because of Harry Fellows, he'd have to be bitter about it. He'd have every reason to hate his former partner."

"And revenge," Jordan added, "can be a powerful motive for murder."

"It puts him in the running, anyway," Richard conceded. "Providing I'm right, that is, and it is the same man in both photographs. There are a lot of years between the two pictures. I only remembered because the guy has such a distinctive look and Anne's story about him is the sort you don't forget."

"But why would he risk showing up at the funeral or visiting Sonia at the house?"

"I suppose because she must have a connection with him, maybe something that goes back to the old days."

Jordan nodded thoughtfully, feeling sorry for the housekeeper if she was somehow implicated in the murders. "The point is, Walter Jessup could be the killer."

Richard shook his head. "Speculating about it doesn't get us anywhere. None of it is evidence. Jessup can wait because right now I'm interested in Father McGuire's sister and his young friend from Chicago."

JORDAN WAS ALONE as the Volvo bumped down the rutted gravel driveway to the farmhouse that Maggie Dennis had rented for the season. Richard had parted from her a quarter of a mile back, intending to circle through the fields on foot to reach the back of the barn. She made an effort not to worry about him, knowing she needed to concentrate on achieving her own results from this visit.

Parking the car under a pair of immense sugar maples, she paused to admire the pleasing composition of farm buildings that must have been built well before the turn of the century. They were wonderfully preserved. The house itself was constructed of squared, dovetailed logs weathered to a silvery gray. Outbuildings to the side and back, including the handsome old barn, were a mixture of fieldstone and wood shingle. It was one of those places that the tourists found so nostalgically charming.

It was also, Jordan noted as she emerged from her vehicle, an isolated setting. There was no sign of its occupant, no sound but the lonely chattering of a windmill. But she was expected, she reminded herself as she mounted the porch stretched across the face of the house.

She started to rap on the door when a husky voice called from off to the side, "Down here, Ms. Templeton."

Jordan moved along the porch, leaning over the rail as two figures appeared from around the corner of the house. They were accompanied by a pair of goats.

The woman stepped forward, reaching up to take Jordan's offered hand in a firm clasp. "Forgive the livestock. They come with the place. I'm Maggie Dennis."

She was much warmer in person, Jordan decided. An attractive woman with intelligent green eyes and premature gray hair she wore very plain and short. Her slacks and shirt were just as severe, but they looked expensive.

"This is Dino," Maggie said, indicating the young man who stood behind her, hanging on to the goats.

He couldn't have been more than eighteen or nineteen, a scruffy youth with a small, wiry body. He had long hair that needed subduing, dusky skin and a wildness in his black eyes. He acknowledged the introduction with a sullen nod.

"All right, Dino," Maggie directed him, "you can put the goats back in the pasture now."

The moody Dino drifted off with his two charges.

Maggie, reading Jordan's expression, answered her curiosity. "He's Romany," she said. "At least, that's what he claims, and I suppose with that complexion he very well could be. He certainly has the legendary Romany wanderlust in him. Showed up here out of the blue the day my brother died. When we heard what had happened aboard the yacht, Dino insisted that Mac would have wanted him to stick close to me. I gave him quarters in the barn, and he has been helpful around the place, but frankly I don't know what I'm going to do about him. I can't very well turn him away. Mac wouldn't have wanted me to do that."

Jordan was concerned for the woman's safety. "You mean your brother hadn't arranged for Dino to be here?"

Maggie shook her head. "Mac didn't know Dino was coming, or he would have told me. Dino won't admit it, but I think the truth is he couldn't stand to be left behind in Chicago without Mac, so he simply followed him here."

"But uninvited—"

"Yes, I know what it looks like. Here I am a widow all alone on a remote farm, and I go and take in this sulky boy I know next to nothing about. But there's more to it than just that."

Maggie moved around to the front steps and joined her on the porch. "Dino was one of my brother's lost souls," she explained. "He has no family, or none that he's willing to talk about, anyway. He had a pretty rough time of it on the streets. Mac was working with him, helping to turn him around."

"And he came to depend on your brother," Jordan observed.

"I think so. Anyway, Mac once discussed him with me. He believed in Dino's worth, and I always trusted his judgment."

Jordan had the impression that Maggie Dennis was an independent, capable woman, but she hoped she wasn't making a serious mistake where the wild-eyed Dino was concerned.

"But none of this is what you came for," Maggie added, remembering. She invited her into the house, indicating a deep sofa loaded with quilted pillows.

"I hope I'm not keeping you," Jordan apologized, settling on the sofa. "You said on the phone you wouldn't be available later this afternoon, and I was a bit late getting here."

"I do have an appointment in town. I'm making arrangements to have Mac's remains sent back to Chicago. But there's plenty of time."

Jordan, trying not to wonder what was happening with Richard, cast her glance around the parlor. It was a warm, comfortable room with country-style fabrics and a generous stone fireplace. Interesting, too. One of its walls was in a construction known as stovewood, a local feature of some of the old farms where roundels of sliced logs were laid up in mortar. She withheld her compliments, however, sensing that her hostess, unlike Sonia Gunnerson, was not susceptible to flattery. Maggie Dennis was the kind of self-possessed woman who would share her knowledge only if she thought you were entitled to hear it.

"Coffee? Tea?"

Jordan shook her head. "Thanks, no. I shouldn't be here at all. Not after your recent loss. It was good of you to let me come."

Maggie, still on her feet, smiled wistfully. "Mac would have understood. That's why I agreed to see you. Sorry if I was a little brusque on the phone, but the media have been pestering me for interviews. So, here are the ship logs right here."

She turned to the fireplace, reaching for a half-dozen ship logs stacked on the mantel. She placed the old journals on a low table in front of Jordan.

"These are just a part of his collection," she said. "Most of his stuff accompanied me when I came up from Chicago ahead of him. I wasn't able to go through all of his boxes to find the rest, but I'll try to do that first thing tomorrow. Then you can use those, as well."

Jordan leaned forward, reverently fingering the pile of faded volumes recording the daily lives of early Great Lakes vessels. "I'm sorry I never met Father McGuire," she said respectfully. "I'm sure he must have had a remarkable knowledge of the lakes and their history."

"It was strictly a hobby with him, of course, but a relaxing diversion from all his duties. And it was Father Mac, never McGuire. That's how he was affectionately addressed by everyone who knew him. Or *was*," she added, "before my brother left the priesthood."

"I didn't know," Jordan murmured.

"Most people don't. He'd only just recently left his orders."

"That couldn't have been an easy choice," Jordan sympathized.

"It wasn't," Maggie confided, perching on an arm of the easy chair facing the sofa. "Decisions like that can be shattering, especially when they involve a crisis of faith. Not that this was really the case with Mac. It had more to do with his conflict with what he perceived as the constraints of the church. He felt that in the end his vows hindered the rehabilitation work he wanted to be involved with on a constant basis.''

"Troubled youths?" Jordan asked.

"That's right," Maggie said. She seemed anxious for Jordan to believe that her brother had in no way failed by leaving the priesthood. "Young people like Dino fighting to survive in the inner city. He helped a good many of them with his counseling and support. I think he would have gone on with his efforts in some other capacity, once he'd had a chance to overcome his personal anguish at leaving the priesthood. That's what this place was meant to do for him."

"A kind of refuge, you mean?"

"Yes, that's why I rented the farm. I thought it would be somewhere quiet and peaceful where he could find a new direction for himself. Of course, I knew he'd love the whole peninsula once he saw it, what with its being the kind of maritime scene that always fascinated him. But now..." She spread her hands in a gesture of painful regret.

"I'm sorry," Jordan said, knowing how inadequate her words were.

"I keep remembering the last time we talked," Maggie said, a faraway look in her eyes, "and how much he was looking forward to being here."

"From the yacht, you mean?" Jordan prompted her.

"Yes, he called me from the yacht to tell me the approximate time of their arrival so I could be ready to pick him up. How did you know?"

"Sonia Gunnerson mentioned it."

"Sonia seems to know everything, doesn't she? Anyway, Mac was already enjoying the experience. Being out on the lake, the chance to pilot a boat like that, the kind of freedom he hadn't known in years. He loved all of it."

"He didn't mind the storm?"

"No, the rough weather wouldn't have bothered him."
She frowned. "There was only one thing troubling his mind
that afternoon."

Jordan leaned forward on the sofa, sensing an important
disclosure. "Something to do with what happened to them
out there?"

Maggie nodded. "No question of it. You see, he knew the
murderer."

Jordan, struggling to curb her excitement, whispered,
"He actually identified their killer?"

"No, he didn't offer any name. I suppose, if they were
introduced, the name had no meaning for him. But the face
did. It was at the end of our conversation that he mentioned it to me. How this someone boarded the yacht on one
of its stops and how Mac felt he looked familiar, that maybe
he'd known him long ago in Chicago. Only he couldn't place
him, and it was driving him crazy. Then Mac said it really
wasn't important, and he laughed about it." Maggie's face
tightened over the irony of her brother's final conversation
with her.

Jordan was appalled. "How awful! If only he'd recognized him, been able to tell you who it was."

"Then we'd know who the murderer is?" Maggie smiled
bitterly. "But you're forgetting we already know. Of course,
it was Richard Davis my brother was trying to remember,
and I've told the sheriff as much. Who else could it have
been? There was no one else."

There was such anger and conviction in her voice that
Jordan knew it would be a mistake to argue with her. Here,
then, was someone else who had already condemned Richard. He wouldn't stand a chance if he was caught, not
without solid evidence to counter his accusers. And if they
failed to obtain that evidence . . .

She shuddered over the possibility.

THE BIG DOOR OF THE BARN was open. Richard checked the area in both directions. There was no one in evidence. Then, as cautious as a fox about to raid the henhouse, he slipped into the dusty gloom.

The place smelled of decades of hay and leather and livestock. But it was deserted now and as quiet as a cathedral with its soaring roof braces.

He didn't have to look very far to locate the area occupied by Maggie Dennis's guest. There was a box stall off to one side, its door standing wide. He peered inside. The possessions of the young man camping here were meager. A cot with a bedroll at its foot, a few clothes snagged on wall pegs and a backpack dumped in one corner.

None of it looked promising. He wondered if there was anything that might interest him in that backpack. If he could just find one new lead, one little bit of evidence that might indicate the kid had been aboard the yacht—

"You don't belong here!"

The challenge came from behind him, harsh and dangerous. Richard whipped around to find himself confronting a wicked-looking pitchfork. The sharp prongs of the fork were leveled at him threateningly, only inches away. The shaft behind them was gripped by a slight figure in grubby jeans. There was a stubble of beard on his jaw, giving him the look of a vagrant.

Richard measured his young opponent and decided that the expression in his glaring black eyes was more anxious than lethal. He dealt with him calmly but emphatically, coolly ordering, "Put the fork down."

"Says you," came the answering growl. "I gotta right to this fork when I find some guy snooping around my things."

Richard had his story ready. "I'm not snooping. I'm a neighbor from down the road. One of my horses got out of the pasture, and I'm hunting for him. I thought he might have wandered in here looking for feed."

"Yeah?"

"Yeah. Now put the fork down, because if I have to take it away from you," he promised, "I will."

The defiant dark eyes meeting his wavered, then fell. The pitchfork was lowered with them.

Richard, no longer faced with the weapon, relaxed. "That's better. You always this hot-tempered?"

"How was I supposed to know?" the young man muttered.

"The next time you might try asking before you snatch up the nearest pitchfork."

Richard watched him. The kid's head was still down. There were gold studs in his ears. One of them flashed in a beam of sunlight that found its way through a high window. He finally raised his face. The rough, menacing look had softened into a youthful vulnerability.

"So, all right," he admitted gruffly, "I get mad easy, but I'm workin' on it. I'm tryin' to remember all the time what Father Mac told me."

"Father Mac?"

"Yeah, he was helping me. Father Mac was one of the guys in white hats. All priests aren't, you know."

"I know. And just what did your Father Mac tell you?"

He shrugged. "Lots of things, but mostly how important it is that I shouldn't get angry at everyone. He said," he went on, pleading for Richard's understanding with a sudden earnestness that was childlike, "I gotta let people know there's other things inside me that count for something."

"Your Father Mac sounds pretty special."

The youth nodded, the toe of one of his boots stirring aimless patterns in the bits of straw at his feet. "Yeah, he was. I hated everyone before Father Mac. Still do sometimes, but I'm better. I don't go around all the time thinkin' I'm no good. See, I was convinced I was a bad operator, and that's just the way it had to be. Only Father Mac made me see that I could change. That I wasn't evil."

"How?"

"For one thing, by telling me he knew what real evil was. He'd met it lots of times. Once it was something pretty awful, about as bad as evil can be. He wouldn't say. I guess he couldn't. But I think it must have been in the confessional, you know."

"Yes."

"Point is, he knew the difference, and I wasn't it."

"I'm sure he did know. A priest would."

"Anyway," he mumbled, suddenly embarrassed by his confidences to a stranger, "I just wanted you to know. I don't have Father Mac anymore, but, like I say, I'm not forgettin' the stuff he told me."

"I think that's pretty smart of you. You go on remembering, and I'm sure you'll be fine."

Another dead end, Richard thought as he left the barn seconds later, heading back toward the crossroad where he and Jordan had agreed to meet. The kid couldn't possibly be connected with the murders. So where, he wondered grimly, did that leave him now?

Chapter Twelve

Jordan was less certain of Dino's innocence as she and Richard reexamined their findings back at the lighthouse.

"Maggie Dennis might not be worried about him, but I keep remembering how you described his threatening you with that pitchfork. And, Richard, I only met him for a moment, but I could see a wildness in him."

He shook his head. "It doesn't make him guilty of anything."

"It could," she maintained, "if it's a wildness capable of uncontrollable rages. *Murderous* rages. And just where was Dino before he turned up at the farm on the day of the killings?"

"I suppose on his way from Chicago to the peninsula."

"Yes, following his Father Mac. Only *how* was he following him? I mean, he could have sneaked aboard the yacht back in Chicago. He could have been lurking on the *Lady Anne*. He could have been the killer who got away in the lifeboat, landed it on the shore along here and hiked to the farm. It is possible."

"Except for one thing," he reminded her. "Dino couldn't have been that unknown someone Maggie Dennis told you her brother was struggling to remember."

"Yes, that's true," she admitted.

She was silent for a minute, thinking about her theory, unwilling to abandon it.

They were sharing the sofa in the parlor. The temperature had dropped with twilight, and Richard had built a fire in the Franklin stove to combat the chill in the room. He had his arm around her, and she relished his warm closeness. It was an occasion that demanded a bowl of popcorn, intimate conversation and easy laughter. Instead, they had to discuss murder. They had to find a way to exonerate him.

"Suppose, then," Jordan offered, "it *was* you who Father Mac was trying to remember. That could still make Dino a candidate, providing he was hidden somewhere on the yacht."

"No good," Richard insisted. "I never met Father Mac before that afternoon on the yacht, either in Chicago or anywhere else. I'm positive about that."

"Then it had to be someone else there he was trying to place." Which meant, she realized with regret, Dino must be discounted. At least for now.

The doors were open on the stove. Jordan stared into the flames consuming a trio of split logs. Pine, she thought. She could identify the distinctive spicy aroma released by the fire's heat.

She glanced at Richard. He, too, was gazing into the fire. But there was no relaxed expression on his face. She knew his mind was once again searching for answers, a way out of his worsening dilemma. The poignancy of his predicament tore at her, deepening her resolve to help him.

Her thoughts centered again on Father Mac and how the knowledge of his renounced priesthood added a new, and intriguing, dimension to the mystery. There was another theory here, one that had been forming in her mind ever since they had left the farm.

"Richard," she asked him suddenly, "what if all along we've been looking at this whole thing the wrong way?"

He turned his head, gazing at her sharply. "What do you mean?"

"Suppose the pilot, the former Father Mac, that is, hadn't been the unlucky bystander who was shot simply because he was there and the killer couldn't leave him alive if his scheme to have you take the blame was to work. Suppose, in fact, that the reverse was true. Do you see what I mean?"

"You're saying," Richard said slowly, managing to follow her, "that *he* was the real target, that Anne and Harry were murdered only because they were witnesses."

"It's conceivable, isn't it?"

"Why? What motive?"

"Don't know, but I can't forget what Dino told you about his Father Mac having met real evil."

"I imagine many priests do sooner or later in their work, only they're not murdered because of it."

"But if he was trying to recall this someone, as his sister claimed, and the killer could see that and had to silence him, maybe for something he'd learned long ago in the confessional—"

"Jordan, priests are bound by holy orders never to reveal anything they hear in the confessional."

"Yes, but he was an *ex*-priest, and— Oh, I see what you mean. Even if he had left the priesthood, he would still honor the sacred confessional. Except the killer might not trust that."

"Jordan, do you really think this is the explanation?"

The breath left her in a soft sigh. "I know. It's all so vague and problematical, isn't it?"

"Besides, where does that leave us with the most likely suspects and their motives?"

She nodded thoughtfully. He was right. Harry Fellows as the murderer's target still made the best sense. There were such strong suspects for that likelihood. Feet tucked under her on the sofa, she reviewed the candidates.

Victor Fellows and his lover, Evelyn, who were protecting some fearful secret of their own. Also, Harry's death freed them to be together openly, not to mention the fortune they probably inherited.

Resin bubbled up on one of the pine logs in the fire, a glob of it landing in the embers with a low, sizzling sound.

Then there was Walter Jessup, Harry's former business partner and now connected somehow with Sonia Gunnerson. He had been sent to prison, possibly because of Harry's wrongdoing. How bitter was the man, how needful of revenge?

The log with the sputtering resin settled into the flames with a soft crash that ignited a shower of sparks against the protective screen.

"Any of them," Jordan murmured in frustration. "Any of them could have been aboard the yacht that day. Any of them could have done it. It's maddening. And so is not being able to remember what I told you earlier. You know, about having seen or heard something that disagrees with the rest of the pattern. It keeps taunting me. Maybe I'm crazy, but I keep thinking it could be essential, and if I could just lock onto it..."

"Don't," he commanded her abruptly, his arm tightening around her. "Don't go on punishing yourself. Tomorrow I'm going to do whatever it takes to learn where they all were that day and whether any of them were involved. But there's no more to be done tonight, so let's just put it aside. Let's try to focus on nothing but ourselves."

She didn't object when he drew her onto his lap and held her there against the wall of his chest. For a long moment that was all he wanted. Just to hold her in silence. Just to savor her soft, fragrant warmth.

Ultimately, it was not enough to blot out all the nightmares swooping around his head like dark birds of prey. He needed to forget them completely, at least for an hour or so. There was a way to achieve this, and he used it to bring an interlude of peace and pleasure to both of them.

Richard leaned into her, his mouth seeking hers. His kiss was light, tender, the tip of his tongue stroking her lips. Then he deepened the kiss, at first with a leisurely care and then with an urgency that demanded a full commitment of their bodies.

"Can you feel how much I want you?" he whispered.

"Yes," she breathed, equally consumed by need, equally ready for him. "As much as I want you."

"Then there's no reason to wait."

"None," she agreed.

Within seconds they were in the bedroom, feverishly shedding their clothes. They came together on the bed, their mouths and hands celebrating each other in a wanton embrace. Jordan reveled in his heat and strength, the dazzling effect of his tongue on her breasts.

He told her she was lovely. Told her she was a joy to him. That he needed her as he had never needed any woman before. What he didn't tell her was what she longed most to hear. He was not yet capable of this. Perhaps would never be. No matter. She loved him so shamelessly that she was willing to settle for what he could give her.

And that, she learned as he covered her, his body joining with hers, was considerable. Through raw, whispered endearments he made love to her with a compelling, bittersweet intensity while Jordan clung to him in a frantic desire to hold back time, to keep him forever with her. To prevent tomorrow and the eventual loss she feared from ever becoming a reality.

Time would not be denied, though. Nor the pinnacle of their passion. In the end, Richard lifted them to a stunning, healing fulfillment. And for the moment, for this vital interval at least, their satisfied bodies were at peace. They slept in each other's arms.

IT MUST HAVE BEEN AFTER midnight when he awakened. He lay there in the darkness of the bedroom, aware of Jordan still deeply asleep beside him. He had urged her to put aside his tangled situation, to forget it until the morning, but he found he couldn't obey his own instructions. He was restless in his desperation, unable to close his eyes again. Useless to just lie here, middle of the night or not.

Careful not to disturb Jordan, Richard planted a featherlight kiss on her bare shoulder and tucked the quilt around her warmly. She didn't stir when he eased away and slid off the bed. He fumbled for his clothes and dragged them on in the dark.

Slipping out of the bedroom, he quietly closed the door behind him and turned on a light in the parlor. The fire had faded to ashes. The room was cold. He added fresh wood and started a new blaze. Then he settled in the single easy chair and put his mind to work.

A half hour later he was still without a plan for tomorrow. There had to be another direction he could try, some way yet he could help himself. What? But it refused to come to him.

He went on sitting there, his blank gaze in line with the worktable. The abandoned contents of the attaché case still occupied the surface of the table. They were no longer important, no longer of any interest to him. Except eventually they reminded him of something about himself. They were plans to guide a boat builder. He was a builder, too. Not that kind of construction but a builder all the same. A conscientious builder who checked and rechecked the details of his projects in order to make certain the finished products were his best work.

It was that same builder's instinct that Richard trusted now. It urged him out of the easy chair and across the room to the worktable. It commanded him to settle at the table, where he began slowly and carefully to reexamine the materials that had been in the case. There was the chance, however slight, that he might have overlooked something helpful, even vital.

He went back through the packet of snapshots, studying each one. Nothing. He went through the specs for the yacht itself. Still nothing. He refused to give up.

It was long minutes later, when he was poring over the design for the yacht's lifeboat, that he found it. Small and seemingly insignificant, easily overlooked at first glance, but there it was. A hidden compartment located within the structure of the engine mount.

Richard smiled with satisfaction at his discovery. It was typical of Harry Fellows that even in his lifeboat he had to include some secret hiding place, whether he ever needed it or not. The question now was, Had the killer been aware of that compartment? Might he have used it to conceal something when he escaped in the lifeboat from the *Lady Anne*? Something like the missing gun that had murdered all three victims? Maybe even something more incriminating than that?

It was foolish of him to be excited over the possibility. If the compartment had ever contained anything, it could very well have been emptied by now. Maybe the lifeboat no longer even existed or was so cunningly hidden he stood no chance of finding it. It was another long shot, only this time even longer than the others. But Richard wasn't going to let that stop him from searching for the lifeboat. It was all he had left.

Two things were in his favor. The lifeboat had to have landed somewhere along this shore because the killer couldn't have traveled any distance in it in the treacherous waters of that afternoon. Secondly, Richard had the outboard that Jordan had rented for him, enabling him to look for the lifeboat.

The fire went on popping in the stove as he reached for her charts of the peninsula's coastline. He found the map he wanted, frowned over it in concentration. Where? Where could the lifeboat have safely landed? North Bay was a strong possibility, except all the activity there following the temporary anchoring of the *Lady Anne* would have revealed its presence.

Wait a minute. He was failing to account for the powerful northeast winds that had been blowing the afternoon of the murders. The *Lady Anne* had been rendered helpless before the killer fled from it, which meant the drifting yacht must have been driven by wind and current considerably southward along the coast by the time Richard regained consciousness on the floor of the cabin. It was not in the vicinity of Cana Island, then, where the lifeboat had beached but much farther northward. But where, exactly? Where would it have found a haven in that storm?

Richard bent tensely over the chart, his finger slowly tracing the coastline on a path reaching above North Bay. There! His finger jabbed at the spot. This was the most likely refuge and, according to his rough calculations, just about the right distance from Cana Island. The secluded Rowleys Bay.

He would take his search there tomorrow morning. One more massive effort. And, something told him, his last chance. No sense in denying it to himself. The manhunt for him was intensifying, and after tomorrow he would have run out of both time and opportunity. The unavoidable had been confronting him ever since their return from the Dennis farm. Jordan, too, had sensed the inevitable, though neither of them had been able to bring themselves to put it into words.

Well, he knew what he had to do if his quest for the lifeboat came up empty. Jordan would hate his resolve, oppose it, but his mind was clear and firm on the issue. That settled, and his final goal established for tomorrow, fatigue overcame him again. Putting out the lights, he returned to the bedroom and stripped off his clothes. He slid under the quilt, turning on his side to draw the sleeping Jordan tightly against him. He tried not to think that this might be the last time he would hold her like this.

THE FIRST PALE FINGERS of daybreak were lighting the sky as Jordan and Richard shared a cold breakfast at the kitchen table. He wanted an early start in the outboard, hoping to scout the shoreline of Rowleys Bay before people were up and about. She thought this was a wise plan and was excited about his late-night discovery.

"We're due for a break, Richard," she assured him. "The lifeboat's *got* to be there."

He nodded silently.

There was something wrong. She could feel his constraint. She'd felt it from the moment he'd awakened her with the sky still inky black outside. She was afraid to ask.

He pushed aside his half-eaten bowl of cereal, his voice carefully even as he disclosed an added intention. "It's still plenty early. Do you think we could find a safe public telephone somewhere before I head out?"

She gazed at him in surprise. "What for?"

"I want to call Chicago. Andrew's school. I'd like assurance he got there safely and is settled in. Which would be the nearest phone you could drive me to that's apt to be deserted at this hour?"

She was confused by his request. "Let me think. There's one in the village hall in Baileys Harbor, but that's not likely to be available at this hour. Anything else is right in the open along the street. Wait, I know. There's a little park along the shore at the end of the village. I think—no, I'm sure—there's an outside phone in there. No one would be down there this early, and the shrubbery blocks it from the street. But, Richard, this is crazy. Use the phone here."

He shook his head stubbornly. "They could be expecting me to phone the school and might be set by now to trace any call I made to there. I'm not going to chance the police tracking my call back to your number."

"Richard, I understand your concern for Andrew's welfare, but you saw him just the other day, and he promised you—"

"No," he interrupted her quietly, "you don't understand. If they'll let me, I need to talk to him again. I *need* to hear my son's voice."

The unspoken fear that had been with her since last evening, and which she had refused to accept, could no longer be avoided. She knew why he had to talk directly to Andrew, but she made him tell her, just the same. Until he put it into actual words it was not a reality.

"Why?" she demanded softly.

"Because it may be a long time before I hear his voice again and because I want him to know, whatever happens, how much I love him and that I'm innocent. He has to hear that from me one more time while I'm still free."

A chill went through her. She understood his intention, could see his obstinacy. Still, she made an effort to reason with him. "But the lifeboat, Richard. Finding the lifeboat could change everything."

"The odds aren't in favor of it, Jordan, and we both know that. Not that I won't give it my best shot, but if it's not there...well, you're still safe from suspicion, and I want to keep it that way. As for me, no more hiding, no more running. I'm not going to look over my shoulder for the rest of my days or have my son grow up living with the knowledge that his father is a fugitive."

"You'll turn yourself in?" she whispered dryly.

"Yes, I'll take my chances in court."

"But the other suspects, Victor and Evelyn, Walter Jessup—"

"Let the experts follow up on them. They have the means and knowledge to check out their alibis and possible motives."

"And what if the police don't? What if—"

The wall phone rang. Jordan would have ignored it, except there was only one person who was, like herself, an early riser who would risk calling her at this hour of the morning. And Jordan needed all the ammunition she could get for her argument with Richard. She turned unhesitatingly to answer it.

"Me." Holly identified herself. "Wanted to catch you before I get ready for work."

Her greeting, lacking its customary cheerfulness, informed Jordan that she was about to be disappointed.

"No luck," her friend went on to regretfully report. "I contacted every one of my sources, and even a few I haven't used before, and they all came up zilch. If a fifth person did board that yacht somewhere on its run, then they were damn secretive about it because no one saw anything. Sorry to go dry on you, kid, but I don't know of anyone else to try."

Jordan tried to keep the discouragement out of her voice. "It's okay, Hol. I know you did your best."

"I don't suppose you'd care to tell me now what this is all about. I mean, I thought you were writing about *past* disasters on the lake, not the stuff of today's headlines."

"It's complicated, Holly. I—I really can't go into it right now."

"Whatever you say. But if you won't satisfy my curiosity in that direction, then you'd darn well better answer my next question."

"Name it."

"What did you go and do to ol' Dwight?" The familiar, fiendish chuckle was back in her voice. "He's been snapping at us like firecrackers ever since he spoke to you the other day."

"Not much. Just made him understand that I am definitely not interested in any offers from him, either professional or otherwise."

"Good for you."

Holly went on for another moment, sharing with her bits of office gossip to which Jordan could no longer relate. That world was far away and no longer real. The only reality for her now was the man at the table behind her, and she was impatient to get back to him.

Managing to end the call, she turned to Richard. She knew from the look on his face that he already understood Holly's failure. "Another door closed," he observed with a wry smile. "Proves my point, doesn't it?"

"Richard," she pleaded, *"please—"*

"No more arguing about it," he insisted. "I have to do what I have to do. Now, will you drive me to that phone?"

She did as he asked. He left her no choice. But she was heartsick about it.

The light was strengthening in the eastern sky as they crossed the causeway and settled in the Volvo. The air was raw, the ground frosted with dew. A pair of cedar waxwings was already busy in the dogwoods. It promised to be a golden morning.

Jordan cared about none of that as they drove through the predawn twilight toward Baileys Harbor. All she could think about, all she could feel was the man who sat silently beside her. She had never been so aware of his solid length, his warmth, even the masculine scent of him. How was she going to stand it when this closeness was gone, no longer a part of her life? Because already she experienced a forlorn emptiness, a missing of something vital.

They didn't talk. There seemed to be nothing to say. They reached the village. The main street was empty except for a stray dog investigating a trash container on the curb.

Jordan turned into the lakeside park at the point where the highway left the village, and parked behind a wall of shrubbery that hid them from the street. They left the car and followed a footpath down the slope in the direction of the beach. They reached an open-sided picnic pavilion. There were public rest rooms close by housed in a small cinder-block building. The phone was mounted on one of its outside walls. The area was deserted.

She waited for him in the pavilion while he made his call. There were gulls roosting thickly on the top bar of a nearby swing set, and she could hear the waters slapping softly on the sandy shore. She watched Richard as he talked on the phone, unable to hear him from where she stood but noticing how earnestly he spoke into the mouthpiece. She could imagine the confusion and yearning of the small boy at the other end. Though maybe not. Maybe Richard had been unable to convince the school to let Andrew talk to him.

No, it must be all right. Richard was smiling now as he spoke. That meant he had his son on the line and, hopefully, Andrew was too glad to hear his father's voice to worry about the rest.

The conversation lasted for several minutes, and then he hung up and joined her in the pavilion.

"Everything all right?" she asked him.

"Yes, he understands. That is," he added, "as much as a boy his age can understand a mess like this."

Jordan nodded. She didn't ask him to share the particulars of his call. That was something private, special between father and son, and she had no right or wish to intrude on it.

"God, how I miss him." He gazed off toward the lake, a note of longing in his voice. "All I want to do after this is all over—*if* it ever does end—is to take Andrew and go far away. Some place where we can forget and start over."

No mention of her in his wish. Well, he'd never made any promises, and she didn't blame him. She was a part of the time and place and events he needed to put behind him. But his failure to include her made her miserable.

Jordan didn't want him to see that. She interrupted his reverie briskly. "Time we got you back to the boat."

"Right." His hand reached out and covered hers, squeezing it briefly, "Thank you."

She wasn't sure what he was thanking her for, and she was afraid to ask. There was already too much finality in this morning.

They left the pavilion and started up the path.

They had no warning to prepare them. No sound of another car turning into the lot, no slam of doors or murmur of voices. Nothing that would have given Richard a chance to retreat or hide. The newcomers had either somehow arrived in silence, or else the thick shrubbery masked all noise and activity. Jordan and Richard were trapped in the open when a familiar figure appeared on the path in the gap between the tall cedars.

"Jordan! I wondered whose car that was in the lot. Are you into bird-watching? They say this is the best time of day for it."

Oddly, Sonia Gunnerson's pleasant face registered embarrassment more than surprise. As though she had been caught at something. Her greeting was too quick and forced, and she even cast a nervous glance over her shoulder. Then her gaze returned to the couple in front of her. Her blue eyes went from Jordan to the man beside her. There was nothing but mild curiosity in her expression.

Then, helpless, they watched the housekeeper's interest turn to shock as she suddenly recognized the man under the sunglasses and baseball cap. "Oh, dear Lord!" she whispered in disbelief, shrinking back against the cedars.

It was Jordan who acted first. She stretched out a hand to steady the housekeeper, who looked as if she was ready to collapse into the shrubbery. Her words were swift and reassuring. "Sonia, it's all right. I promise you it's all right."

The trembling woman shook off her hand. She looked frightened and uncertain.

Jordan pleaded for her understanding. "Remember, Sonia, how you told me you couldn't believe Richard did it, that you always liked him. You were right. He didn't do it. Please don't give him away. *Please* give him a chance to prove his innocence."

"Jordan, don't." Richard checked her. "You're only scaring her. Sonia, I—"

"Got it!" announced a satisfied voice from the other side of the shrubbery. "I knew I had an extra one buried somewhere in the trunk. You're going to wear it, too, love, because if it's this cool up here, it's going to be really chilly along the beach. Hello, where did you get to?"

Startled, Jordan and Richard watched a lanky figure swing through the opening in the cedars. He was triumphantly bearing a cardigan sweater. He stopped when he discovered them.

"Oh," he mumbled, "I guess we're not alone."

Jordan found herself looking into a long, deeply creased face with a hawkish nose. Not an attractive face but a striking one. The expression on it today was less intense, much more pleasant. The mystery man from the funeral, she realized. Harry Fellows's former partner, Walter Jessup.

Sonia's angular face, she noticed with a fast glance, was deeply flushed with his appearance. Walter, suddenly aware of the awkward silence in the group, must have sensed something was wrong. He moved protectively to the housekeeper's side, draping the sweater around her shoulders.

"What's up?" he demanded. When no one answered him, his eyes went from Richard to Jordan. Then they flew back to Richard, uneasy, shrewdly probing. "Hey, the picture in the news. Aren't you—"

"Yeah," Richard admitted hoarsely, "the man the whole peninsula is looking for." He paused to clear his throat, then went on slowly, persuasively, "I think we need to talk. That's all I'm asking for, just a few minutes to explain myself. Then you can do whatever you feel you have to do, and I swear I won't try to stop you. Will you give me that much?"

Chapter Thirteen

The hard red disk of the sun rose off the lake. Its splendor went unnoticed by the four people who tensely occupied the rough table in the picnic pavilion. Sonia and her companion shared a bench facing Jordan and Richard seated across from them.

Jordan studied the older couple as Richard, leaning forward earnestly, told them his story. The sharp breeze off the water stirred the thatch of Walter's handsome white hair and lifted curling wisps of Sonia's own silvery blond hair. She kept tucking them back in place.

The two of them were well past middle age, Jordan observed. But they were more than just friends. She could see that in the way Walter occasionally touched her and in the soft glances Sonia directed his way. It didn't matter how they had come to be involved. What counted was that Sonia was romantically attached to a man probably regarded as unacceptable by the family who employed her. That being the case, Jordan prayed, then surely the housekeeper could relate sympathetically to her own situation with Richard. Be understanding enough to grant his vital request.

But Jordan was in no way certain of the outcome of this scene. Sonia and Walter had reluctantly agreed to listen to Richard's version of the murders, but their expressions remained guarded as he presented his case. Jordan, from time to time, tried to add her own convincing explanations.

"And that's it," Richard finished at length. "The whole thing. Now the choice is yours. You can go to the phone right there and call the sheriff's department, or you can give me this one last opportunity to locate that lifeboat. And if I fail, I'll turn myself in just as I planned to do."

He sat back. Jordan, pressing his hand under the table, waited tautly with him for the couple's decision. Sonia, who had been nervously tracing weather-worn initials carved into the surface of the table, raised her eyes, searching her companion's face. The two of them exchanged their uncertainty.

It was Walter in the end who urged, "I say we give these young people their chance. I guess I know what it's like to have the world not believe you and to pay for something you never did."

His reference to his long-ago conviction for arson and insurance fraud convinced Sonia. She nodded slowly. "All right. We won't say anything."

Jordan sagged with relief. She could feel Richard's own relief in his quick squeeze of her fingers. They all relaxed as the strain at the table eased.

It was Walter now who bent forward, wanting to know. "What about suspects? You haven't said a word about suspects, either of you, and you must have at least one somebody in mind if finding this lifeboat is so urgent."

Jordan's and Richard's uncomfortable gazes must have strayed in Walter's direction before they could prevent them. Sonia noticed their looks and was immediately indignant.

"Whatever Walter felt about Harry, he had nothing to do with their deaths. How could you even consider it?"

"I'm sorry," Jordan apologized to Walter, "but when I spotted you at the funeral you looked so—"

"Like someone who could commit murder? Yep, I guess I did, all right. Shouldn't have turned up there like that. Sonia didn't want me to, but..." He hesitated, then shrugged. "Well, I guess the truth is, there was something inside me that needed to be sure the bastard really was dead.''

"Walter, you promised!" Sonia censured him.

"Sorry, love." He beamed at her affectionately. "She wouldn't talk to me after I showed up at the burial. I had to sneak up to the house that afternoon and demand to see her in the kitchen before she'd let me apologize.''

Which explained his mysterious presence at the Fellows estate, Jordan realized.

"But, of course," Sonia added, "my seeing Walter at the house is a bit awkward.''

"So," he continued, "we meet elsewhere. Like this morning. We were going to walk the beach here, and it had to be early before she was needed back at the house.''

"It's convenient," Sonia said, "because Walter is staying in the motel just across the highway.''

No wonder, Jordan thought, there had been no sounds of arrival to alert Richard and her. Their cars must be parked at the motel.

Walter grinned sheepishly. "We're working on my old bitterness toward Harry. Sonia says it's all water under the bridge, and unless I put it behind me she won't accept my proposal of marriage. Well, she's right.''

The housekeeper blushed becomingly. "We knew each other years ago, before all the trouble with that first factory that burned and when my Gus and Walter's wife were still alive. Naturally, we were just friends then.''

Walter winked at them. "Don't you believe it. I had a secret crush on her even then. Didn't learn her husband was gone until just a few weeks ago, and then I wasted no time in renewing old ties.''

"Well," Sonia admitted happily, "one thing did sort of lead to another, though we haven't told anyone about us yet. You're really the first to know.''

Jordan was glad they had found each other again. Sitting there, hands touching like a pair of young lovers, they made a winsome couple. But it was a disappointment to learn that Walter Jessup had to be struck from their painfully short list of suspects.

Sonia, perhaps sensing her thought and wanting to remove any last residue of doubt, defended her companion. "Anyway, Walter was nowhere near the yacht that day. He couldn't have been because he was with me. We were having lunch together at the White Gull Inn in Fish Creek, and there was a roomful of other diners."

Walter was amused by her protectiveness. "Sorry, folks, but it looks like that leaves me out." Face sober again, he asked Richard, "Who else have you got in the running?"

Richard shook his head. "Seems like the list has just shrunk to Victor and Evelyn. I'm afraid they're the only possible candidates."

"No!" Sonia said, refusing the notion.

Jordan tried to explain to her what she had seen and heard at the estate and why Harry Fellows's son and widow could be responsible for the murders. But the housekeeper was emphatic in her denial.

"You don't understand," she said. "They have alibis for that afternoon."

"You're positive about that?" Richard pressed her.

Sonia nodded. "Yes. They left the house before noon that morning. Drove away together in Victor's car. Evelyn was looking anxious, but naturally it wasn't my place to ask them why or where they were going."

"Then," Jordan objected, "if you didn't know where they were—"

"Oh, but I do know. There was a phone call in the afternoon before they returned. It was after I got back from lunch with Walter. It was from a receptionist in a doctor's office down in Green Bay. She said Mr. and Mrs. Fellows had just left following their appointment, only Evelyn had forgotten her sunglasses in the waiting room. They were expensive designer sunglasses, and she wanted Mrs. Fellows to know they were safe. I told the woman Mrs. Fellows's husband couldn't have been with her. She described him, and of course it was Victor. I never got the chance to tell Evelyn about the sunglasses because, by the time they got back, we'd heard the *Lady Anne* was missing."

Richard was perplexed. "A doctor? What kind of doctor?"

"I don't know. It was never mentioned." The look on her face said she was too loyal an employee to have pursued it. "I do have my suspicions about it," she conceded, "but they don't matter here. What counts is that they both have alibis that can be easily verified if anyone checks."

Jordan, too, suddenly had her suspicions about the kind of doctor Evelyn had consulted, but this was no time to go into them. The sun had cleared the horizon, and she was worried about getting Richard away. If Sonia and Walter had wandered into the park and recognized Richard, others could do the same. Only *they* wouldn't be tolerant about it.

"We should go," she murmured to Richard.

He nodded. They rose from the table, thanking the older couple, who wished them luck. Minutes later they were in the Volvo and headed back to Cana Island.

"I guess that eliminates Victor and Evelyn," Richard said, fighting discouragement.

"Unless they hired a killer. That's possible, isn't it?"

He shook his head. "I don't think so. Whoever was on board and behind that cabin door was someone Harry invited there. Someone he was familiar with and trusted."

"Then we just have to learn who it was."

But she shared his disappointment. Victor and Evelyn had been a last hope. Now they, too, were out of the picture. There seemed to be no one left. Worse, there was almost no time left. She kept remembering Sheriff Matthews's passionate determination to catch Richard and Richard's own intention to turn himself in if this final search failed. She was scared.

The village behind them, they drove now in silence along the deserted road twisting through the forest. Jordan's thoughts were centered on their imminent parting. She couldn't do it, she decided. She couldn't let him go off alone in that outboard. If they were to be separated after this morning, perhaps not to see each other again, then she wanted to share every last precious minute with him, whatever the outcome. And as for her terror of small boats...well, somehow she would overcome that. She *had* to.

Her announcement was abrupt and decisive. "I'm going with you in the outboard."

He wasn't surprised by her declaration. Maybe he even expected it. And he was prepared with a swift refusal. "Not even discussable."

"Why, when all the other times we—?"

"Weren't out in the open." He cut her off. "This one will have to be, and it would put both of us clearly together. You've been into enough risky situations already because of me. This is one too many."

"It's my choice, damn it, and if I'm willing—"

"But I'm *not* willing. How do you expect me to live with myself if I'm taken and you're there beside me, accused of being my accomplice?"

"That's an exaggeration. I wasn't there on the yacht."

"No, but they'd charge you with sheltering and aiding a man wanted for murder. Your Sheriff Matthews would be so outraged over your deceiving him that he'd see to it you were taken into custody as an accessory. You know he would."

"I'm not worried about that."

"Well, I am. It's bad enough now that Sonia and Walter know you've been helping me. At least we can trust them not to talk about it. But it's got to stop here before anyone else learns you're involved."

If he cared about her, *really* cared about her, Jordan reasoned illogically, he would want her there beside him. But that was the problem. Maybe he didn't care enough.

She was miserable over his opposition, but no argument would move him this time. He was coldly silent by the time the road ended at the causeway. The outboard was waiting for him on the shore.

She watched him as he readied the boat, hating it that they were parting this way. What if she never saw him again? What if her last memory of them together was their anger? She couldn't stand it.

He was in the boat now, ready to shove off. She had to win one last promise from him.

"You won't do anything rash, will you? I mean, if the lifeboat isn't there, you won't just march up to the nearest telephone and surrender yourself? You will come back here first?"

He considered her request, then nodded. "In any case, I'll need to bring the outboard back here to the trailer so that it can be returned to the rental."

Is that all he cared about? she thought bitterly. Preserving the damn boat so she wouldn't be charged for it?

He didn't kiss her goodbye. Maybe this was his way of letting go, of making it easier on both of them. Wise or not, she hated that, too. She wanted to cling to him, hold him tight. Of course, she didn't.

A moment later she found herself alone on the hard shingle, watching the outboard as it grew smaller in the distance and willing herself not to cry.

She went on standing there, one hand holding her wind-whipped sable hair back from her face as she squinted against the brilliance of the day. The waters were a hard blue laced with whitecaps. She tried not to think about her grandfather last summer or all the potential dangers of being on the open lake in a small boat.

It wasn't a rational concern, anyway. She had a much greater fear for the man out there beating up the coast in a vulnerable outboard. What if this time he was recognized and taken? There would be no way she would know. She'd be waiting all day at the lighthouse, conjuring up unbearable images.

Well, she wasn't going to sit uselessly like that, sick with worry and wondering if she had lost Richard forever. There was an alternative.

Walter Jessup might no longer be a suspect. Nor Evelyn and Victor Fellows. But there was still someone else. One last possible candidate whose actual whereabouts on the afternoon of the murders had yet to be established. Dino, the mercurial young man staying with Maggie Dennis. Father Mac had befriended him, but the troubled had been known to turn on their saviors. There could also be an explanation in connection with Dino for that mysterious someone the ex-priest had been struggling to remember. Whatever Richard's impressions about him, Dino could have been on the yacht and then fled it after some insane rampage. It might account for his turning up at the farm out of nowhere.

Then there was that discordant scrap of knowledge that had been preying on a dark corner of her mind for the past twenty-four hours, and which continued to elude her. Was it somehow related to Dino? Here was something else for her to learn.

The sun was well up by now, but it was still very early. Maybe too early for her to be calling at the farm. Jordan didn't let that stop her as she climbed back into the Volvo. She would tell Maggie that she just happened to be passing the farm and wondered if she'd had time to dig out the rest of those ship logs from her brother's belongings. Then, if Maggie wasn't annoyed by her presumptuous arrival, maybe she could engage her in another conversation that would produce results. She might even risk telling Maggie the whole story, enough of it anyway to coax her full cooperation regarding Dino.

It might have made better sense, Jordan realized as she turned the car and headed inland again, to go back to the lighthouse and phone the farm first. But she was in no mood

to be sensible. Richard had settled on his own version of a
search for his salvation. But this one, she told herself firmly,
belonged to her. It was her own last stubborn measure to
save him.

SILENCE. SO COMPLETE a silence it was eerie. Jordan was
immediately aware of it as she stepped out of the car. Nothing stirred. The windmill, now that the breeze had dropped,
was still. There were no sounds from the goats out back, and
the farm buildings that only yesterday had looked so
charming seemed forlorn this morning. As though the place
was deserted.

Well, maybe it is, Jordan thought, telling herself that she
was being imaginative about the silence. Maybe it simply
meant no one was at home, and she had come for nothing.

Whatever the explanation, she couldn't seem to shake her
sense of uneasiness as she mounted the porch and paused at
the front door. The screen door was closed, but the inner
door was open, though it wasn't a warm morning. It should
have been a warning to her that something was wrong, but
she chose to view it as evidence that Maggie must be home,
after all.

The screen door rattled in its frame when she rapped on
it. A jarring sound. She waited, but no one answered her
knock.

"Hello," she called through the screen. "Anyone there?"

The silence persisted.

Hands on either side of her face to block off the glare of
the sun, she pressed her nose to the screen and peered into
the shadowy parlor. And that was when she understood the
fearful silence that gripped the farm.

She lay sprawled facedown on the floor of the parlor. A
woman with short, iron gray hair. Maggie Dennis. She was
twisted at an unnatural angle and perfectly motionless. But
even then Jordan was unwilling to accept the horrifying reality, preferring to believe Maggie's position was the result
of illness or an accident and that she needed help.

Without hesitating or considering the risk, Jordan snatched open the screen door and flew into the room. She knelt beside the inert form. That was when she saw the blood staining the braided rug, noticed that its source was a gun wound on the back of the gray head. She knew then that Maggie Dennis was beyond help. Knew that she was looking on death and that the death was murder.

Jordan was too stunned to move. Unable to stagger to her feet, get to her car and safety. She went on crouching there, staring at the body and fighting a sudden rush of nausea. Somewhere under her shock she was aware of Maggie's outstretched hand clutching a ragged scrap of heavy paper. There was enough of it left in her rigid fingers to identify it as the corner of a glossy photograph. The rest, the important part, had been torn from her tight grasp.

Jordan's head whipped around in alarm as a step sounded on the porch. The screen door was ripped open, and then Dino was in the room, gaping at her, gaping at Maggie on the floor.

With a cry of anguish the young man raced across the room and dropped to his knees on the other side of the body. Paralyzed, Jordan watched him bend over Maggie, as though in an attitude of prayer.

"Don't touch her!" she warned him, startled by the ferociousness in her voice.

Dino obeyed her. For a long moment he didn't move. Then he slowly lifted his head. There were tears in his eyes.

"I came to the farm looking for Father Mac," he whispered fiercely. "And when I found out what happened to him I stayed on. I stayed on to protect Maggie. Father Mac would have wanted me to protect her. Only I blew it, didn't I? Damn it all to hell, I blew it!"

Jordan didn't answer him. Their gazes met across the body, and the suffering in his eyes turned into a trapped look as he understood the accusation in her stare.

"No," he said, shaking his head. Slowly at first and then with quick, violent jerks. "No, I didn't do it! I wouldn't have done it! Not Maggie! *Never!*"

"It's all right," she said, soothing his wildness. "I believe you."

And suddenly she did believe Dino. She wasn't sure why, but she believed in his innocence. Or maybe she did know why. Maybe she finally realized that his involvement in the murders had never made any real sense, that she'd considered him only out of desperation. Or maybe…maybe it was because the awful truth, the actual explanation, was at last beginning to surface in her mind. But there were veiling shadows that remained. Perhaps Dino had the knowledge to lift them.

"Come away," she instructed him, getting to her feet.

She went out onto the porch, and he followed her numbly, tugging at his long, shaggy hair, his black eyes fastened on her, seeking her directions.

She faced him, in control of herself again. She had to be. The situation was crucial. "Where were you when it happened?" she asked him directly.

"Down the road to a neighbor's. Maggie sent me."

"What for?"

"She wanted me to bring Milt Johnson back here. His place is a couple of farms down."

"Milt who?"

"Johnson. He's a sheriff's deputy."

"Why was she asking for a sheriff's deputy?"

He shook his head. "She wouldn't say. I just know she looked funny when she told me."

"Funny how?"

"I dunno. Kind of all uptight, I guess. She was all right over breakfast, joking with me, even, and then just a little bit later she was all changed."

"Something must have happened to cause that. What was it?"

"Nothing happened. Nothing major, anyway. Shouldn't we be calling somebody about Maggie?"

"Not yet. Dino, this could be very important. *Think*. What did she do after breakfast?"

"She went into the back bedroom to unpack more of Father Mac's things. Said she was going to find the rest of those ship logs for you. I was out here stacking the firewood there. Next I knew she came out on the porch. That was when she told me to go bring the deputy."

"Wait a minute. This doesn't make sense. Why wouldn't she just phone the sheriff's office, ask them to send an officer directly to the farm? Why send you down the road for a deputy?"

"I asked her that. All she'd say was, 'Go get Milt Johnson. No one else, Dino,' she says. 'Just Milt Johnson and tell him it's urgent.' Except he wasn't there. His wife said he was due back after his shift any time. I waited, but then when he didn't show I got worried about Maggie. I told his wife to send the deputy when he turned up. That's when I came back here."

"And while you were gone someone arrived at the farm. Someone killed her."

"Yeah." His face contorted with grief and rage. "Why would someone do that to Maggie?"

"I think, Dino," Jordan said softly, "it must be because of what she discovered in that back bedroom. Something the murderer couldn't let her share with anyone."

His black eyes narrowed. "The picture, you mean?"

"Then you noticed it, too, in her hand. Or, anyway, the little corner that was left of it after the killer snatched the rest of it."

"Didn't mean that. I didn't notice there was a piece of it still left in her hand. What I meant was I remember she was carrying it when she came out on the porch to find me."

"She had the photograph with her then?" A chill of excitement raced up Jordan's spine. "It *was* a photograph, wasn't it? Dino, did she show it to you? Did you see it?"

"I could see it, all right. She held it out to me. 'This is going to shake up a few people, Dino.' That's what she said, and she had this tight look on her face when she said it."

"What was in it?" she urged him tautly.

"Nothing important. Not to make her say what she did. It was just an old picture of a basketball team, maybe guys in high school or a little older. You know how they pose 'em, all lined up and lookin' out at the camera."

"Did you recognize any face? No, of course not. How could you?"

"Yeah, but I did. He was a lot younger then, but it was him."

"Who?"

"Who else? Father Mac, of course. He was the team's coach, I guess. Anyway, he was right in there with them. And they must have just won some championship or other because there was this big ol' trophy down on the floor in front of them."

Dino's words were a strobe light flashing on the dark corner of her brain that, until this second, had refused to yield its vital morsel of information. The elusive *something* that had been worrying her since yesterday was suddenly no longer elusive. Jordan *knew*.

"What is it?" Dino demanded, baffled by the stunned expression on her face.

She shook her head. She couldn't afford to stop and explain it to him. Couldn't permit herself to be further shaken by Maggie's gruesome death or even pause long enough to provide Dino with the comfort he deserved. Because if she was right, and she was confident now she was, then every second mattered.

She gave the young man swift instructions, digging through her purse as she talked. "Stay with her, Dino. Wait for the deputy, and when he comes tell him everything."

"You're leaving?"

"I have to," she insisted, regretting the necessity of deserting him in his bewilderment. "It's vital. Here, I'll give you a note for this Milt Johnson."

The familiar disorder in her purse finally surrendered a pencil and an empty envelope. It was the only paper she could find. She held it against one of the posts on the porch, scrawling rapidly across its back.

"If there's any question of his believing you," she told Dino, "this ought to assure him I was here and where I've gone. I just hope he's not too long."

She finished the note and thrust it into Dino's hand. "I'm sorry to leave you, Dino, but it's important, believe me." She gave him one final caution. "Whatever happens, don't give this to anyone but the deputy. *No one else.*"

Not waiting for his promise, Jordan was down the steps and tearing across the yard to her car. Within seconds she was on the road and headed in the direction of Rowleys Bay. Her mind hummed with her startling knowledge as she sped northward.

Those speculations last evening she had shared with Richard were no longer improbable. It *was* the ex-priest who'd been the murderer's target, and Harry Fellows and his daughter had died simply to provide a cover for a cold-blooded killer.

John McGuire had been silenced probably because of something threatening he knew, just as his sister, Maggie, had been destroyed because she'd recognized a face in that old photograph. The same face out of the past that her brother had been struggling to remember aboard the *Lady Anne.*

None of it, without further information, was a certainty. But enough of it was there to convince Jordan she was right. Right enough, anyway, to make it imperative that she intercept Richard at Rowleys Bay. Because if the murderer was who she believed he was, then the man she loved was in mortal danger.

Chapter Fourteen

Richard tried to keep his mind off Jordan, to concentrate on nothing except his vital pursuit of the lifeboat. But the outboard was no powerful cruiser, and it was a long haul to Rowleys Bay. He couldn't help thinking about her, regretting his brusqueness in their parting. The worst of it was he'd left so much unsaid that needed saying, and now it might be too late for it.

Maybe, he thought, he'd been wrong not to let her join him in this hunt. Maybe, after all her risk and effort on his behalf, she was entitled to share in this final critical effort. She had already proved to him, again and still again, that she was a resourceful woman who knew how to handle a challenge. Had he neglected to respect that, failed to treat her as the equal she deserved to be? He wasn't sure. He just knew that she meant too much to him to chance her wellbeing.

Rounding the last point, Richard was relieved to put his uncertainties about Jordan behind him. He had arrived at Rowleys Bay, and there was no time for personal frustrations.

Slowing the motor to an idling speed, he took a moment to survey the scene, comparing the actual situation to his memory of it in the charts he had studied last night. His recollection was accurate and matched the reality.

Spread before him was the shallow bay, nearly a mile across at its greatest width and almost solidly framed by forest. Midway along the left side of the bay was a spit of land occupied by a few summer cottages. Beyond that the bay narrowed into the Mink River, which was not a proper river at all but a deep, winding inlet. An inlet, he recalled from the maps, that was largely a wilderness area bordered by unbroken woods and marshes.

He'd been right. The bay offered the perfect haven for any craft running from rough seas on the open lake. Just as the lifeboat must have streaked for shelter on the afternoon Richard's world had collapsed around him. But this was a large sea. It could be anywhere in here, if at all.

He was in for a long search, no question of it. And that presented a problem. The outboard didn't consume much gas, and he had an extra can with him. But it had been a long trip from Cana Island. He couldn't expect to cover both the bay and the inlet and then get back to the lighthouse without refueling.

Just off to his left, tucked behind its own snug little harbor, was the tiny settlement of Rowleys Bay. There was a good dock there, a cluster of shanties and a bait-and-tackle shop that served fishermen. A sizable resort was nearby, and Richard knew it was risky landing so close to it. The sunglasses and baseball cap didn't provide him with much of a disguise. But it was still early, almost no one around. Anyway, he had no choice.

Minutes later, after negotiating the approach along a safe channel clearly marked by buoys, he cut the engine and coasted into the dock. There were two people on the pier. One was a boy, who paid no attention to Richard. He was perched on a piling, a pole in his hand and an expression of concentration on his narrow face. He apparently took his fishing seriously. The other was an elderly man wearing a tattered baseball cap and glowering at the herring gulls that swarmed around the dock. He seemed only mildly interested in Richard's arrival, but he came limping along the pier as Richard moored the outboard and climbed onto the landing.

"Want something?" It was more of a growled challenge than a greeting.

Richard nodded at a pump located along the edge of the dock. "I need to fill up on gas. Anyone around to help me?"

There was no immediate response to his request. A pair of rheumy eyes in the creased face regarded him suspiciously for a long minute. Richard, fearing his disguise was being penetrated, tried to maintain an attitude of nonchalance.

The cantankerous old fellow, tugging at his battered cap, finally acknowledged the question and grunted, "That'd be me. Haven't opened it yet for the day. I'll need to get the key."

He shambled off in the direction of the weathered shanty that was the bait-and-tackle shop. Richard, watching him go, knew he'd feel a lot more comfortable once he got his gas and headed out of here. Restless with both concern and his long confinement in the outboard, he paced along the length of the pier, welcoming the opportunity to stretch his legs.

He eyed the boy on the piling. He was older than Andrew and looked nothing like him. It didn't matter. He still made Richard think of his son. He'd never gone fishing with Andrew. It was something they had missed. What he wouldn't give right now to share a few lazy hours with Andrew and a pair of fishing rods. He hated to think that might never happen after today.

The boy, perhaps sensing his longing, glanced up from his occupation with the pole. Unlike the old man, he wore a friendly grin as he observed in the outboard the fishing gear that Richard had borrowed from one of the lighthouse sheds to provide a cover for his search. "You gonna try your luck out in the bay?"

"I thought I might."

He shook his head, offering the grave advice of an expert. "I wouldn't bother. Best fishing is up along the Mink River. That's where I'd be if I had a boat."

"Sounds like you know your fishing grounds."

"Yep, I'm really into it. Never miss a day hanging out down here in season. Saturdays like this I'll spend the whole morning, and on weekdays this is the place I head to soon as the school bus drops me."

"*Every* day?"

"Sure. Good weather and bad. Doesn't make a difference, I'm here. My dad says I'm gonna grow gills and fins if I don't give it a rest."

Richard's curiosity had been nothing but casual until this minute. But the kid's claim fired a sudden inspiration. It was just possible... He encouraged the boy. "*All* kinds of weather? You couldn't have been down here on an afternoon like the other day's when it was so wild."

"Heck I wasn't," he boasted. "Worst of the storm had passed through, but I was here, all right."

"The waters out there would have been awfully rough, I guess."

"Not bad on the bay, but they were really kicking up over the lake."

"You must have been all on your own down here," Richard probed. "At least, I suppose there were no boats out on the water that afternoon."

"Naw, it was pretty lonesome, all right." He lifted his pole to check his bait. "Except for that one crazy boat, anyway."

An excitement began to burn in Richard. "Crazy how?"

"'Cause he wasn't much bigger'n your boat there, and he came in off all that heavy stuff on the lake. Boy, was he tossing!"

Richard tried to control his eagerness, to preserve a tone of idle conversation. "Bet he made straight for the safe harbor here."

"Uh-uh. Think he was headed for Mink River. Least-ways, he kept out in the middle of the bay." The youngster lowered his line again into the water, adding with uninterest, "Not so far out, though, I couldn't tell who it was."

"You *knew* him?"

"Jeez, they're not bitin' at all today! Yeah, pretty sure. I was with my uncle once when he gave him a speeding ticket down in Sturgeon Bay."

"Who?"

"The guy we're talkin' about," the boy said impatiently. "You know, Sheriff Matthews."

Richard was dumbfounded. *Con Matthews!* Was it possible?

"You ready for that gas, mister?"

Richard swung around. The old man had returned with the key. There was no chance to question the boy further. His mind seething with the shocking thing he had just learned, he followed the limping fellow along the pier to the pump.

The man filled his gas tanks, glancing up at him sharply from beneath a pair of shaggy eyebrows as he worked. "Heard what the kid was telling you. Lot of bull."

"Oh?"

"You can count on it. I know Sheriff Matthews, and I know he wouldn't go anywheres near the lake in rough weather. Man gets seasick in anything choppy. Does keep a little runabout for hisself in a boat shed he's got somewheres up the Mink, but he only uses it for once-in-a-while fishing on the quiet backwaters along there."

"I'll take your word for it," Richard said, assuming an attitude of supreme indifference.

"There's your gas. Anything else today?"

"That's all." The man was still considering him suspiciously as he paid him. Richard tried to cover himself by sounding casual. "I'm off to the Mink River for a little fishing of my own. Hope to land a coho."

The excitement that he couldn't afford to show throbbed now in his veins as he lowered himself into the outboard and started the motor. He was finally getting the break he'd prayed for! Whatever the old fellow claimed, Richard was confident that somewhere up the Mink River, probably concealed in that shed, was the missing lifeboat. And much more astonishing than that, Sheriff Con Matthews had put it there!

THE OLD MAN, eyes narrowed, watched the outboard chug across the bay on its way to the inlet. He spat off the dock and muttered, "Coho, my behind!" Anybody who understood anything about fishing these waters knew there were no lake salmon to be taken off the Mink River.

Mind made up, he headed for the telephone in his shop. Seconds later he was calling the sheriff's department in Sturgeon Bay.

"Sheriff himself is off duty right now," the dispatcher informed him.

"Well, I need to talk to him personally," the old man insisted. "Something I think he ought to know."

"He just checked in a few minutes ago from his car phone. If it's important, maybe you can still reach him there."

The dispatcher gave him the number. He dialed it with bulldog determination. It was picked up almost immediately.

"Sheriff Matthews," the deep voice identified himself.

"Sheriff, this is Ed Grace out at Rowleys Bay. Got something that might interest you. There was this guy just here in his outboard buying gas and asking some peculiar questions."

The old man went on to describe Richard's visit, ending his account in a disdainful voice. "Went off toward the Mink. Fishing, he says. Ask me, he don't know beans about fishing."

There was a pause, and then the sheriff asked calmly, "What did he look like, Ed?"

The old man gave him a brief description of Richard. "Hey, you think he could be this bird you guys are hunting for?"

"Oh, I doubt it, Ed. The description isn't really right. Probably just another tourist being curious, but I'll see it gets checked out. Sure do appreciate your being so alert, though."

"Yeah, well, like I say, I did tell him there was no way you'd of been out on the waters that day."

The sheriff laughed. "That's right, Ed. The last place I would have been. You take care now, and be sure to give my love to Vi."

The old man hung up, satisfied that he'd made his report. He could forget about it now.

Several miles away, seated behind the wheel of his heavy-duty pickup parked outside the Pioneer Store in Ellison Bay, Con Matthews finished the can of soda he had stopped to buy. The stuff was biting on his tongue, just the way he liked it, and he relished the last drops.

He looked relaxed as he sat there, a reassuring image of the self-confident local sheriff. People trusted that kind of thing. They voted for it. He wasn't relaxed. Not yet, he thought with a little smile. But soon, real soon, he could genuinely relax. The intolerable strain he had lived with these past couple of days was coming to an end. Richard Davis, the last threat to everything he valued, was almost his.

Pity he'd left him alive aboard the yacht. But he'd had no choice about that, though it had resulted in considerable worry with Davis on the loose. Now it seemed Davis had managed to get onto him, had even picked up an outboard somewhere. He'd have to take care of that before it was too late, just as he'd taken care of all the rest.

Of course, he would have to handle it with care, make certain that he covered all aspects of the situation before he destroyed his enemy. But Con knew how to do that. He had always seen to it that he came out on top since those early, miserable days in Chicago.

Crushing the empty soda can in his hand, just the way he would crush Richard Davis, he started up the engine and swung onto the highway. He aimed the pickup toward Mink River and the rough, isolated track that led to his boat shed.

DON'T LET ME BE TOO LATE. Let him be where I can still reach him.

Jordan held fast to this silent plea as the Volvo rushed down the last sloping mile to Rowleys Bay. She cleared the trees, and the spreading sheet of the bay sprang into view. The road leveled here, dividing at the water's edge. The right branch swung off toward the tiny settlement hugging the harbor. The left curved around the side of the bay toward a spur of land where a few cottages huddled under the pines.

Jordan braked at the fork, left the engine running and charged across the road. Standing on the shore, she anxiously scanned the expanse of the bay. She found it almost at once. A lone outboard plowing a steady path away from the direction of the open lake. Even at this distance she could recognize the figure in the stern.

Hands cupped to her mouth, she lifted her voice in an urgent shout.

"Richard! Here! Over here!"

Her only response was the mewing of the swooping gulls. Useless. He would never hear her above the sound of his motor. He was too far out in the bay.

Frantic, she watched the small craft cutting its purposeful way in the direction of the low headland. She knew the bay from past fishing excursions with her grandfather, and she thought she understood Richard's destination. The Mink River was in there beyond that headland. Once he cleared the point, the mouth of the inlet with all its swampy growth would swallow the outboard. She would lose him. Her only hope was to try to intercept him out at the point.

Diving back behind the wheel of her car, she sent the Volvo hurtling along the roadway that skirted the bay, heedless of the condition of a surface that was graveled now and rutted. But neither the clouds of dust raised in her wake, nor the blare of her horn she laid on repeatedly to capture Richard's attention, made any difference. Though she managed to keep the outboard in sight between the intermittent groves of trees, the boat never hesitated in its determined course.

She was on the point now, tearing past unoccupied summer cottages that frustratingly blocked her view of the bay. She could no longer see the outboard. The lane abruptly ended. Her foot punched the brake, bringing the car to a rocking standstill. Then she was racing down to the shore.

Too late? No, she had beat him to the point. The outboard was almost abreast of where she stood. She waved her arms wildly above her head and shouted, trying to hail him. No good. He was still too far out, keeping well away from the shallows and concentrating on nothing but the channel.

What could she do? In another minute he would be crawling past the point, leaving her behind him. It was the sun striking sparks off the waters of the bay that answered her desperation.

Slinging the purse off her shoulder, Jordan clawed through its contents and found her pocket mirror. It took several tries before she had it angled properly to catch the sun, but she finally managed to trap the light and send it back across the waters in shimmering flashes.

It worked!

The white dazzle instantly alerted Richard. He swung his head, puzzled, searching for its source. He found her standing on the shore signaling him. With relief she watched the outboard slow and then turn for the beach.

She waited anxiously as the boat slid toward her, the motor angled now to protect its prop in the shallows. Then the nose of the craft crunched on the hard shingle, and Richard scrambled ashore.

"Jordan, what in the name of—"

He never got to finish expressing himself over her startling arrival. The breath was knocked out of him as her body slammed into his. Her arms went around him, locking him in a death grip. He wasn't sure whether he was being attacked or embraced. Either way, there was a definite pleasure involved in the experience.

"I was so scared!" she confessed in a breathless rush. "I thought I wouldn't get to you in time to warn you!"

He managed to loosen her choking hold on him. There was a mixture of amusement and concern on his face. "Sweetheart, what's going on? What's this all about?"

"Don't you dare laugh at me! I know I'm being emotional, but this is serious!"

Actually, he was damn flattered by her possessive hug, but he immediately sobered. "Tell me."

And she did, leaving nothing out of the account of her shattering visit to the farm, including her certainty that Con Matthews was the killer. Richard, in turn, rapidly related his own discovery back at the dock.

"Now we both know it's true," she insisted. "He *is* the one. That's why Maggie Dennis sent for the deputy instead of calling directly for the sheriff because it must have been the sheriff himself she recognized in that old photograph."

Richard shook his head. "At this point we're still only half sure. There's nothing absolutely positive."

"Oh, but there is," she informed him triumphantly. "One little something I haven't explained."

One of his thick eyebrows lifted in wry wonder. "Would you care to share it?"

"Remember how I told you I was convinced there was something I saw or heard that just didn't feel right, only I couldn't place it? Not until Dino described that photograph to me. It was when he said the basketball team was posing with a trophy that I finally realized what had been nagging at me since yesterday. In fact, since we went to Sturgeon Bay, only I wasn't able to pinpoint the actual time and place before now. I mean, it was such a tiny little thing. That's why it didn't fall into line for me. A small detail but, as it turns out, vital."

She was making no sense. "Jordan," he interrupted her impatiently, "what has some old basketball trophy got to do with—"

"No, Richard, listen. It doesn't have anything to do with this situation. The point is, the mention of the trophy triggered my memory of another trophy."

He was thoroughly puzzled. "What trophy?"

"The yachting trophy aboard the *Lady Anne,* of course. The one that belonged to Harry Fellows. Richard, you were very descriptive that first morning when you told me about everything that happened on the yacht. How Harry was sitting there polishing his trophy while you argued with him about Andrew. And how, afterward, when you found their bodies in the salon the trophy was on the floor, and you picked it up and set it on the bar."

"Go on," he urged.

"Then when Con was talking to me in Sturgeon Bay he remarked how difficult it was for him to investigate the murder scene, that his friend, Harry, was still clutching his prized trophy. Only he couldn't have been because you'd left the trophy on the bar."

"You're right." Richard realized the truth with a sense of increasing excitement and dread.

"Which means," Jordan said, "he was really recalling where the trophy was when he shot him, because only you and the murderer would know that Harry was polishing that trophy just before he died."

"So," Richard agreed, "Con Matthews slipped up when he told you about the trophy."

"Yes, but it's been his only real mistake so far. He's cunning, Richard. And he's desperate. He has to be to have killed four people like that. It must be something awful he's determined to hide."

"Whatever it is, he's still a homicidal maniac."

"That's the whole point. I kept remembering all the way here how passionate he is about catching you. It was bad enough before, but knowing now just what he is and how much he has at stake..." She shuddered over the possibility of Con Matthews cornering Richard. "I think he'd do anything to make certain you took the blame."

"You're right. He has to keep the guilt focused on me."

"That's why I rushed to warn you. If he should learn you're onto him, he won't be satisfied with your capture. He'll kill you like he killed the others and then say you turned on him and that he had to shoot you in self-defense. That way he's safe forever. No questions, no suspicions."

"Except he doesn't know I'm onto him."

"Richard," she pleaded with him, "don't risk it. I've left the note with the deputy. Now let him handle it."

He shook his head. "Jordan, it's no good. Matthews has a powerful reputation on the peninsula, and this deputy is one of his own men. Whose word do you think he's going to trust?"

"We can't count on him to help us, can we?" she realized dismally.

"Not without some evidence to link Matthews to the murders. With the photograph gone, that lifeboat is still the only hope. If it's there, I have to get to it and get to it fast."

"Not alone," she resolved. "Not this time."

"Jordan, no! Matthews is prowling out there somewhere, and—"

"All the more reason for you not to go in there by yourself. Richard, you've got to have a lookout while you investigate that boat shed. Or don't you think I've earned the right?"

"Yes, over and over," he admitted, and his admiration of her had never been stronger.

"Then don't shut me out. Let me be there for you. Besides," she appealed, offering him a compelling argument, "I think I know where that boat shed is. I fished with Casey on the Mink a couple of times, and I remember an old shed along one of the channels. I could lead you to it. Otherwise, you might never find it."

There was no time for further discussion. Richard had to make a decision. "Get in the boat," he said hoarsely. And God help him, he thought, if this was a mistake he would live to regret.

Jordan, without hesitating, clambered into the outboard. She seized one of the oars, thrusting it against the hard shingle to help launch them. Richard shoved at the bow, hopping aboard as the boat slid free of the beach. It was when he started to move around her to reach the motor that he remembered her irrational fear of boats since her grandfather's death. She was already settled in the front, perched there rigidly on the seat, hands folded together tightly in her lap.

"You all right?" he asked.

She nodded stubbornly, her nervousness evident now that they were afloat.

"Sure?"

"Positive. Let's go."

She fought her tenseness as the motor kicked over seconds later. Gathering speed, the outboard swung toward the main channel. *I can do this,* Jordan promised herself, determined to conquer her phobia. *I have to do it.*

Uneasiness threatened her as the shore receded. She resisted it, concentrating on something else. She thought of Richard close behind her at the tiller. Thought of how much she loved him. And Richard? How deeply did he care? He had seemed more than just pleased by her fierce embrace, and he had finally allowed her to join him. That had to mean something. But she couldn't forget his yearning to have all this behind him so that he and Andrew could go off somewhere together and forget. She hadn't been included in that longing. So the shadow of uncertainty was still with her.

There was one satisfaction. Her focus on their relationship, however frustrating, did help to lessen her fear of being out on the water. She might not be cured, but she found herself relaxing considerably as the outboard nosed into the mouth of the Mink River.

The landscape closed in again as the open bay fell behind them. There was an abrupt change in the vegetation. Marsh grasses and thick reeds bordered the channel, infested with clouds of gnats. The woods were massed behind the grasses, ranks of young poplars and the taller spars of larches. Jordan could scent the rich tang of balsams and the spicier aroma of pines. The forest in places was a graveyard of dead trees where the swamp waters had invaded. Someone had mounted nesting boxes for wood ducks on the raw trunks. It was the only visible indication of man.

It was a lush wilderness, but the naked limbs of the ghost trees depressed her with their gauntness. Or was it the mood of the sky? It, too, had altered. It was overcast now, marking one of those sudden changes in weather that were common on the peninsula. The air, without the cheerful sun, was much cooler. Jordan shivered. Or maybe it wasn't the temperature, either. Maybe it was anticipation of what lay ahead.

"Which way?" Richard called from above the throb of the engine behind her, which seemed muted now that the wilderness had squeezed in on them.

"Keep straight ahead," she answered him. "We have to look for a side channel off to the right."

Jordan had promised to lead him to the boat shed. Now she prayed that she could remember the way. Shifting her position, she lifted herself to her knees on the seat in order not to miss the turning. Straining forward, she searched the heavy growth along the muddy banks.

Moments later she spotted a break in the vegetation that defined the narrow mouth into the channel. This was it! Using her hands as signals, she directed Richard into the opening and along the winding branch.

The channel was perhaps two hundred yards or so in length, a dense forest undergrowth ranged along both its edges. Cautious now with their approach, Richard eased the outboard around a sharp bend masked by cedars. And here the channel ended in a broad, still pool.

He cut the engine, and they drifted on the tannin-dark waters. The sudden silence was eerie. No doubt about it, Jordan thought. It was an isolated, secretive place.

On the far side of the pool, straddling the bank, was the boat shed—a sagging affair with flaking green paint. Whatever its sorry condition, it was still solid enough. Wide doors opened directly over the water, the kind that were securely barred from inside. Richard knew there would be no easy way to gain access from this side.

"What now?" Jordan whispered. It was the sort of spot that commanded whispers.

In answer, he picked up one of the oars and pointed it toward a gray, rotting pier jutting into the pool just off to their left. Then, dipping the single oar like a canoe paddle, he maneuvered them with quick, efficient strokes into the side of the pier. There was a crudely fashioned cleat on one of the timbers, and as they bumped against a piling, Jordan snugged the outboard's line around it.

"Look," Richard directed softly, coming to his feet beside her. He indicated a rough track that led to the pier and boat shed through the woods. The outboard's position offered a perfect view of the lane. Jordan would be able to see, as well as hear, any vehicle well before it reached the shed. There was no sign of such a vehicle in the area now. The whole place wore a mood of complete desertion. But he was taking no chances.

"I'm going around on foot to the back side of the shed," he instructed her. "There has to be another door there or the land side, or maybe a window. I'll probably have to force my way inside. I don't want you to leave the outboard. If you see anything, or hear anything, slap one of the oars against the pier just as hard as you can. I'll know to get out of there fast. And, Jordan?"

"Yes?"

"If anything happens, or if I'm not back in, say, twenty minutes, I want you to take the outboard and get out of here. Promise?"

"Richard—"

"Promise."

"All right."

He was gone then, scrambling out of the boat, negotiating the dilapidated pier, trotting through the trees. Seconds later he disappeared from sight around the corner of the shed. Jordan was suddenly alone, and she didn't like it.

Except for a solitary sandpiper on a mud bank, there was no other sign of life in or around the pool. The waters were flat, but there had to be a current stirring beneath the surface. It made a slow, persistent sucking sound under the peeling doors of the shed. She listened to it and found it unnerving as she kept watch on the lane. Then suddenly it subsided. There was nothing now but the stillness, hushed and ominous.

Chapter Fifteen

Richard used a clasp knife from the outboard's fishing gear. The lock was a simple, old-fashioned one, a matter of a few minutes' work. It yielded with a dull snap, and the door was free. Depressing the thumb latch, he spread the door inward.

The place was in heavy gloom, its single window boarded over. He doubted there was any electricity. In any case, he couldn't afford to waste time searching for switches. If he left the door open, the light from outside would be sufficient.

Eager now, and yet vigilant, he entered the shed, pausing just inside to permit his eyes to adjust to the dimness. His nose tested the air like a wary animal. He could identify the odors of gasoline and mildew. Nothing alarming.

Then, as his vision improved, he could see he stood on a wide platform overhanging the dark, oily waters. The dust-covered piles of clutter lurking in the shadows on both sides didn't interest him. It was what was berthed below the platform that captured his attention.

There were two craft moored side by side. One was a small motorboat. The other, recognizable even in the murky light, was the lifeboat from the *Lady Anne*.

Richard's breathing quickened in excitement. His search had been rewarded. Here was the evidence that Con Matthews had fled the yacht the afternoon he had ruthlessly murdered three people. Still, it was not irrefutable proof of his guilt. Richard needed something more solid. Hopefully, he would find it in the lifeboat's hidden compartment.

Without hesitation he lowered himself into the boat and went straight to the mount where the engine was still in place. It took him a moment to locate the catch concealed under the mount. When he released it, a section of the structure swung out into view, revealing a kind of deep drawer. There was a single, flat object in it. Richard lifted it out and angled it toward the light, bewildered by his finding. This was totally unexpected.

Resting in the palm of his hand was a pocket-size recorder, the kind people routinely carry to enter reminders to themselves. He checked and found a tape inside. There was evidently a long message on it, since he had to wait impatiently while it rewound. Then, depressing the Play button, he listened eagerly.

He heard a man's low voice speaking slowly and carefully. *"Ab imo pectore, Gervais..."* It was gibberish. Either that or some obscure foreign language. Richard didn't understand a word of it. He started to turn up the volume and then checked himself. Wait a minute. There *was* a recognizable quality about it. Latin! He was almost certain of it now. He was hearing Latin, and there was only one explanation for that. Roman Catholic priests, at least the veteran ones, were familiar with Latin. And that meant Father Mac. Had to be.

Exactly what the ex-priest had recorded, or why, would have to wait for someone else to translate. Right now Richard needed to look for further evidence. He couldn't count on the contents of the tape. It might produce no more than prayers. Except why had the thing been hidden?

He thought about pocketing the recorder but decided that, for safekeeping, it was better to return it temporarily to the compartment. That accomplished, with the drawer concealed again, he began to examine the rest of the lifeboat. There were oars, also life jackets and a supply of emergency flares. Nothing that could be defined as incriminating. Then, secured far under the bow seat, his fumbling fingers located a metal box. He freed the container, lifting it from its hiding place.

The light was too weak down in the lifeboat to properly inspect the contents. He climbed back onto the platform and knelt on the boards, placing the box in the path of light from the door and lifting its lid.

It was what he expected it to be. The lifeboat had been equipped with a first aid kit. All the usual stuff inside. But there was something at the bottom wrapped in black plastic that was not familiar. He took it out of the box. Its weight alone was an indication of its identity.

He quickly unwrapped the plastic, peeling back the folds while careful not to touch the object itself. And there it was! Harry Fellows's Colt .38 automatic. The weapon that had been used to kill him.

But why hadn't Con Matthews secreted the gun in the same drawer that contained the recorder? Must mean he didn't know about the compartment under the mount or the recorder, which the ex-priest could have placed there himself before his death. For that matter, why hadn't Matthews disposed of both the pistol and the lifeboat? But these were questions to be answered later. Right now it was enough that Richard had his evidence.

His elation made him careless. It made him unaware of the rapid, silent movement behind him. He was still leaning over the gun when the butt of a revolver came crashing down on the back of his skull.

CON GAZED DOWN in contempt at the sprawled body of the man he had just rendered unconscious.

So Davis had found the lifeboat he'd come looking for. Not that it would do him any good. Because, by the time Con was finished, there would be nothing to connect either the lifeboat or the Colt automatic with him.

It had been risky keeping the boat and the gun, even locked away like this. But there had been no time to properly dispose of them. He had been too busy chasing Davis. Now he wondered if some latent instinct hadn't urged him to hang on to the boat and the gun, sensing their further usefulness. Both of them would be the means of destroying Davis and whoever was out there waiting for him.

That's right, he decided confidently, he could always count on his voice of self-preservation. It was what had instructed him to leave his pickup concealed off in the woods, to lock the door of the shed behind him, to wait here patiently in hiding for Davis to arrive. And he'd gone on hiding, waiting for a chance to strike while Davis wasted time scrabbling around the lifeboat. Sounded as if he'd been muttering to himself, too. But what Con had never figured on was the companion. It didn't make sense. Davis was supposed to be alone.

Never mind. He would take care of that. Pity he had failed to bring handcuffs with him. They were back in the cruiser. But he had what really mattered, his service revolver. Anyway, there was plenty of strong cord in the shed. He'd better hurry before the friend decided to investigate.

Swiftly and silently he bound Richard's hands behind him. Then, grunting softly, he hauled his inert body across the platform, dumping him facedown in the lifeboat. Time now to check on the other one.

There were cracks between the boards forming the shed walls. Revolver in hand, and the Colt tucked in his belt, Con pressed his eye to one of the narrow gaps. He'd heard their voices out there at the pier less than a hundred feet away, had even decided one of the voices was a woman's. What he had never guessed was the identity of the woman he could now recognize huddled tensely in the outboard.

His shock was profound. But only momentary. Rage replaced it, deep and powerful. Peering through the crack, he silently cursed her for the cheating, lying little bitch she was. He had actually cared about her, and all along she must have been hiding Davis, helping him. He would see to it that she paid for the treachery with her life.

NOTHING, JORDAN THOUGHT as she kept her gaze on the track cutting through the woods. No glimpse of an approaching vehicle. No warning sounds, though she thought she detected some muffled noises from the shed that indicated Richard must have managed to get inside.

But her uneasiness persisted. It was more than just the danger of this situation, the tension of wondering what he was discovering and waiting for his return. It had to do with the mood of the place. It was evil in a way she couldn't discern. Then, scant seconds later, she understood.

Mist. Traces of mist stealing like smoke around the outboard. Jordan's head whipped around, the familiar panic leaping inside her. She hadn't noticed. Her attention had been fixed on the woods. And all the while the vile stuff, born in the swamps, had been sneaking up behind her, creeping in thin veils along the channel. Now it was steaming around the perimeter of the pool.

No doubt about it. It was thickening, threatening to coalesce into her old enemy—the fog.

She checked her watch. The twenty minutes was almost up. She looked anxiously in the direction of the shed. The insidious current beneath the surface was active again, lapping under the shed doors. One of the doors creaked. Then it began to swing open, drifting out over the water. She thought for a second that the current must have tugged it loose.

An instant later one of the boats inside slid through the gap. It rocked gently on the pool and then slowly turned. She could read the letters on the side. The *Lady Anne*. It was the yacht's lifeboat!

No sign of Richard, though. What was happening?

"Richard!" she called.

Silence. She couldn't stand it. She had to investigate. Her hands reached for the line. She freed the outboard from the pier, then snatched up the oars. Her nerves made her awkward, but she managed to paddle to the side of the lifeboat.

She was shaken to discover Richard down inside the boat, his limp body stretched across the floor of the bow, his hands tied behind him. Sick with dread, she gripped the side of the lifeboat, prepared to go to him.

"Stay where you are."

Jordan froze, heart slamming against her ribs.

"No, he isn't dead, but he will be soon enough."

She dared to turn her head, to look. He was behind her on the edge of the pool, a tall specter in the gathering fog. A specter with a service revolver in his hand and a vicious grin on his mouth.

"Simple, huh," he taunted her. "All I had to do was shove the boat out, and you fell for it."

She stared at him, at the vapor licking around him, knowing she was trapped and wondering how she could possibly help Richard or herself.

"Easy, now," Con ordered her. "Don't make me shoot you. Not yet."

He had a boat hook on the ground beside him. He used the long pole to catch the front of the outboard, dragging it to the bank where he stood. She had no choice but to sit there and let him capture her.

"Out!" he commanded. On trembling legs she got to her feet and stepped ashore as he held the gun on her. "Turn around, hands behind you. That's right."

Her skin crawled as his hands made contact with her. He bound her wrists tightly, then roped her to a birch.

"Are you leaving me here?" she demanded, fearing he was about to separate her forever from Richard.

"Wouldn't think of it. Patience, Jordan. I'll only be a few minutes."

Her position permitted her to watch him with growing horror as he calmly, efficiently made his preparations. He talked to her as he worked, explaining his intentions like a doctor describing to his patient the surgery he expected to perform.

"We're going on a little voyage," he said, catching the lifeboat with the hook and drawing it to the bank beside the outboard. "Just the three of us."

"Where?" she croaked, tugging uselessly at the rope that held her to the tree.

"Out," he replied in a silky-smooth voice as he busied himself with the removal of the motor from the lifeboat. "Way out on the lake, Jordan, where we can be private together. No interruptions, no chance of any witness. It has to be that way. I can't risk anything messy here. You can understand that, can't you?"

He was going to kill them, ruthlessly and without conscience. She had no doubt whatever of his brutal purpose. Her mind searched for a way to stop him. Should she tell him that she had alerted his deputy, that Milt Johnson was probably on his way? No, a mistake. He wouldn't wait if he thought that. He'd shoot them here and now, then find some way to cover himself. Time was all they had on their side, and there wasn't much of that.

Con came to his feet, bearing the weight of the gasoline engine. "You'll excuse me, won't you? I won't be long."

He took the engine and vanished inside the boat shed. Jordan strained forward and was just able to glimpse Richard down inside the lifeboat. He hadn't stirred, was still unconscious, maybe even seriously injured from the blow Con had delivered to the back of his head. She couldn't go to him. She was alone. Alone and deathly afraid.

Con hadn't gagged her. But they both knew there was no point in her screaming. There was no one within hearing. And if she did try to cry out, he would deal with that. Wiser of her not to arouse him, to remain conscious and alert. Wait for any possible opportunity. Would there be one?

The deputy. He was their only hope. But not a very strong hope. Even if he'd finally turned up at the Dennis farm, trusted her note, he didn't know about the Mink River. They were on their own, and the loathsome fog, growing thicker by the moment, was against them.

Con knew it, too. He explained it all with satisfaction on his face when he brought from the shed a trolling motor and the heavy-duty engine batteries to power it. "Slow but silent," he said, crouching in the stern of the lifeboat as he mounted the equipment. "No one to hear us on our way out, no one to interfere. And the beauty of it is—" he paused to direct at her a smile of pure evil "—the fog covers everything. Lucky, isn't it? But then, I've always been lucky like that."

Trolling motor in place, he used strong line to lash the outboard to the side of the lifeboat. "Return transportation," he said, indicating the outboard. "Because, you see, three of us are going out, but only one of us is coming back."

Jordan didn't react. She refused to let him see how effective his torment was.

He returned to the shed, fastening its doors, leaving it as though no one had ever been here. "Now," he said, approaching the birch, "now I think we're ready to leave." He freed her from the tree, but her hands remained bound behind her.

"Into the lifeboat, please," he directed her, waving the barrel of his revolver. "No, not there in the middle. Up front. I want a safe space between us. That's right, on top of your boyfriend. Uncomfortable ride for you, but he's in no state to mind."

Jordan found herself sprawled awkwardly on Richard's back.

Con laughed. "Or maybe you'll enjoy the closeness with him. Will you, Jordan?"

She didn't answer him.

His laughter abruptly ended. He stared at her pinned to Richard, snarling maliciously, "You chose the wrong man, Jordan." Then he settled himself in the lifeboat's stern and switched on the current. The electric trolling motor began to hum, the prop delivering a silent thrust that swung the double craft in a wide arc. Seconds later they had cleared the pool and were gliding at a steady pace along the fog-shrouded channel.

Con, managing the steering lever with confidence, let himself be guided by his familiarity with the route. He watched her, his unnerving little smile back in place.

"I wonder," he said softly, "if you have any idea how much of a disappointment you are to me? I liked you, Jordan. Well enough to think you might have enjoyed a relationship with a man who's about to become a state senator. And who knows? Together we might have achieved a lot more. But I made a mistake, didn't I? I trusted you. Now I have to correct that mistake."

She gazed at his burly figure with distaste. The upright sheriff of Door County. He had managed to deceive everyone with his caring and his concern, her included. Except for his predatory eyes, she realized. They had always made her slightly uneasy. Now she understood why. There had been something calculating in their depths, something his hearty smile hadn't been able to entirely conceal.

Eyes like the fog, she thought, sickened by the similarity. Gray and cold and treacherous. A worsening fog from which she couldn't escape, drawing her deeper into the hideous nightmare of last summer.

She was experiencing it all over again—the taste and smell of the clammy stuff, the raw terror of her helplessness. Only this time the fog, together with the agony of her situation, threatened her with an uncontrollable hysteria. In another minute she would be shrieking like a madwoman. In another minute—

No. She forcefully denied her panic. She wouldn't give in to it. She wouldn't let it defeat her. She was scared and she was cold, but if she surrendered to complete irrationality she would be destroying any possible chance to help either Richard or herself.

They were turning into the main channel now. The fog here was a solid wall. Con had to concentrate on feeling a course for the lifeboat. Jordan used the opportunity to fight back with the only method available to her.

She began to struggle against the bonds on her wrists. He still had both guns, but neither one was trained on her now. They were down at his side. If she could free her hands, somehow reach those weapons while his attention was occupied with navigating...

It was useless. She couldn't begin to loosen the cord. It was so tight it cut into her wrists. Shifting her position against Richard, she squirmed in unbearable frustration. She felt ready to explode.

And then it happened. The tingling contact of Richard's flesh against her flesh. His bound hands pressing against her bound hands. Her body subsided, went very still as slowly, carefully his fingers wound around her fingers.

A thrill licked through her like lightning. He was conscious! He was with her! For a moment she thought his squeezing fingers were relaying a message of comfort. And then she understood what he was silently telling her. She couldn't free her own hands, but her fingers were in a position to work on his bindings.

It was a difficult task. She realized that at once as she began cautiously picking at the knots on his wrists. Her attitude was a cramped one requiring considerable exertion and a massive self-control. It was going to be a long process. Would there be enough time?

But the real problem was concealing her surreptitious activity from Con. The silence alone was against her. Except for the muted whirring of the trolling motor, there was a heavy, suffocating stillness intensified by the fog. It had to make him more aware of any wrong sound or movement.

She knew it was true when she tried to ease herself into a more favorable position. He had been absorbed in their tricky passage through the channel, but his head immediately swiveled. He cast a long, suspicious glance at her.

Jordan pretended she was merely wriggling into a more comfortable posture.

She had to do something to cover her operation, to keep him from discovering that Richard was conscious and a potential threat. She needed a distraction. There was an obvious one, and she used it.

"Why?" she challenged him. "Why did you kill them?"

He gazed at her with those penetrating gray eyes. Did he suspect again that she was trying to deceive him? "Entertainment for the long trip?" he asked her slowly. "Is that what you're looking for, Jordan? Or maybe you think if you're going to die, you have a right to know what for."

She ignored his sarcasm, pressing him for his account of the grisly carnage he had committed aboard the *Lady Anne*. "You were aboard the yacht," she prompted him, "but nobody was supposed to know you were there."

He considered her again, then decided there was no reason she shouldn't know. "That's right," he admitted in a chillingly detached voice as the roped boats crawled onward through the fog with Jordan laboring furtively over the knots. "Harry arranged it like that. He was backing me in my race for the state senate. Our meeting had to be secret because it involved illegal campaign funds."

"And the yacht was the perfect place for that meeting, wasn't it?" she encouraged him. "Out on the waters, safe from any observation. You must have been careful about driving down from the peninsula, leaving there without anyone's knowledge to join the yacht on its run. Where did you slip aboard, Con? Milwaukee?"

"Clever little detective, aren't you?" he said harshly. "What else have you figured out?"

"Enough to guess that Harry Fellows probably deliberately avoided having a proper crew on the *Lady Anne*, staff who might talk. The only necessity was a pilot. He chose Father Mac for that. A casual friend from Chicago with no knowledge of Wisconsin politics, I suppose. In any case, he would have been busy at the wheel."

"Father Mac," Con muttered viciously. "*Ex*-priest, and the one man anywhere I *didn't* want to encounter. How's that for irony, Jordan?"

"You knew him from long ago," she said, urging him to go on, pretending a loathsome fascination while she struggled with the knots on the back of Richard's wrists. "It must have been a bad shock for you meeting him again after all these years."

"I recognized him straight off," Con said with a biting resentment. "He hadn't changed much. But *I* had. I wasn't much more than a kid back then, and the years made a difference."

"And another identity?"

"That, too. But I could see he thought I was familiar and that he was trying to place me. Sick. It made me sick inside. I'd put the past behind me, buried it. Now here was Father Mac, no longer a priest and with the knowledge to send me to hell."

Jordan, fighting for their release, went on working intently at the knots. They were tight and damp from the fog, resisting her efforts. Her fingers were slipping. She had to try to forget they were trapped here with this monster. She had to maintain a self-discipline. Think of Richard, she ordered herself. The enormous restraint he must be exercising to keep perfectly still. Let him be your inspiration.

There was still Con. She had to keep him occupied, emotionally off balance with his hate.

"Why?" Jordan demanded. "What did Father Mac know about you?"

The gray eyes bored into hers as he considered her question. There was a sadistic little smile on his mouth as he finally shook his head. "Tempting. But, no, Jordan, not even for you. I made the mistake once of confessing all that. I won't make it again."

She was glad, after all, that he had decided not to tell her. She knew it must be something unspeakably obscene. But that still left her needing to bait him.

"Something you'd shared with him in the confessional, wasn't it?" she insisted. "But now Father Mac was no longer bound by holy orders. He didn't have to obey an oath of silence. All he had to do was remember who you were, and everything you'd struggled for would be finished."

"A question of time," Con said reluctantly. "It was only a question of time before he *would* remember."

Jordan knew she was making some progress with the knots and she tried not to let herself grow careless with her sudden excitement. But was there enough time left? The Mink River was already behind them. She could sense the openness of Rowleys Bay. They were crossing the bay now through the curtain of fog. Con was keeping their roped crafts off to the left, well away from the settlement behind the harbor. He was taking no chances.

"So you decided to keep out of Mac's way," she said.

"I had to give myself a chance to think. I had to figure out how to take care of him."

"And you hid yourself away in the master cabin."

"Harry knew how rough waters could make me seasick, and it was getting rough by then. I wasn't seasick, though. I had a prescription that took care of that."

She almost had it now. Richard was nearly free. Con was looking at her suspiciously again. Her fingers froze on the knots. She had to buy more time, prevent him from investigating.

"You listened from the cabin when Richard came aboard at Two Rivers, didn't you?" she accused him swiftly. "You overheard him arguing with Harry and Anne and realized that he would be blamed for the whole thing, that he could be charged with the perfect motive."

"All the pieces, huh, Jordan? You've got all the little pieces laid out and ready to put together. All right, that's how it was. How it *had* to be. I couldn't risk waiting. Mac was too close to remembering, and I had too much to lose if I didn't silence him. The hard part was Harry and Anne.

But I had to sacrifice them. It wouldn't have worked otherwise."

His eyes blazed with a corrupt pleasure as he explained it to her. Jordan shuddered. He was a man totally without morals or scruples. Was this what it meant to be insane? But she couldn't concern herself with that question. Con's preoccupation meant she was able to concentrate again on the knots. She had to hurry. They must be almost outside the bay.

"Too good to miss," she said angrily. "The whole situation was too good to miss, wasn't it? Even the gun was there in the cabin where you probably realized Harry kept it. And no one knew you were on the yacht."

"No one I would leave alive, that is," he added. "It was easy. Davis was down and out before he knew what hit him. I surprised the others in the same way. The storm was so wild by then it covered everything I was doing. Then I crippled the yacht, made sure I left no evidence of my ever being there and got away in the lifeboat."

The cord fell away, sliding from his wrists. Richard was free. Jordan's fingers, aching with strain, quivered in triumph. Richard's hands grasped hers, relaying another message. She understood and kept still as he began to attack her own bindings.

"But you made one error," she reminded Con. "The raft. You didn't check for that. Richard was supposed to have been trapped on the yacht, found there with the bodies. Instead he got away."

"And washed up on your beach, didn't he? Then you helped him. The two of you have given me a bad time. But that's about to end. We're almost there, Jordan."

They were on the open lake now. Even with the fog, Jordan *knew* they were on the lake. She could hear the bleat of a foghorn from somewhere in the nearby strait off the end of the peninsula. A haunting, lost sound. She could *feel* the awesome depths of the waters beneath them. Panic surged through her again, the panic of last summer when she'd been buried in fog and Casey had died. A fearful thing threatening to paralyze her.

Deny it, she ordered herself fiercely. Help Richard to help you. Hang on until he frees you. It can't be much longer.

Richard had an advantage over her, she realized. She'd had to be careful not to reveal any betraying movement, to preserve the secret activity of her fingers behind her. But her body shielded Richard's, permitting him greater freedom as he worked at her knots. Even so, she had to stall for him. She had to fill the silence.

Pretending she didn't know about Maggie Dennis's death, Jordan, convincingly desperate, challenged their captor. "You won't win. They'll bring you down in the end. I met Father Mac's sister, I talked with her. She's suspicious. Maggie Dennis has—"

"Already been taken care of," Con assured her mildly. He lifted his shoulders in a dismissive shrug. "I had no choice. Ever since she reported her brother's phone call I've been keeping an eye on her. When I stopped by her place this morning to check on her, ready like the responsible sheriff I am to ask her if she'd remembered anything more about that call, I found her with one of Mac's old photographs. She denied making the connection between the boy in that picture and me, but I could see the accusation in her eyes. She had to be eliminated. Now there are only three people who know the truth, and two of them are about to join Maggie Dennis and the others. We're there, Jordan."

He cut the motor, and there was silence. Nothing but the soft lapping of water against the joined boats, the monotonous hoot of the remote foghorn.

Con gave them no time to act. He snatched up the service revolver at his side and leveled it at them, saying briskly "You can both sit up now."

Jordan didn't stir, but she could feel Richard tensing with readiness beneath her.

Con waved the weapon in his hand impatiently. "No more games. Do you think I wasn't aware of what you wer up to the whole way out here? I realized all along you were untying each other." He chuckled malevolently. "Why should I have bothered to stop you when it turns out you've accommodated me? Now I don't have to risk the contact of untying you myself."

He paused, glancing quickly away to the left where the far-off land appeared faintly through the vapor like a phantom coastline. That it was visible at all was evidence that the fog was beginning to lighten.

"Move!" Con ordered.

Jordan obeyed him, rolling away from Richard and easing herself onto the seat. Richard turned over and levered himself to a position beside her, his hands clenched into angry fists.

"That's better," Con said, keeping the revolver aimed at their huddled figures. "You have to be untied. That's the way it all works. And it will work," he promised them.

The fog undulated over the dark waters, alive and sinister. The horn in the strait went on wailing. And Con explained how he intended them to die.

"I suppose Maggie Dennis's body must have been discovered by now. My department will be busy investigating. Publicly I won't forgive myself because I wasn't available. No, I was on the trail of Richard Davis, trying to follow a tip of a sighting that came in from the dock at Rowleys Bay. Of course, the fog prevented me from overtaking Davis. How was I to know that the maniac snatched Jordan Templeton from her rented outboard found drifting along the shore, which is where I'll leave it when I return. That he took his hostage out on the lake and killed her with the same gun he'd used on the yacht to execute the others. That in desperation, finally knowing it was hopeless, he shot himself. There will be questions, of course, speculation about why Maggie Dennis died and where Davis was hiding himself and the lifeboat, but nothing that the sheriff of Door County can't remorsefully handle. Yes, I think my luck will hold."

"But it won't hold!" Jordan retaliated, sick with dread but determined to buy them time. She was prepared now to tell Con about the note she'd left for his deputy, that it would do him no good to kill them when his secret was known. "Your luck has already run out—"

"No more talk!" he demanded, plainly nervous over increasing signs of the fog breaking up.

"She's right," Richard said, attacking his weakness. "The fog you're depending on is going. It won't be here much longer to cover your dirty work."

"But long enough," he informed them brutally, "to shut both of you up for good."

Richard pressed protectively against Jordan, ready to cover her with his body as Con leaned slowly forward, his hand groping for the Colt automatic down by his side. They went rigid with anticipation as his fingers neared the weapon that he would use to destroy them.

In that crucial second a harsh explosion rent the air. Not gunfire, Jordan realized in dismay. Then, in a flash of recognition, she understood. It was no more than the raucous screech of a gull tearing out of the blind fog bank just behind Con. But it was enough. Startled, his head went whipping around in alarm.

It was the chance Richard had been waiting for, and he didn't hesitate. From his seat in the bow, he launched himself like a lethal missile. Too late Con turned and staggered to his feet to meet the charge. Before he could use the revolver still in his hand, Richard was on him, grappling for the gun.

Jordan rose to her feet and then found herself fighting for her balance in the wildly rocking craft as the two men, cursing and straining, struggled for the advantage. She was barely conscious of the line that lashed the two boats together snapping under the stress. In that moment, when the outboard parted and broke away from the lifeboat, the figures locked in combat went hurtling over the side, the service revolver flying with them.

With a cry no less shrill than the gull's, Jordan rushed toward the stern where the two men had plunged into the cold lake. The waters here were churning in a frenzy as they went on battling each other. Then both of them sank out of sight.

Jordan remembered the Colt automatic Con had been reaching for. She went down on her knees, searching for it frantically. But when Richard had punched into him, his foot must have involuntarily kicked it away. She couldn't see it anywhere.

Arming herself with one of the oars, she scrambled to her feet. She searched the waters where they had disappeared, prepared to attack if the wrong man surfaced. The oar was raised in her hands as she peered tensely into the depths.

Richard, where are you? Don't die! Live for us!

There was a rush of breaking water behind her from the other side, then an icy, wet hand seized her powerfully by the ankle. Jordan screamed and twisted around, losing the oar. Con Matthews, his streaming face contorted with demonic rage, began to drag her overboard.

Before she could recover the oar, Richard shot to the surface beside him, roaring ferociously, "You will not hurt my woman!"

The fist he slammed into the side of Con's head had an impact so savage that it rendered the sheriff senseless. The sudden relief they both felt was so vast that neither of them knew how to express it.

"I should let him drown," Richard gasped after a moment, clinging to the side of the boat with one hand and supporting the sagging body of Con with the other. "It's what he deserves. But I suppose I have to save the bastard for his own jail."

Jordan helped him to heave Con's limp body into the lifeboat. Then he drew himself into the boat and collapsed on the floor, taking a few seconds to recover his wind. Jordan searched again for the Colt and found it this time under the pile of flares. She handed the gun to Richard.

She longed to ask him about his shouted fury down in the water, his words that had thrilled her even in her terror. But this was hardly the moment. Besides, she feared that his outburst had been merely a kind of masculine announcement of his assault rather than any genuine declaration.

All she could manage to say was, "Are you all right?"

"Yeah, all right," he assured her, "though damn worried there for a minute when he got away from me under the boat."

He sat up and started to reach for her. Jordan never knew whether he meant to embrace her or simply to use her to steady himself as he climbed to his feet. They were interrupted in that instant by a launch speeding toward them with a purposeful urgency from the direction of Rowleys Bay. Through the rapidly parting fog they could distinguish several male figures in the boat. One of them, already on his feet and hailing them, wore the uniform of a sheriff's deputy.

"Cavalry to the rescue," Richard observed with a wry grin. "This is getting to be one hell of a party."

Chapter Sixteen

He was driving her crazy. He had been up since daybreak, so tense with expectation that his nervous energy was turning the house into a chaos. He had started in the kitchen, strewing the table and counters with dismembered newspapers along with mysterious sketches and scrawled lists, none of which had any meaning for her.

When Jordan asked for an explanation, he mumbled something about tie beams and trusses. Okay, she wasn't a complete ignoramus. She could tell that meant his efforts were connected somehow with his construction business. Exactly how she didn't know.

At the moment, having just gotten off the phone after a long conversation with Deputy Milt Johnson, who was now acting sheriff for the county, she stood in the doorway, observing the parlor with dismay. With every available surface in the kitchen exhausted, Richard had simply moved his disorder into the parlor. Her worktable, over which he was currently hunched, groaned with his litter. Face it. The man might be a joy to her in nearly every respect, but neatness wasn't high on his priority list.

Sensing her in the doorway, he glanced up from his work just long enough to check the clock across the room. "Is that clock right?"

"Yes," she answered him patiently, having already offered this assurance twice already, "the clock is right."

He grunted and returned to his column of figures.

Poor Richard. This waiting was very hard on him. But his son was being rushed to him just as swiftly as was humanly possible. An apologetic Victor Fellows was having Andrew flown up from Chicago on the company plane. He and Evelyn had insisted on personally delivering his nephew to the island as soon as the plane landed in Ephraim.

That could be at any moment, Jordan realized, but in the meantime she had to distract Richard from his restless occupation. The house had suffered enough.

"Are you ready now," she demanded, "to hear what Milt Johnson had to say?"

He swung away from the table. "I'm listening."

Jordan wasn't so sure. Now that Richard was absolved, and Con Matthews was behind bars with the evidence mounting against him, she had the feeling Richard wanted to put all of it behind him as rapidly as possible. His interest was already focused elsewhere, and she was reluctant to examine that direction too closely, fearing it didn't include her.

Leaning against the doorway, she began to relay what Milt Johnson had shared with her. "You were right, Richard. The message on the recorder *was* in Latin, and it was Mac who taped it. Sheriff Johnson had it translated at the university in Green Bay. Turns out it was a voice letter for Mac's friend and former bishop. They must have studied Latin together long ago in the seminary."

"Revealing stuff?"

Jordan nodded. "Very. It seems that just before the end Mac *did* remember who Con Matthews was, except he wasn't altogether certain or maybe he would have acted on it in another way. Trouble is, he didn't realize just how dangerous Con had become, though he must have been cautious enough about him to slip out on deck and stick that recorder in the lifeboat for safekeeping."

"And, of course," Richard added, "Mac would have known about the concealed drawer. Harry trusted the priest and probably showed it to him, along with everything else they inspected when they visited the yard while the yacht was under reconstruction. But why Latin instead of English?"

"Because the letter had to be confidential, for the bishop's ears only. And even then, disclosing everything to no one but another priest, he was violating the sacred confessional. That's what he must have felt, anyway, even if he had left the priesthood. He was undergoing a terrible moral struggle and needed to share the story with the bishop."

"Con never did tell us what he'd done back in Chicago all those years ago."

"No, but Mac did on that tape. Richard, it's pretty vile. Father Mac had organized and coached this neighborhood basketball team. Street kids, smart and tough and good enough to win an inner-city tournament. Con was one of them, and he celebrated afterward. Then he wanted another victory. He was a hero, and this girl was supposed to accommodate him. Only she resisted and then afterward threatened to send him to jail on rape charges. That's when ... when he killed her brutally."

"And was maybe still half-drunk," Richard said, anticipating the sequence of events, "when he confessed to Father Mac afterward. And what could Mac do about it? He was a priest then. He couldn't tell."

"No," Jordan agreed, "but once Con was sober, he must have decided to leave. He put Chicago and his identity behind him and made another life for himself up here."

"And the rest we already know."

"Except for one thing. Richard, I've been thinking about Father Mac...."

"I know what you're going to say. You believe that in the end he would have gone on honoring the secrets of the confessional."

"Exactly. I'm probably being fanciful since I never met John McGuire, but after everything that's happened I feel like I knew him. At least, the kind of man he was. I'd like to think that he wouldn't have disobeyed his vows of the confessional. That, instead, he would have found some other way to defeat Con Matthews's evil."

"We'll never know but it's a good way to remember him. At least Matthews will pay for his death now that all the pieces are sorted out."

All but one, Jordan thought unhappily, remembering his words in the water when he had defended her against Con's attack. *Am I his woman?* She wanted to ask him, yearned to know. But she was a coward, still afraid. She was waiting for Richard to approach this topic, but he hadn't yet. Maybe never would.

Right now the sound of a saw in the yard captured his attention. He waved his pencil in the direction of the window. "How's our friend doing?"

Jordan crossed the room, checking through the glass. Dino was out there laboring cheerfully to clear away the limbs the storm had brought down on that wild afternoon. The young man, more of a lost soul than ever since Maggie Dennis's death, had turned up unexpectedly at the island this morning. Neither Richard nor Jordan could bring themselves to send him away.

"Still stubbornly at it," she reported. "Richard, what are we going to do about Dino?"

He suddenly lifted his pencil high in the air. "Listen!"

"What?"

"Wasn't that a car horn?"

"I didn't hear anything."

"Well, I think it was a car horn."

Jordan moved decisively to the table, removed the pencil from his hand and tossed it down on his clutter. "Come on."

"Where are we going?"

"Out to the causeway. You can pace up and down on the rocks while we wait for Andrew. It'll make a nice change from tie beams and whatever."

As it turned out, the rocks were spared the grooves she was convinced he would have worn in them. Seconds after they reached the lip of the causeway, a dark blue Cadillac emerged from the woods on the other side. The driver barely had time to brake at the road's end before a rear door shot open. A small, sturdy figure spilled out of the car and charged without pause along the stony causeway, shouting as he ran. Richard raced toward him from his end.

Father and son met in the middle, catching each other in a wild embrace. Jordan, hanging back to allow them the privacy of their moving reunion, found herself threatened by emotional tears.

"Looks just like his pa, doesn't he?" observed Dino, who had joined her on the shore.

"They make a pair, all right," she agreed, thinking with a smile that in another few years Andrew would be a real heartbreaker. Even from here she could see he already had his father's strong appeal.

Richard, an arm slung happily around his son's shoulder, turned and called for Jordan and Dino to join them out on the causeway. When they arrived, he proudly introduced them.

"Andrew, this is our new friend, Dino. And this—" he took Jordan's hand, drawing her forward "—is the special lady I told you about on the phone."

Andrew blushed, betraying a shyness. "I remember. Jordan Templeton, right?"

She beamed at him, offering a quick wink. "I won't ask you to tell me all the terrible things he said about me, Andrew. I'll just welcome you to Cana Island."

He grinned, shyness suddenly forgotten as he scanned the woods and shoreline behind them. "Wow, your own island!"

"Well, not really. But I do get to live here, and it is a lot of fun."

Eyes shining with exuberance, Andrew gazed longingly at the lighthouse tower rising above the trees. "Can we go up to the top?"

"Naw," Dino answered. "I already tried that. It's strictly off-limits, except for emergencies. But I could show you a great spot for swimming on the other side."

"Dad," he pleaded eagerly, "could I go see it?"

"I'll watch him," Dino promised them.

Richard playfully cuffed his son. "Go! But look only, swim later."

"Okay."

The two of them took off in the direction of the beach on the other side of the lighthouse.

Richard, watching them go, laughed. "How do you like that? After almost losing each other, all he can think about is swimming."

Jordan nodded. "I believe it's called being seven years old."

By this time Victor and Evelyn, following from the Cadillac, had reached them on the causeway. The two men shook hands.

"Thank you for delivering my son."

"My pleasure," Victor said warmly, all trace of his earlier hostility forgotten.

Evelyn, too, seemed anxious to be friends. "Sonia sends you her love. She wanted to be with us, but Walter's daughter has come up from Chicago to meet her. Sonia is praying it goes well. They're planning to get married."

"Oh, I'm glad," Jordan said. "I could see how right they are for each other."

Victor slid an arm around Evelyn's waist. "Theirs won't be the only wedding," he confided. "We're getting married ourselves. As soon as it's decently possible, that is."

Evelyn looked faintly alarmed by his disclosure. "Victor, maybe we shouldn't be—"

"No more secrets," he insisted, squeezing her against his side.

She nodded. "You're right." She gravely lifted her chin. "What Victor is trying to tell you is that I'm pregnant."

"*We're* pregnant," he corrected her with a pleased grin.

"The doctor in Green Bay!" Richard exclaimed.

Jordan didn't share his surprise. She had guessed, from the moment Sonia had provided alibis for them for the afternoon of the murders, the kind of specialist Evelyn and Victor must have been consulting.

"It's been awful hiding the whole thing," Evelyn confessed. "I knew people would think the worst, that I cheated on my husband with his son. But my marriage was such a farce. You see, Harry was...well, impotent and couldn't have another child. I could have lived with that, but not his abuse. I know it was wrong, Victor and I falling in love, but—"

"Enough," Victor interrupted her. "We're putting all that behind us, and we've got a baby to help us do it."

Wise, Jordan thought, wishing them well when they departed a moment later.

"Let's go find Andrew and Dino," Richard suggested as the Cadillac vanished into the woods.

They turned and made their way back through the trees, emerging on the lawn at the side of the house. They lingered by one of the lilac thickets, watching Andrew and Dino down on the beach. The two young people, with shoes off and pant legs rolled to the knees, were splashing through the sun-bright waters.

"Devious pair of mutts! I told them not to go into the water."

"Uh-uh," Jordan corrected him. "You told them not to go swimming. Nothing was mentioned about wading."

Richard chuckled. "Fair enough." He was quiet for a minute, feasting his eyes proudly on the figure of his son. Then he asked eagerly, "So what do you think of my kid?"

"I think he's someone that I'd like to get to know a whole lot better," she said warmly. She paused for a second, then decided she was through being a coward about the subject. "The thing is," she added meaningfully, "will the two of you be around long enough for that to happen?"

"Hey, what's this? You wouldn't be trying to chase us away already, would you?"

"Never! But, Richard—" she struggled for the words "—you told me yesterday in the park that, when it was all over, all you wanted to do was take Andrew and go far away. Some place where you could start over, you said."

"And you thought—" He broke off, seizing her by the hand and drawing her around the lilacs, out of sight of the beach. Then he turned to face her squarely. "It's true, what I said. I do want to take Andrew away and start over. Away from Chicago, that is."

"Then you meant—oh!"

"Now you're getting it. The mess I made in the kitchen and the parlor was because I was hunting through the local real estate listings for properties I could fix up and sell. That's what all the sketches and figures were about. I was looking at what it's going to take to move my operation up here. I thought you understood."

"I do now. A fresh beginning, huh?"

"Yeah. Like settling down right here, I thought. Like becoming a local businessman, I thought. Like marrying the woman I love, I thought. So now, what do *you* think?"

"What I think," she informed him solemnly, "is that I wouldn't object to a demonstration of your intentions."

He promptly obliged her with a pair of arms that held her close and a mouth that silenced any further questions. No doubt about it. The man she loved knew how to kiss. Thoroughly, deliriously.

Afterward, resting in his arms, Jordan was aware of the lilacs against which they were pressed. They had opened overnight on the island and were in their full glory. Masses of bloom that had never been so heavy, so riotously purple, so richly fragrant. Or did they just seem this way because she was so wonderfully happy?

Richard, however, was interested in something more practical. "Got an idea. You suppose there's any chance of our getting Dino interested in the construction business?

sense potential there, if we can convince him to stick around long enough to try it. I could really use the help because you'll be busy. You've got a book to write.''

"We'll work on him," she said confidently. "After the last few days, there isn't anything we can't manage."

"Together," he said.

"Together," she agreed.

On the most romantic day of the year, capture the thrill of falling in love all over again—with

Harlequin's

Bachelors

They're three sexy and *very single* men who run very special personal ads to find the women of their fantasies by Valentine's Day. These exciting, passion-filled stories are written by bestselling Harlequin authors.

Your Heart's Desire by Elise Title
Mr. Romance by Pamela Bauer
Sleepless in St. Louis by Tiffany White

Be sure not to miss Harlequin's Valentine Bachelors,
available in February wherever
Harlequin books are sold.

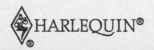

HARLEQUIN®

Don't miss these Harlequin favorites by some of our most distinguished authors!
And now, you can receive a discount by ordering two or more titles!

HT#25577	WILD LIKE THE WIND by Janice Kaiser	$2.99	☐
HT#25589	THE RETURN OF CAINE O'HALLORAN by JoAnn Ross	$2.99	☐
HP#11626	THE SEDUCTION STAKES by Lindsay Armstrong	$2.99	☐
HP#11647	GIVE A MAN A BAD NAME by Roberta Leigh	$2.99	☐
HR#03293	THE MAN WHO CAME FOR CHRISTMAS by Bethany Campbell	$2.89	☐
HR#03308	RELATIVE VALUES by Jessica Steele	$2.89	☐
SR#70589	CANDY KISSES by Muriel Jensen	$3.50	☐
SR#70598	WEDDING INVITATION by Marisa Carroll	$3.50 U.S. $3.99 CAN.	☐
HI#22230	CACHE POOR by Margaret St. George	$2.99	☐
HAR#16515	NO ROOM AT THE INN by Linda Randall Wisdom	$3.50	☐
HAR#16520	THE ADVENTURESS by M.J. Rodgers	$3.50	☐
HS#28795	PIECES OF SKY by Marianne Willman	$3.99	☐
HS#28824	A WARRIOR'S WAY by Margaret Moore	$3.99 U.S. $4.50 CAN.	☐

(limited quantities available on certain titles)

	AMOUNT	$
DEDUCT:	**10% DISCOUNT FOR 2+ BOOKS**	$
ADD:	**POSTAGE & HANDLING**	$
	($1.00 for one book, 50¢ for each additional)	
	APPLICABLE TAXES*	$_____
	TOTAL PAYABLE	$_____
	(check or money order—please do not send cash)	

To order, complete this form and send it, along with a check or money order for the total above, payable to Harlequin Books, to: **In the U.S.:** 3010 Walden Avenue, P.O. Box 9047, Buffalo, NY 14269-9047; **In Canada:** P.O. Box 613, Fort Erie, Ontario, L2A 5X3.

Name:_____

Address:_____ City:_____

State/Prov.:_____ Zip/Postal Code:_____

*New York residents remit applicable sales taxes.
Canadian residents remit applicable GST and provincial taxes.

HBACK-JM2